"*Red Center* is for hard-core spy novel junkies. It has a little of everything....I hadn't come across Frederick Nolan before, but I'm looking for more of his work now!"
—*Arizona Daily Star*

"Nolan knows his politics, crime, tradecraft, and people, but most of all he knows how to keep readers turning pages in this riveting, witty, even stylish treat."
—*Publishers Weekly*

"Nolan displays a keen awareness of how intelligence agents operate....EXCITING."
—*Wilmington News Journal*

"This violent, fast-paced spy thriller provides an irresistible combination of international espionage and drug trafficking, *Miami Vice*-style....A TENSE, ACTION-PACKED TALE."
—*Booklist*

Also by Frederick Nolan
published in paperback
by St. Martin's Press

WOLF TRAP

RED CENTER

Frederick Nolan

ST. MARTIN'S PRESS/NEW YORK

RED CENTER

Library of Congress Catalog Card Number: 86-26250

ISBN: 0-312-90961-6

Printed in the United States of America

First St. Martin's Press mass market edition/March 1988

10 9 8 7 6 5 4 3 2 1

This is for
Christian and André

PROLOGUE

The Chief Intelligence Directorate of the Soviet General Staff—*Glavnoye Rasvedyatvelnoye Upravleniye*—is smaller and less well known than its sister organization. The GRU does not advertise itself. Its head office is not a tourist attraction like the old insurance office building on Dzerzhinsky Square which houses the KGB, but is hidden away in a suburban backwater by the Central Airport, the old Khodinka Field. It is no less deadly for that.

Patrolled night and day by armed guards and killer dogs, the area itself is bordered by restricted buildings, among which are the offices of three leading aviation firms, the Military Aviation Academy, and a rocket construction firm. On the fourth side of the rectangle formed by these buildings lies the Institute of Cosmic Biology.

The entrance to the central enclave, again guarded by dogs and electrified sprung-steel S-wire, is down a narrow lane named for Richard Sorge, a famous Soviet spy. It leads through a blind wall ten meters high into the GRU complex. The main GRU operations executive building is a nine-story extended rectangle, surrounded on all sides by a two-story structure, the windows of which look down upon a central courtyard. The external walls have no windows at all, which may account for its being known, sardonically, as the Aquarium. No car—not even that of Marshal Sokolov, the minister of defense—is permitted to enter this restricted area. No one may take inside any metallic object, not a cigarette lighter, or a belt buckle, or still less a briefcase. Everyone entering or leaving, regardless of rank, is required to pass through a sophisticated electronic security check.

Most of the GRU's staff are based in the Aquarium, but its chief executive, Colonel General P. I. Ivashutin, spends four or five hours of his eighteen-hour day in the rather less forbidding administration building on Znamensky Street, just across the Yauza River from Moscow's famous Sokol'niki Park. Between the hours of ten and midday, Ivashutin holds his daily briefings. These are invariably followed by a private conference with his first deputy, Colonel General A. G. Pavlov, which lasts until one. Sometimes, not invariably, they lunch afterward in the ornately gilded dining room on the top floor, where the food is said to be the equal of anything in Europe.

It was ten twenty-three precisely, a brilliant June day. The morning sun shone brightly through the tall windows of the conference room. Around the beautifully polished conference table, on which, in 1914, the czar of Russia and his generals had signed the declaration of war against Germany and Austria, sat Ivashutin's eight deputies. With the exception of Pavlov, they were all in full uniform.

"You have all read the intelligence digests I circulated for your attention?" Ivashutin asked, lighting a cigar. The cigars were a personal gift from his old friend Fidel Castro, specially flown in each week by Aeroflot. Someone had told Ivashutin that Castro had given them up to encourage young Cubans not to smoke. Sometimes Fidel was a damned fool, the Russian thought.

Of course, "the Grandfathers" replied, immediately. The digests confirmed that the United States was developing a new generation of space satellites hardened against radiation and hostile laser beams and capable of evading Soviet attack. These satellites, the report continued, would hover twenty-two thousand miles in space, part of a worldwide network called Space-track, which would provide around-the-clock surveillance of all satellites in deep space. Five stations would track the satellites: one in New Mexico, another in Hawaii, a third in Korea. The fourth was under construction on the British-owned island of Diego Garcia in the Indian Ocean, and work on the fifth, in Portugal, would commence shortly.

"I am sure you all appreciate, then, the significance of the setbacks the Americans have received in this area recently," Ivashutin said. "Allow me to refresh your memory. On August 28, 1985, an advanced Titan 34D rocket exploded at Vandenberg Air Force Base in California, destroying what we believe to have been an $800 million satellite. On January 28, 1986, the space shuttle Challenger exploded soon after takeoff, killing everyone on board. On April 18, a second Titan 34D, carrying what the Americans call a 'Big Bird' satellite, blew up five seconds after takeoff at Vandenberg, wrecking two launch pads in the process. On May 3, a Delta rocket carrying a weather satellite broke up and was destroyed."

The Grandfathers nodded, saying nothing. Ivashutin was going somewhere; when he was ready, he would tell them. Inside nine months, Ivashutin went on, three of the four means the Americans had available to put heavy military payloads into orbit had failed. The fourth, the Atlas-Centaur, shared much of the Delta's engine design and was therefore suspect.

"Flights of all four have been suspended indefinitely. Even the most optimistic NASA planners do not foresee a resumption of the American space program until mid-1987, and possibly it will be a great deal longer. Meanwhile, their surveillance capability is severely inhibited, presenting us with a unique opportunity to preempt their plans to dominate space with what they childishly insist upon calling 'Star Wars' hardware."

He looked at each of them in turn. No one spoke, although he knew they had all guessed what was coming. Ivashutin permitted himself a frosty smile before continuing.

"In the light of these developments, we have been invited"—
he paused on the word just long enough to make them smile at
his irony—"to submit this agency's recommendations, with es-
pecial reference to our own supersatellite, to the general secretary and the Secretariat."

The Grandfathers looked at each other. They had tried pre-
empting the American Strategic Defense Initiative once before,
with an ultrasecret assault satellite nicknamed Smert Ptyetsa
(Death Bird) by the Space Agency scientists. Conceived as a
means of ensuring the West could never place in orbit any satellite deemed inimical to Soviet interests, the Death Bird had been
identified for what it was by American satellite surveillance
the moment it had appeared at the launch site two years ago.
The result had been an eyeball-to-eyeball confrontation with the
Western powers, who delivered an ultimatum: launch, and take
the consequences. No one who remembered those tense meetings when the American missile-carrying F-16s were standing
by to scramble, or the embarrassing climb-down by the general
secretary which ensued, wanted a repetition of that debacle.

"What about the Neighbors?" Pavlov asked, using the GRU
nickname for the KGB. "Do they also know of the secretary's
request?"

"Of course," Ivashutin said smoothly. "And in their usual
subtle way, they have promised the Central Committee a scenario guaranteeing that it will be us, and not the Americans,
who achieve domination of outer space."

"And?" Pavlov prompted.

"Comrade Secretary Gorbachev replied, as is his wont, 'Do
you honestly believe what you are telling me?'"

The Grandfathers around the table roared with loyal laughter.
The chief's impersonation of General Secretary Mikhail Gorbachev was wickedly accurate. Ivashutin held up a hand for
attention. His deputies at once fell silent.

"I need not tell any of you that there is a wind of change
blowing in the Kremlin," he said. "And I propose that we shall

profit by it. We have in this matter an opportunity once and for all to demonstrate we are not only the equal but the superior of any espionage organization in the world!''

He laid his hand firmly on the table, giving his words more emphasis than if he had slammed it down hard.

''It was we, not the Neighbors, who ran Sorge in the Great Patriotic War,'' Ivashutin said, ''we, not they, who obtained the atomic bomb from Nunn May. It was we who stole the American Sidewinder missile at Zell-am-See in 1967, we who obtained the plans of the French Mirage fighter. This new task is work we can do better than the Neighbors. Better than anyone!''

He paused, looking at each of them individually, as if assessing them. They sensed the anger in him, the ambition. Times were changing, and Pyotr Ivanovich Ivashutin was not a young man. He needed a coup, a big success. They said of Mikhail Gorbachev that he had a nice smile but iron teeth. He had already flouted Kremlin protocol by reconstituting the Politburo, by replacing Gromyko, by putting Viktor Chebrikov, Yuri Andropov's handpicked successor—and therefore, by definition his own, since he had been a protégé of the former KGB chief—at the head of the KGB. Providence had sent Ivashutin an opportunity to show the general secretary that no stodgy, cliché-spouting party hack from Dnepropetrovsk could hope to compete on equal terms with a man who had given his whole life to the Great Game.

Ivashutin nodded abruptly, a mannerism they all knew well. It meant he had come to a decision.

''The Americans are in disarray. They have only one major surveillance satellite in orbit. If it is neutralized long enough for us to put Smert Ptyetsa into orbit, the Americans will be helpless. I want a scenario, gentlemen. An initiative so devious that the Neighbors will not even smell it. I want the very best brains put on this job, and the very best men to carry it out. Understand me—the best! Everything is to be subordinated to this task, everything! I want to go to the chiefs of the General Staff and tell them that we—we, no one else!—have found a way to make the undetected launch of our satellite possible. Is that understood?"

"But . . . Comrade General!" one of the deputies protested. "The National Security Agency spends more than a hundred million dollars a year protecting its computer network. That's more than our entire budget for hardware. What you are asking is impossible. It can't be done."

"It will," Ivashutin said. "It must."

PART ONE

READY

1 It took David Caine about twenty minutes to get from National Airport to Arlington. He paid the cab off outside the courthouse and walked south to Fourteenth. At an office building in the twenty block, he inserted a plastic ID card into the slot in the wall beneath the plaque which read INTERNATIONAL SECURITY SYSTEMS, INC. A buzzer sounded behind the solid oak door. He pushed it open and went inside.

The carpeted hallway was discreetly lit; several of Hugh Casson's distinctively economical watercolors hung on the burlap-covered walls. Caine went across to the reception desk and handed his personal ID to the athletic-looking Ryan O'Neal clone behind the desk. Beyond it, separated from the hallway by a smoked-glass wall, he could see the desks of the genuine security firm behind whose cover his own secret organization operated. They didn't look very busy.

"Thank you, Mr. Caine," the young man behind the desk said. "The director is expecting you."

Caine nodded and went across the hall to the elevator. There were no stairs in the front of the building. It was impossible to get from the reception area he had entered to the upper floors without using the elevators, in which concealed cameras with fiber-optic lenses kept all visitors under surveillance.

The soft chunter of electronic machinery and the muted chirr of telephone bells met him as he stepped out on the third floor into a small hallway decorated with the same green burlap. On either side, unmarked swing doors led into corridors with offices on either side. Miles Kingly's office was at the far end of the one on the right. To get through it, you had to pass through an outer office occupied by Kingly's personal assistant, Betty Torre. She was a lively, handsome woman in her mid-thirties who had been working for Kingly since he came to Washington from Berlin in 1983.

"Hello, David," she said. "That's a fine tan you've got."

"The sun shines bright on my old Kentucky home," Caine replied. "How are you?"

"Ginger peachy," she said, and made a gesture with her head toward the door of Kingly's office. "He's expecting you."

"So I'm told," Caine said. He knocked and went in.

"You got here fast," Kingly said, looking up.

"Delta was ready when I was." Kingly grimaced, and Caine instantly regretted his mild humor. He had forgotten Kingly's dislike of anything smacking of flippancy.

"Sorry I had to rush you," Kingly said with no trace of regret. "No choice, really. Sit down, sit down."

He was nearly fifty now, with a hairline that had not yet receded enough for him to be called balding, and an out-of-condition body not yet quite flabby enough to be called fat. He wore an immaculately cut gray lightweight houndstooth suit from his Sackville Street tailor, a silk shirt, a Traveller's tie, and shoes handlasted in St. James's. Not for the first time, Caine wondered how Miles could afford it, even on a station director's pay.

"What's the panic?" Caine asked. It must be something of more than usual importance for Control to have pulled him in out of the field. All but the most sensitive assignments were handed out through the liaison desk, right here in Arlington.

"Priority signal from Station One," Kingly told him, sliding a sheet of paper across the desk. "A service job."

"Is that all?"

A "service job," in ISS jargon, was an in-depth check on an

individual working within American intelligence. It was normally a very routine business, certainly nothing to fly to Washington for.

"This one would appear to be special," Kingly said. "So I thought I'd better brief you personally."

"Who's the subject?" Caine said, turning the briefing sheet around to read it.

"A Company operative working undercover in Miami. Name of Genevevo."

"Antony Genevevo, Clandestine Services," Caine read. "I thought they weren't allowed to operate domestically."

"He's attached to Domestic Ops," Kingly explained. The Domestic Operations Division was one of fifteen or so separate components of the CIA's Clandestine Services, or to give it its official title, the Directorate of Operations. Domestic Operations was, in essence, an area division, conducting its clandestine activities inside the United States. Caine's attention sharpened. If DOD was operating in his territory, he wanted to know a lot more.

"Why don't London just ask the Company for sight of his dossier?" he asked.

"The inference is that Sam mustn't know of our interest."

Kingly never called the Americans "the Cousins," as most people in the Service did. He said the terminology had been debased by journalists and thriller writers.

"It says we're to concentrate on any links Genevevo might have with the Comrades," Caine noted. "Do they think he's turned Red?"

"It's possible. DGI"—the acronym stood for Dirección General de Inteligencia, the official title of the Cuban intelligence service—"is very active there, and we all know the Cubans are just a branch office of Red Center. Would you like some coffee or tea?"

"Coffee would be fine," Caine said. Kingly pressed a button

■ 11

on his desk as Caine asked another question. "Have we got any background on Genevevo?"

Before Kingly could answer, the door opened and Betty Torre came in.

"Coffee for David, tea for me," Kingly said. "And let's have some of those biscuits from Fortnum's."

"Germaine Greer, where are you when I need you?" Betty said to the ceiling. Kingly didn't smile. He waited till the door was closed, then swung his feet up onto the desk.

"Last summer, Six brought over a big one. A GRU colonel. Second Directorate, no less."

"Quite a catch," Caine observed, and it was true. GRU defectors were very much rarer birds than KGB men. A colonel in the Second Directorate, which dealt with the Americas, Britain, Australia, and New Zealand, was a real prize. DI6, the Secret Intelligence Service, would really have their tails up.

"They brought him out through the consulate in Berlin. Cheeky buggers, even flew him back on a commercial flight. They'd never have got away with that in my day."

Kingly had been the station director in Berlin for six years prior to this posting. He talked about it as if it had been the best time of his life, although as far as Caine had been able to ascertain, Kingly's achievements there had been less than spectacular.

"They gave him a code name: Viktor," Kingly went on. "Put him in intensive care."

More jargon: "intensive care" meant nonstop, relentless debriefing which went on nine hours a day for week after week after week. Everything the defector said was checked, cross-checked, and double-checked. They usually took them to a military establishment first: Saltdean Barracks outside Brighton was one of the more favored places. Later, he would be taken to the safe house at the corner of South Audley Street and Adam's Row, and later still, to the secluded Winterbourne Hotel at Bonchurch on the Isle of Wight.

"They kept him to themselves as long as they could, of course," Kingly went on. "Wanted to be sure they'd emptied him out. But once the expulsions started, Sam knew we had a talker."

The preceding September, Britain had ordered twenty-five Soviet officials out of the country—diplomats, embassy staff, trade officials, and journalists. The Russians, calling this "an unwarranted action of unfriendly character," riposted by kicking twenty-five British officials out of Moscow for "engaging in activities incompatible with their status." The formal expulsion of spies from any Western country was a sure sign to other intelligence agencies that a Soviet defector with a wide knowledge of field activities was talking. It was clear now that it must have been "Viktor," the GRU colonel.

"So now Sam is asking for equal time?"

"Right," Kingly said. "But Six won't be in any hurry to hand him over."

"What's Viktor got to do with Genevevo?"

"Ah," Kingly said, swinging his feet to the floor. "Here's the tea."

Betty Torre put the silver tray on the otherwise empty desk. "Note: biscuits, not cookies," she said to Caine. "Flown in by diplomatic pouch."

"Proper treasure, you are," Caine said.

"Ain't it de troot," Betty said, and went out. While Kingly poured his tea into a pretty Minton cup, Caine looked around his office. It was L-shaped and unadorned, almost austere. Tinted windows kept out the glare of the Washington sunshine. The walls were covered with the same green burlap, the floors with the same darker green carpet as the outer offices. Kingly's desk stood in the lower horizontal of the L. Behind it stood floor-to-ceiling bookshelves of Malabar teak, packed with government publications, military digests, and intelligence reports. The other part of the office contained a reproduction Regency table, and chairs, for Kingly's briefing meetings. There were no pictures, no personal touches. The only thing hanging on the walls was a large-scale Rand-McNally map of the United States.

"You were going to tell me what Viktor has to do with this Genevevo," Caine said, watching Kingly munch the biscuits like a kid in a candy store.

"Ah, mm, yes," Kingly said. "One of Viktor's gifts to Six was a chap in D15's F Section called Clive Jamison. Nasty little bugger. He'd made contact with the Comrades in London, and they flew him out to Vienna a couple of times to make sure he was kosher. He'd given them some Beta-level stuff: Five's assessment of the KGB order of battle in England, GRU infiltration of the IRA, that sort of thing. Viktor blew the whistle on him, and K Section took him to pieces. One of the people he named as an informant was Genevevo. The Joint Chiefs wanted to know more, but apparently preferred not to ask Sam direct. Which resulted in its being handed to ISS."

International Security Systems, Inc., Arlington, was part of a genuine worldwide network of security consultants with head offices in Lincoln's Inn Fields in London. Its business, the supply of security equipment and expertise to government and private agencies, was a perfect cover for the organization to which David Caine belonged.

Dating from the signing in 1947 of the still-secret UKUSA agreement, it had become a sine qua non of Western intelligence that America and Britain did not spy upon each other. Since the UKUSA agreement brought together under a single umbrella the SIGINT (Signals Intelligence)-, HUMINT (Human Intelligence)-, and ELINT (Electronic Intelligence)-gathering facilities of America, Britain, Canada, Australia, and New Zealand, such surveillance was theoretically rendered unnecessary.

Then in 1982, a wretched pedophile named Geoffrey Prime confessed to his wife that he had been supplying the Soviets with secret documents from GCHQ, the British cipher center at Cheltenham where he had formerly worked. His wife, Rhona, informed the police, and Prime was arrested.

It transpired that Prime, possibly alone, or possibly in concert with another man killed in an unexplained glider accident near Cheltenham ten days later, had turned over to the Comrades not only thousands of pages of secret material relating to the most sensitive U.S.-U.K. spy-satellite projects, but also details of the even more secret Sambo project, a detection system used to locate Soviet submarines.

American reaction was Draconian. Claiming that British security was as "leaky as an old scow" and that Government Communication Headquarters was a "negative asset," General Lincoln D. Faurer, head of the American National Security Agency, clamped down on the flow of information passing to Britain, and his formerly cordial relationship with Sir Brian Tovey at GCHQ deteriorated to one of utmost formality. The same reticence became apparent in Five and Six's dealings with Sam. A solution was sought, and found—the ISS organization.

Through a Hong Kong-based consortium managed by the Properties Division of the Department of the Environment, a controlling interest was acquired in the long-established London company. Funds approved by the Permanent Secretaries' Committee on the Intelligence Services were made available for the establishment, at each of the existing offices of ISS, of a separate, secret section whose task was to monitor American intelligence activities around the world.

The covert staff of ISS was recruited over a two-year period from every branch of the security services. In Caine's case, it had been Army intelligence. He had been given a six-week crash course at the DI6 school in Borough High Street and posted to the American branch as soon as he had completed it. ISS had come on stream late in 1985, working alongside, but not for, D16. Its director, Major General Sir James Bamford, DSO, MC, listed in *Who's Who* as "semi-retired, on attachment to MoD," reported only to the chairman of the Joint Intelligence Chiefs and the Prime Minister's COBRA committee.

"You say Jamison named Genevevo as a source?" Caine asked. "A source for what?"

"Jamison did some liaison work with the Americans on Operation Nightingale, which was set up to investigate heroin and cocaine smuggling between Florida, Nigeria, and London," Kingly explained. "He went to Miami, and the DEA people there put him onto Genevevo. This was before Genevevo went undercover, obviously. Apparently, Jamison convinced him that he could crack the ring at the British end if Genevevo would feed him the names of the people running drugs across the Atlantic out of Miami."

"And they gave them to him?" Caine said incredulously.

"It was more like a swap. In return, Jamison gave the Americans some D15 assessment papers on graft in the Bahamas that made their Blue Lightning operation possible. Rather neat, really, a new twist on false-flag recruiting."

"Genevevo thought he was helping British intelligence to catch drug smugglers—"

"—while in fact Jamison was also passing the names of every federal undercover agent he got direct to his Soviet case officer, Arkady Semionov."

"Who in turn, no doubt, passed them straight to the Cubans."

"Something like that," Kingly said. "So one has to wonder, had Genevevo merely been duped, or turned?"

He pushed a six-inch-square envelope across the desk. Caine slid out the floppy disk and read the coded formula on the label: ISS/1/IT 300386/BABY—STATUS VIPAR. This told him that the interrogation transcript had been prepared at ISS/1, London, on March 30. Jamison's code name was "Baby," and the security classification meant its contents were highly restricted.

"I'd like to study this for a while," he told Kingly. "Can I use the visitor desk?"

"Get Betty to fix it," Kingly said. "Anything else you need?"

"No, nothing," Caine said. Kingly stood, ending the interview.

"Must get on," he said. "I've got a lunch date."

"Anyone interesting?"

Kingly gave him a frosty smile and Caine shrugged. Kingly had always been extremely cagey about his contacts, just as he was almost paranoid about leaving sensitive materials in plain sight. That was why his desk was always empty. Either that or he didn't trust even his closest associates, Caine thought. He picked up the file and went out, wishing now he'd taken another biscuit.

2 Caine spoke briefly to Betty Torre and then ambled along the corridor to the liaison office. The blue card in the slot outside the door told him the duty officer was Dick McClelland. He went in, and McClelland came across to meet him, smiling. He was like a jolly bear to look at, a big, grizzled man with a grin a yard wide. But the jolly-bear appearance was utterly deceptive: McClelland was one of the most astute officers in the Service.

"How are you, Dick?" Caine asked. "How's the book business?"

McClelland's wife, Diane, ran a bookshop which specialized in modern first editions. Caine had once bought a complete set of Ian Fleming's James Bond novels from them, all fine in mint-condition dust wrappers. Dick was always trying to buy them back.

"Prices keep going up and up since Joe Connolly wrote that book. I should think those Flemings of yours—"

"Save your breath, Dick." Caine smiled.

"Always worth asking." McClelland grinned. "What can I do for you?"

"Apart from a mint first of *The Godwulf Manuscript*, not a lot," Caine said. "Betty said I can use the visitor desk."

"I assume she'll have already cleared it with Arthur?" Arthur Cotton was head of Security. His responsibilities ranged from the use of the "safe room" to the maintenance of the twin remote-controlled Mossberg 500 Bullpup shotguns behind the reception desk.

He walked with Caine to the safe room at the end of the corridor, unlocked the door, and let him in. The room was simply furnished with a teak desk, a Naugahyde-covered swivel chair, and a desktop PC. There were no windows and no other exit.

"Anything else?" McClelland asked.

"See if you can raise Tom Crandon in Miami for me, will you?"

Caine closed the door and sat down. Switching on the IBM, he slid in the disk and waited while the computer hummed and buzzed. The screen lit, the cursor blinking on a warning: *Awaiting Authorized Access.*

All secret information stored on disks was scrambled. This meant that it would appear on the screen as a meaningless mess unless it was used in conjunction with a Cryptag security key like the one that Betty had given him. It was a resin block, six millimeters thick, which contained a radio receiver, transmitter, and microprocessor. He inserted it into the interrogator unit, keying in his own personal password. Because the tag was interactive, the computer would now have a record of who had used it and how much information had been requested.

The green-tinted screen filled with lines of information. Caine read the entire interrogation transcript through once, fast, then returned to the beginning and read it again, this time more slowly. He was into the fourth reading when the telephone on the desk beside him purred quietly.

"Miami," McClelland said.

"Secure the line," Caine told him. "Hello, Tom."

"Where are you?"

"Head office," Caine said. "Can you meet me tomorrow at your end? Fifteen hundred hours, Rendezvous Three?"

"No sweat," Crandon said. "You got something for me?"

"See you tomorrow," Caine said, and hung up. Tom Crandon was the ISS "specialist" in Miami. Within the firm, ranks were referred to in civilian terminology. Heads of sections (there were seven in the United States) were called "consultants." Each consultant controlled five intelligence officers known as "specialists," who in turn controlled a minimum of two, a maximum of six field agents called "technicians." Caine's section, F, covered the southeastern United States, with headquarters in Louisville, Kentucky, and specialists in Miami, Memphis, Birmingham, and Atlanta.

Caine hung up, then lifted the phone to call Eastern Airlines. He booked a one-way coach seat to Miami on EA 197, leaving National Airport at five-thirty. Next he called Sheraton and reserved a room at the River House near Miami International Airport. There was a Budget Rent A Car office a few blocks from the hotel. ISS expense accounts didn't run to renting cars at airport concessions.

He spent the rest of the afternoon reading and rereading the interrogation transcript. By the time he was finished, he could have recited everything Clive Jamison had told the K-7 interrogation team—dredgers, as they were known in the trade. K Section, which operated from an anonymous-looking building at the Euston Road end of Gower Street, was the liaison branch of D15 and D16. K-7, counterintelligence, was headed by the man who had brought Caine into the service, Colonel Peter Harland.

Caine switched off the computer and took the disk back to Kingly's office. Betty Torre told him Miles was still out. She took the disk and put it into the security slot which fed it directly into the safe, for which only Kingly had the combination.

Turning down Dick McClelland's offer of a lift, Caine checked out of the office and took a cab to the airport. It was three forty-five when he left; Kingly had still not returned from lunch. If the espionage business ever dried up, Caine thought, Miles could always get a job in publishing.

3 The midafternoon traffic was fairly light, and Caine made good time in the rented Omni. He paid the toll and rolled across the Rickenbacker Causeway toward Key Biscayne. Cormorants wheeled above the Marine Stadium. Sunshine glittered on the roofs of massed cars in the huge parking lots on the oceanside. The divided highway was lined with graceful coconut palms. Shortly after it became a two-way, Caine turned right on Harbor Drive and right again into the parking lot of the Yacht Club.

Despite its exclusive-sounding name, the bar and restaurant were open to the public. The bar looked out across the bay. It was decorated Trader Vic-style, with lobster baskets and cork floats. Tom Crandon was already there, sitting by the window and gazing pensively at the sailboats on the bright blue water.

He was a tall, well-built, good-looking man of thirty-three, with blond hair and blue eyes. He wore one of those shirts with no collar, a tan lightweight suit, and loafers with matching tan woven tops. He turned as Caine came in, and a wide grin banished the thoughtful expression.

"David!" he said, coming across to shake Caine's hand. "Let me get you a drink."

"I'll take a Beck's," Caine said to the bartender, a hulking young fellow with a Sundance Kid mustache and the beginnings of a beer gut. The bartender put the bottle and glass on the counter without a smile.

"Two fifty," he said.

"That include service?" Caine asked.

The bartender didn't answer. He took Crandon's five, banged the change down, and went back to his cronies down the bar. Caine grinned.

"Oops," Crandon said. "You hurt his feelings."

"I'm old enough to remember when people were polite down here," Caine said, pouring the beer.

"You think this is bad?" Crandon said. "Try the airport."

"I already did," Caine said. "Even the British are rude out there. What are they trying to do, give New York a good name?"

"You snowbirds are all the same," Crandon said. "Bitch, bitch, bitch. Why don't you stay up North where you belong?"

A snowbird, in local jargon, was one of the pale-skinned, pudgy creatures who flew down to Florida at the first sign of cold weather up North. "North" was a moveable feast: to a Miamian, Cape Canaveral was up North.

"They used to have ads in the papers, 'When you need it bad, we got it good,'" Caine said. "You remember that?"

"I'm too young," Crandon said. "I don't even remember the Beatles. Come on, let's go sit at a table."

The dining area was filled with round tables covered with checkered tablecloths that were supposed to give the place the atmosphere of a bistro. It was empty, as they had expected it to be. Nobody came here to eat at this time of day. The bleached-blond beach boys at the bar were talking spinnakers and trapezes, and evinced not the slightest interest in them.

"Okay," Crandon said, sipping his beer. "What's the panic?"

"A service job," Caine told him.

"You flew here from Washington to tell me you want a service job?"

"It's a special."

"It would have to be. Who's the subject?"

"CIA undercover operative, name of Tony Genevevo."

"What's special about him?"

"He might be a Comrade."

"What do we know about him?"

"He's Cuban-American. Born here in Miami. Divorced, with grown-up children. I've got a dossier for you."

He didn't tell Crandon anything about Jamison, or what Jamison had told K-7 about Genevevo. Crandon needed to know only the identity of the surveillance target.

"Okay, we can check him out. If he's Cuban, could be La Dirección has got an armlock on him."

Tom was using the nickname local Cubans used for DGI, the Cuban intelligence organization. Although it kept pretty busy in the Miami area, "La Dirección" was little more than a branch office of the KGB. Headed until 1985 by Ramiro Valdez, it was best known for its prize alumnus, Carlos the Jackal, who had been trained at a DGI camp in the Contramaestre Mountains in Cuba prior to being sent to Patrice Lumumba University in Moscow.

"How's your workload?" Caine asked.

"The usual," Crandon said. "Four or five legit jobs. You know about them. The rest's routine, mostly to do with drugs. You in Co-Caine city, babe."

"Anything special going down?"

"Word on the street is that there's a big one in the works. Which means big-big. It has to be, these days. Three years ago, a kilo of snow fetched between sixty and seventy-two thou. They're landing so much of the stuff now, the going price is down to between twenty and thirty, depending on the quality."

"Any idea who, what, where?"

"Nothing definite, but it doesn't seem to be any of the Colombian families."

"Why would the Company be interested?"

"Everybody else is," Crandon said. "We got the Florida Cocaine Task Force, the Drug Enforcement Agency, FBI, armed forces, state police, Christ alone knows who else down here, all falling over each other. It figures the Company would be in there someplace. I can find out.''

"How soon?"

Crandon looked at him judiciously. "A few days?"

"Be like Avis—try harder."

"Oooh, I get goose bumps when you're mean." Crandon grinned. "Okay, sooner. Earn my pension, right?"

"You won't live to draw a pension," Caine told him. "You'll screw yourself to death before you're forty."

Tom grinned. He had no ties, no wife, no mortgage, not even a steady girlfriend. He drove a very expensive car, he snorkeled in St. Martin, he skied in Zermatt, spending his money as fast as he earned it, sometimes faster. The all-American male: Hugh Hefner would be proud of him, Caine thought. Tom's life-style was a long way from being a low profile, but there were all sorts of covers, and Tom's seemed to work.

"That's the trouble with you old men," he said. "You see us younger guys living out your fantasies, and you're eaten up with jealousy."

"I don't have fantasies," Caine said. "I'm saving myself for Susan Silverman."

"Think she'd give you a tumble with me around?" Crandon scoffed, getting up out of his chair. "Fat chance."

They were both keen readers of Robert B. Parker's Spenser novels. Caine was trying to put together a set of first editions. Last time someone had offered him an early Parker they'd wanted a couple of hundred dollars for it.

"You want another beer?" Tom asked.

"Not at these prices," Caine said. "Let's get out of here, Tom. I want to get started on this Genevevo thing right away. The works: friends, politics, money, sex life. Whatever."

"Wouldn't all that be on his dossier at Langley?"

"We didn't pull it. Don't want to tip off Sam."

They walked out into the spring sunshine. A light breeze

came in off the bay. The steel-and-glass towers of Miami shone flat and hard across the water. It was the kind of day when shipping clerks dream of being millionaires.

"I might need to put on some extra people, David," Crandon said. "That okay?"

"Use your own judgment," Caine told him. "I want it fast, but I want it good."

"I'll get right on it. You want to have dinner later?"

"Fine."

"How does Joe's Stone Crab sound?"

"It goes *'eek, eek, eek.'*"

"You got a sense of humor like the Incredible Hulk," Crandon said. "I'll pick you up, okay? Where you staying—the River House again?"

"I'm kinky for fat tourists."

"You went to the right place." Crandon walked across to his car, a silver gray Porsche 944. All part of the golden-boy image, like the beach apartment, the four-hundred-dollar suits, the gold Oyster Perpetual. Caine smiled as Crandon revved the engine and roared away. He got into the little Dodge and headed back across the causeway to Miami. Two cars behind him, a couple of Cuban-Americans in a tan Thunderbird carefully matched their speed to his.

"You got trouble," Crandon said. "Right here in
River City."

It was Caine's third full day in Miami.
Hamstrung by Kingly's injunction not to alert Sam, there was
little he could do except cool his heels at the ISS office on
Biscayne Boulevard while Tom Crandon set up surveillance on
Tony Genevevo.

The office was a suite of three rooms in a fairly new building
opposite the public library. It was furnished in a style which
Crandon referred to as Filing Cabinet Modern, the walls decorated with photographic blowups of security equipment. Facing
the entrance was a roster of some of the Florida companies for
whom ISS acted as genuine security consultants. Crandon had a
small personal office across the hall from the "front." It was
functional and uncluttered—a desk, a divan, a low table, a couple of easy chairs, the usual electronic gadgets.

"What kind of trouble?" Caine asked.

"We're not the only ones watching Genevevo," Crandon
said.

"What?"

"That's exactly the way I felt when I found out. I thought
this was going to be a nice, simple service job, David. In, out,
easy-peasy."

"So did I," Caine said.

The preliminary investigation into Genevevo's background

had run into a brick wall. Crandon couldn't even get anything out of his police contacts downtown. Then he realized why: Genevevo was working for Pedro Avranilosa, a Cuban-born middleman who acted as ambassador for the South American cocaine dealers, putting them together with local buyers. Which meant one of only two things: either the Company had their man Genevevo in deep, deep cover, or he had gone over to the other side and the Americans knew it.

In such circumstances, putting Genevevo under surveillance was a very delicate operation: if he was working undercover and they blew him, they could get Genevevo killed. Avranilosa was dealing in ten-figure sums. Wasting an informer was small-change stuff.

The surveillance itself could not have been more difficult to set up if Genevevo had deliberately set out to frustrate it. His house was on South Lake Drive, facing the lake. There was no way to keep a van on the street for more than an hour or two at a time. The same applied to "sidewalkers": they stood out like spiders on a whitewashed wall on the wide, empty residential streets. Fortunately, Crandon's team had gotten lucky and obtained a short-term rental on a two-bed apartment on the next street, from whose back windows it was possible to obtain a clear view of Genevevo's house.

After all the bad luck, they got a break: on the third day of their surveillance, Crandon's watchers filmed a meet between Genevevo and his control, a Domestic Operations Division officer named Frank Forsyth. Domestic Ops involvement indicated that Langley suspected that El Gordo, Fat Man Avranilosa, might be involved with what Domestic Ops liked to call "foreign institutions."

"So Genevevo's watching Avranilosa, who is probably working for the Cubans. Okay," Caine said. "Then who is it watching Genevevo? His own people?"

"They're not Feds, David. It's not local cops either. I know most of the local boys. These guys are all Cubans. I don't know who the hell they are.''

"DGI? You think maybe the Fat Man's got his people checking Genevevo out?''

"It's possible.''

"Is Genevevo onto them?''

"He's doing a hell of an acting job if he is.''

"How did you spot them?''

"Pure accident,'' Crandon said. "Take a look.''

He pressed a button on the TV remote control. The big Mitsubishi rear-projection screen flickered to life, and the videorecorder began to turn. The video camera had been positioned inside a parked vehicle. Genevevo, a good-looking, compactly built Cuban-American, came out of his house and down the path to a blue 1985 Dodge Daytona. The camera stayed on him as he got into the car. His dark hair was cut very short and lay flat on his scalp like a yarmulke. He wore a seersucker jacket and dark blue slacks.

"Now watch,'' Crandon said.

Genevevo's Daytona rolled away down South Lake Drive, and then, from behind what would have been the cameraman's right shoulder, a black Lincoln Continental slid into the picture and moved off after the Dodge.

"The limo was a rental,'' Crandon said. "It was hired by a man who gave his name as Luis Echeverría, with an address in Hialeah. And in answer to your next question, no, nobody of that name lives there.''

"Didn't he show ID when he hired?''

"Driving permit.''

"Forged, of course. How did he pay? Credit card?''

"Stolen. They're pros.''

"Cubans. Pros. It's got to be La Dirección.''

"Say it is. Why are they watching Genevevo?''

"Because Avranilosa called them in?''

"If he suspected Genevevo, he'd just take him out. Why waste time having him watched?"

"There's a reason," Caine said. "We just haven't hit it yet. What else have your people come up with? Were you able to get peeps or sneakies into his place?"

Sneakies were listening devices, and peeps were cameras with fiber-optic lenses no bigger than the head of a pin, which could be pushed through the cracks in walls or the joints in floorboards.

"Didn't even try. Genevevo's a pro, too, David," Crandon reminded him. "We put an induction tap on his line, just in case, but he's not going to use the phone for anything sensitive."

"What are you using at the apartment?"

"I'm having to use shotgun mikes. They're not particularly effective, but at least they tell us when he's in the house."

"So what have we actually got on Genevevo?" Caine asked.

"He's got himself in like Flynn with the Fat Man. He handles all Avranilosa's collections, and that is *dinero, hombre*. No special male friends we've been able to spot. He lives high on the hog, higher than he could ever hope to live on a government salary."

"What about women?"

"He plays the field. Only one he sees regularly is a woman called Lynda Sanchez, who runs a restaurant over on Key Biscayne."

"And nothing to indicate he might be playing Comrades?"

"Nothing you could nail down."

"What have we got on Avranilosa?"

"El plenty," Crandon said.

Pedro Avranilosa was the son of an American sugar importer and a Cuban woman. Born in Santiago in 1938, he had attended Havana High School and gone on to the university.

"His family knew the Castros well. Pedro was a real

Fidelista,'' Crandon went on. "He was only twenty when they kicked Batista out. Then like a lot of others, he became disenchanted when Fidel started cozying up to the Russians. The U.S. government airlifted him out in 1965. The Company vetted him, of course—I've seen his records. He came in clean, but he's been playing dirty ever since. The local cops have rounded him up a few times on drug busts, but he's always walked away free.''

"And now Domestic Ops is interested. Why?"

"Could be a lot of things. Remember I told you there was word on the street that a really big deal is going down soon? That could be why Genevevo is in there. The Fat Man is a middleman, a fixer. Maybe he's connected to someone the Company is interested in. Maybe they think he's working for La Dirección.''

"Possible, I suppose," Caine said without enthusiasm. Cuban intelligence frequently filtered their agents into mainland Florida. That might explain Domestic Ops' interest in Avranilosa, but it provided no clues at all to why someone in London thought Genevevo was working for the Comrades.

"Guilt by association?"

"He wasn't working for the Fat Man then."

"What about this Lynda Sanchez you mentioned—have you talked to her?"

"Didn't want to tip Genevevo," Crandon said.

Caine sighed. "So we look at the surveillance films again."

"Ready when you are, C.B.," Crandon replied. He switched on the video again, and for the next four hours they watched Genevevo at work. As Crandon had said, their man was living the lush life. He went to all the glitter palaces in Miami Beach and Coconut Grove, and the smiling welcome he got everywhere indicated he was a big tipper. He had a private box at the Hialeah track, a boat at the Miamarina, a light plane at Opalocka.

"Who wants to be a millionaire?" Caine said.

"I do," Crandon replied.

They watched Genevevo going about his—or Avranilosa's—business. Hotels, used-car lots, pool halls, motels—like the trained operative he was, Genevevo made much use of bars, all-day porno cinemas, and massage parlors. Crandon's watchers were very good: they only lost him a couple of times.

"Here's the meet with Forsyth," Crandon said.

The film showed a man walking down a street. He was about fifty-five, stocky, undistinguished-looking. He wore a dark suit, a white shirt, and a neat tie. The only flamboyant touch was the bright ribbon hatband on his narrow-brimmed straw Stetson. Caine watched him duck into a massage parlor. The sign outside said WHO SAYS YOU CAN'T HAVE IT BOTH WAYS?

A few minutes later, Genevevo's blue Daytona pulled up. Genevevo got out, looked around casually, and then went inside. The clock superimposed on the top right-hand corner of the frame moved another ten minutes. Then Forsyth came out. Meet concluded, drop made, Caine thought.

"What do we know about Forsyth?" he asked.

"Been down here since 'eighty-two. The scuttlebutt is, he was drinking heavily and got demoted for insubordination. Around the same time, his wife walked out on him. If he'd kept his nose clean, he'd probably have his own station by now. But he's too much of a loner. You want me to switch this thing off?"

"It isn't telling us much," Caine said.

"I know," Crandon replied gloomily. "The trouble was, David, you told us to watch Genevevo, not to see if anyone was watching him."

"Have you got a cigarette?"

"I quit. I thought you did, too."

"I did," Caine said. "Only sometimes I get the urge to—" He sat up abruptly, staring at the screen. "Stop the tape."

"What?"

"Run the film back, Tom. Take it from the sweep of the street, before it picked up Forsyth."

When making surveillance films, the watchers usually "swept" the scene, so that the locale could be easily identified. Caine waited impatiently as Crandon rewound the tape and switched the machine back to play.

"Slow it down when you come to the pan," Caine said, leaning forward. "Now . . . wait . . . there. Freeze it."

The image on the screen was that of a short, wiry Cuban-American, walking toward the stakeout car. He had long sideburns and a gunfighter mustache. He wore mirror sunglasses, a cheap straw hat with the brim turned down all around, and a pink shirt with a domino motif instead of a breast pocket.

"That shirt," Caine said. "That domino shirt. I've seen it before."

"Jesus!" Crandon said. He knew what that meant. "Shall I run it through from the beginning?"

"No, wait," Caine said. "Give me a minute."

His head was spinning with the implications of what he had just seen. He pinched the bridge of his nose between his fingers and forced himself to concentrate. "The art gallery," he said. "Go back to the art gallery."

"Grove House," Crandon said, snapping his fingers. "I know the one you mean."

He pressed the eject button, took out the cassette, slid in another, waited while it sighed metallically into the slot, then put it on fast forward. Figures flickered across the screen like the chases in Keystone Kops one-reelers.

"Here it is," he said.

"Slow motion," Caine told him. The tape advanced jerkily, in single frames, the resolution poor. The camera was panning across the junction of Main and Poinciana Avenue. A tan Thunderbird turned into a parking slot a few bays ahead of the vehicle from which the film was being shot. A man got out of the T-bird and walked toward and past the cameraman's point of view.

"Shit!" Crandon said disgustedly. "It's him. Domino Shirt."

"When was this film shot?"

Crandon looked at the logbook. "Yesterday morning."

"Who took it?"

"Butch Young. Len Wurzel was driving."

"Where are they now?"

"At the apartment. Coral Way Village."

"Are they armed?"

"What the hell would they be armed for?"

"I think we'd better pull them out, Tom," Caine said. "I don't like the way this is shaping up."

"No sweat," Crandon said, but he was sweating and so was Caine. He dialed the apartment and let the phone ring just once, then hung up. That would tell his men to leave the place immediately and call in from a public phone as quickly as they could.

They waited.

Nobody called. After ten minutes, Caine stood up.

"We're blown, Tom," he said.

He grabbed his jacket and the ASP Smith & Wesson M39 combat pistol in its shoulder holster, then ran out of the room and down the stairs, not bothering to wait for the elevator. Behind him, he heard Crandon yelling into the phone.

5 The sleek white Lincoln Continental Mark VII slid onto Broad Causeway and across the narrow neck of Biscayne Bay. It headed through Bay Harbor Islands and on until it reached the ocean at Collins Avenue.

The man in the rear seat was a good-looking Cuban of thirty-two or thirty-three, with dark hair and coffee-colored skin. He wore a pale blue Gianni Versace cashmere jacket, dark blue slacks of imported mohair, a pale blue open-necked silk shirt with a monogram on the breast pocket, and neat Bruno Magli loafers. On his wrist was a heavy gold Cartier watch with a crocodile strap; around his neck was a fine solid-gold chain.

At first glance, he might have been taken for one of the new breed of successful Cuban-American entrepreneurs who have grown rich with the latinization of Miami: he had that same, sleek "made-it" confidence. But Saturnino Baca was no run-of-the-mill businessman. That was why, nestling in a spring clip beside him in the door recess, was a 9mm Smith & Wesson automatic pistol. All perfectly legal, of course—Florida law permitted residents to carry handguns in their cars—but in Baca's case, a necessary precaution, even on an errand as ostensibly safe as this. For Saturnino Baca, "Mr B." as he was known on Calle Ocho, was head of the most powerful Cuban family in Miami, and his businesses were those of extortion, prostitution, and drugs.

The limo rolled on through picture-postcard scenery of languid coconut palms and lush tropical greenery. The sky was a brilliant blue, with hardly a cloud in sight. Past Balfour the driver made a left and came to a stop at the entrance to the Bal Harbour Estate, a palm-thatched wooden gatehouse with a striped pole like a frontier post. A red-and-white octagonal sign said STOP HERE.

The security guard came out of the gatehouse. He wore a white shirt with dark blue epaulettes, white slacks, and a white pith helmet. On his left sleeve was a shield-shaped patch which bore the name of the security company he worked for. Around his bulging middle was a tan leather belt and a holster holding a .357 Magnum Mark III Lawman Colt. He bent down as the chauffeur rolled down the tinted window.

"Hi, Chico. Hello, Mr. Baca," he said, touching the brim of his helmet. "Go right on through. You're expected."

The man in the back of the car nodded, and they drove on. The whole estate was like a park, maintained without regard for cost. The sidewalks were litter-free, and there were no fallen coconuts or palm fronds in the road. Antispeed ramps kept the big car to a ten-mile-per-hour crawl. Here and there, sun-stark white walls peeped through high hedges or banks of flowering plants. Once in a while, they passed an ornate wrought-iron gate, or a driveway leading toward a large mansion half-hidden behind palmetto and buttonwood trees.

"You see the piece that asshole at the gate had, Chico?" Baca said to his driver.

"I seen it, Mr. B," Chico grinned. "Old fart ever fire that thing, it gonna break his arm."

The limo turned left into Hibiscus Close, following the road until it ended in a cul-de-sac, then stopped at a pillared gateway. The chauffeur got out, taking a telephone from a recess in the pillar. He listened, spoke, nodded, and put the phone back on the hook. The heavy gates swung open. A CCTV camera watched them as they drove in.

The house was huge, all white, with red roof tiles and green shutters on every window. The drive led to a turning circle with a covered walkway leading to the house. The garage doors were open: inside stood a Mercedes 300SL convertible and a Bentley Mulsanne. A smiling Chinese manservant came out of the house.

"Good day, Mr. Baca," he said. "This way, please."

Baca followed him up the walkway, through a foyer, and out to the huge patio at the rear of the house. Wide fieldstone steps sloped gently down from it to an Olympic-sized swimming pool set among manicured lawns that stretched all the way down to the boat dock fronting the bay. Across the glittering water, the skyscrapers of Miami stood stark against the empty sky.

The rear part of the house was a wall of glass, fifty feet wide and eighteen feet high, open now so that the inside and outside living areas were one. The floor of the enormous room inside was of imported marble. Twelve thousand square feet of house, with four and a half acres of land around it enclosing tennis courts, staff quarters, guest cabins. For a guy who had never taken a risk in his life, Baca thought, Avranilosa was doing all right. His host came out of the living room, a drink in his hand and a smile on his face.

"Nino!" Pedro Avranilosa said. "Good to see you, hombre."

He was a big man who had gone fat. He had black hair, dark brown eyes, and the swarthy skin of a mestizo. He wore a La-Coste sport shirt, tan slacks, and Gucci loafers. On his wrist was a solid-gold Rolex Explorer. A diamond twinkled on his ring finger as he beckoned the waiting houseboy.

"Lemme have a Pisco sour," Baca said. As the servant padded away, Avranilosa waved a hand toward a table and chairs in the shade. They were made of white-painted metal, with brilliantly colored cushions on the chairs. A huge beach umbrella with the same pattern was bent at an angle to keep the sun away.

"Listen, Nino, I want to thank you for coming out here," Avranilosa said. "I appreciate it."

"You said it was urgent."

"Damn right, it's urgent," the Fat Man said. "I got a big problem, Nino. I just found out Tony Genevevo is a cop. A goddamn Fed."

"What?"

"It's true. That's why I called you."

"I don't believe this," Baca said disgustedly. "I don't believe what I'm hearing here. You're telling me the last— what?—fifteen, eighteen months, right?—the fuckin' Feds have had a line in here? Thanks to somebody you brought in?"

"Nino, listen to me," Avranilosa pleaded. "I know what you're thinking, but it's not as bad as it looks."

"You think so?" Baca snarled. "We're talking a sixty-million-dollar deal, the Feds are listening to every word, but you don't think it's as bad as it looks. Is that what you're saying?"

Avranilosa silently cursed Havana for getting him into this. It was like walking on razor edges. But he danced to Havana's tune just as Havana danced to Moscow's music, and if Havana wanted this Frederic Drosdow introduced to Baca as a Turkish cocaine dealer working out of Bogotá, Avranilosa didn't have much option but to do it. He had once asked Drosdow what the deal was all about. Drosdow just looked at him. "You don't need to know that," he said. "Just do it."

"Nino, listen," Avranilosa said placatingly. "I talked to Drosdow. He says if we play this right, it can still go down."

"Drosdow wants me to buy sixty mill of snow with some fuckin' cop taking pictures?" Baca said angrily. "What are you, crazy?"

Avranilosa held up a finger as the Chinese houseboy came out with Baca's drink. They waited until he had gone back into the house.

"When Drosdow told me Genevevo was a Fed, I told him he

was out of his tree," Avranilosa said. "I brought him in off the street, taught him the business. He was good. You said so yourself, Nino."

"I know, I know," Baca said grudgingly. "And it was true. I never seen anyone could keep the peace between our people and the Colombians like Tony Genevevo. You say Drosdow fingered him? How the fuck does he know so much?"

"Drosdow said his source was impeccable," Avranilosa said. "I couldn't afford not to check it out. I put some of my people on him, and they spotted him making a meet with a CIA field man name of Forsyth. My first instinct was to waste him."

"Uh-uh," Baca said. "The Feds react very bad when one of their people gets blown away."

"I know. But I figured it was my responsibility. I brought him in. I was still thinking about it when my people picked up a secondary surveillance."

"On Genevevo?"

"I didn't believe it myself at first. But it's true: some rent-a-cop outfit called International Security Systems has a team watching Genevevo."

"What the fuck is this, Pedro? What the fuck is goin' on here?"

"I don't know. All I know is somebody's paying a security firm to watch Genevevo. The Feds got more undercover agencies in Florida than the rest of the country put together. It could be anyone: DEA, Task Force, Miami cops, state police—"

"It could be Disney fucking Enterprises," Baca said impatiently. He stood up, getting ready to go. "It doesn't make any difference. You tell Drosdow I'm out, *comprende*?"

"Nino, listen, don't fly off the handle," Avranilosa said placatingly. "Let's try to find a way through this. I talked to Drosdow. He says—"

"Drosdow, Drosdow!" Baca said impatiently. "That goddamned go-between! What the fuck does he know?"

"Give me a minute," Avranilosa pleaded. "A couple of minutes of your time. Is that too much to ask?"

Baca looked at the skyscrapers across the water, as if the view could help him decide. He shrugged and sat down again. "All right. What?"

"There's a way through this, Nino. A way we take out Genevevo, shake off these other people, and come out of it clean."

"He's a Fed. You waste him, they'll take Miami to pieces. Didn't you read about that DEA agent that got killed in Guadalajara?"

"There's a way," Avranilosa said. "If you still want to go through with the cocaine deal."

Avranilosa watched Baca carefully. He knew Baca needed the cocaine deal desperately: the Colombian families were making heavy inroads into what had formerly been exclusively Cuban territory. Baca nodded, indicating he should continue.

"Here's what we do," he said.

Going slowly, making sure Baca understood every nuance, Avranilosa told Baca what Frederic Drosdow had instructed him to tell the gang boss. It figured Genevevo had already passed the word to the Feds that a deal was going down, he said. That was okay: Genevevo didn't know how big the thing was yet. He watched Baca closely as he went on, outlining the way the whole thing could be handled. Baca nodded, wary interest in his eyes. Maybe Drosdow had been right, Avranilosa thought. Maybe Baca would go for it after all. He'd told Drosdow there wasn't a chance in hell he would, but it was beginning to look like Drosdow had been right and he had been wrong. The trick, Drosdow had told him when they'd discussed the proposition earlier that day, was to tell Baca everything he needed to know, but not *every*thing.

"How will Baca react to the news about Genevevo?" Drosdow had asked.

"He'll want to walk away from the whole deal."

"That can't be permitted," Drosdow said flatly.

"Now all we got to do is convince Baca," Avranilosa said. Drosdow stared at him with those empty blue eyes, and Avranilosa instantly regretted his jibe.

"Suppose we terminate Genevevo," Drosdow said. "Would that satisfy him?"

"Take Genevevo out and you'll have ten thousand cops up your ass before you can say FBI," Avranilosa said scornfully.

"Not my way," Drosdow said.

"What have you got in mind?"

"Chaos," Drosdow said.

He explained his plan. There was no doubt it would work, he said, if they could get Baca to go for it. As long as the Cubans didn't stage one of those Marielito chain-saw massacres they were so fond of, they could do their deal and walk away from it clean, with no DGI involvement and nothing to tie them to it.

"That's the way I want it," Drosdow said, as if daring him to argue. "You sell it to Baca."

Avranilosa nodded his agreement: not that he had much choice. He wished he had the courage to tell Drosdow to take a flying fuck at a jumping marlin, but he did not dare. One word from this cold-eyed *sinvergüenza* and Pedro Avranilosa would spend the rest of his life cutting sugar cane back on the island.

He did not like Frederic Drosdow, nor did he trust him: if any of this went wrong, it was for Pedro Avranilosa that Saturnino Baca would come looking, not Frederic Drosdow, who would by then be long gone. It was quite one thing for Nino to suspect but tolerate Avranilosa's "connection" to Cuban intelligence in Havana. It would be quite another if Baca thought he himself was being manipulated by them.

"Well?" Avranilosa said now as he finished laying out Drosdow's plan for Baca. "What do you think?"

"I like it," Baca said. "Chaos. That's good. I like it."

"Do I tell Drosdow to go ahead?"

"Yeah," Baca said. "Tell him we can handle our end. Tell him to just make sure he handles his."

"I'll pass the word," Avranilosa said, hoping he was concealing his relief. "How long do you think it will take to set up?"

"Coupla days," Baca said. He shook his head, chuckling. "Chaos. You got to hand it to that fucking Drosdow. He knows the way we operate."

If you only knew, Avranilosa thought, remembering how sure Drosdow had been that Baca would take the bait. There was no way you could overestimate a Marielito's greed, Drosdow had said. Avranilosa could still hear the contempt in his voice.

Crandon's Porsche was an easy car to follow. Caine knew that. He also knew it made him very hard to catch if he didn't want to be caught. It was about three times faster off the mark than an American car, particularly one as soft-sprung and power-steered as the Buick Electra which was following him now.

Just past Flagler Memorial Park, SW Fifty-fifth Avenue Road cut diagonally away to the left. Caine made the left and rolled down to a junction where six streets met: Fifty-sixth going north-south, Second going east-west, and the road he was on cutting diagonally across the intersection. He stopped at the junction and checked his mirror, smiling as he saw the Buick coast to a stop by the curb a hundred yards back.

He put the Porsche into gear, floored the gas pedal and spun the wheel, using the handbrake to execute a 135-degree turn onto Fifty-sixth Avenue, pointing north. A block up, he turned left onto 1st Street and then left again on Fifty-seventh going south. He was half a mile away before the driver of the Buick even worked out which way he might have gone. At the bottom of Red Road—the old name for Fifty-seventh—he turned right into Fortieth, sped past Tropical Park Garden, and took Seventy-fifth across the canal and onto the man-made island.

It was early evening. He drove as slowly as a pensioner toward the apartment block on SW Seventy-second Court, half expecting to encounter flashing police lights, but apart from a mother pushing a baby buggy loaded with groceries, the street was empty. The curtains in the first-floor apartment were still drawn. Young's VW Rabbit was still in its slot.

Caine got out of the car, leaving it open. Nothing for it but a blind walk-in, he decided. If there were Foreigners in the apartment, he would have to handle it. He glanced at his watch: seven-ten. He unbuttoned his jacket for easier access to the shoulder holster, then went into the building. The apartment was on the right at the head of the stairs. Using his own keys, he opened the door.

Silence.

Easing his ASP out of its holster, Caine moved into the corridor which bisected the apartment. The door of the living room was on his right. Taking a deep breath, he grasped the handle firmly, then went in all at once, fast and low and with the gun up ready.

There was no one there.

He stood upright, his breath coming raggedly now in the reaction. There were no signs of a struggle. The surveillance equipment was all where it was supposed to be. He checked the videotape boxes. They were all empty, as were the tape spools on the Akai. There was no film in any of the cameras.

Swiftly, silently, he checked the other rooms. All were empty, their tidiness mocking him. He went to the window and checked the street outside. It would not be long before whoever had been tailing him figured out his probable destination. They might have even put a beeper on the car: he'd had no time to check.

He ran downstairs and got into the Porsche, driving as fast as he dared off the island and down to Bird Road, the local name for Fortieth Street. He pulled into a Mobil station and ran for the phone booth.

"Any word?"

"All hell's broken loose, David," Crandon replied. "Where are you?"

"Near Tropical Park. Tell me."

"Genevevo's been lifted."

"What? When was this?"

"Couple hours back, near his home. Six heavies, all Cuban. They were driving—"

"Never mind that!" Caine said. "Who's on them?"

"Pete Lavery," Crandon told him. "He just called in. Says they took Genevevo to a warehouse up near the airport. Acme Novelty, 1888 Northwest Twenty-ninth Street."

"Tom, the shit's hit it. The apartment has been sanitized. No sign of our people."

"Jesus, David, you think—?"

"I'll back up Lavery," Caine said.

"I'll meet you there."

"No, Tom!" Caine said. "Stay put!" He hung up before Crandon could argue. He ran for the Porsche and burned rubber getting back onto the street. When Crandon thought about it, he would realize he had to stay where he was: with both of them on the street, no one at ISS would know what was going on. He drove fast and decisively, praying no rookie cop with a low arrest record would pick him up. Heavy traffic in Coral Gables slowed him down, and he cursed in frustration, willing himself back under control. The easiest way to total a motor was to drive with your teeth clamped together.

He turned north on Douglas and was able to make better time on the wide avenue. Off to his left, the lights of the hospital gleamed brightly in the growing twilight. He turned left at the Tamiami bridge and saw the frontage of the Sheraton River House looming up ahead. On his right lay an industrial area, with single-story units that housed building firms, cleaning companies, and storage warehouses, all girded by the tracks of the Seaboard Coast Line railroad.

He parked the Porsche out of sight behind a building and walked up to Twenty-ninth Street, keeping in the shadows. The street was deserted and dark, except for one building on the opposite side. ACME NOVELTY, he read on the sign above the entrance.

A small sound caught his attention, and he saw Lavery in the dark entrance to a garage alongside an office building. The agent was wearing a Parrot Jungle T-shirt, oil-stained chino pants, battered Nike training shoes, and a plastic baseball cap from Disney World. Lavery, a thin-faced beanpole of a man, looked and sounded like anything but what he was, a cum laude graduate of the University of Miami who had chosen security work in preference to being the token black in a WASP law practice.

"They're in there, boss," he said, pointing at the lighted windows on the second floor of the Acme Novelty building.

"How many of them?"

"Six in the car. Other cars there already. What's happenin', man?"

"They took Genevevo in there?"

"Right. He was in no shape to argue."

"You didn't see anyone else?"

"Like who?"

"Lennie Wurzel and Butch Young are missing."

Caine scanned the building opposite, wishing there was something he could do. A shotgun mike would have been useful: at least they might have been able to hear what was going on inside. As it was, there was no way of getting closer to the Acme building without being spotted.

"Got any suggestions, Pete?"

"Bet your ass," Lavery said in the darkness. "Less get the fuck out of here."

"You looked around already?"

"Some," Lavery said. "Nothing special about the place. It's L-shaped, long side facing the street. Parking in back, seven-foot wire fence topped with barbed wire in back of that. Freight yard beyond it. See that furniture place next door? There's a alley runs between the two buildings, used as a freight entrance. Dead end. That's it.''

It was black-dark now. Once in a while, a big jet roared up into the sky from Miami International, its navigation lights winking like moving stars. An hour went by. Nothing happened.

"I could kill for some coffee," Lavery said.

"Where's your car?"

"End of the street, near Le Jeune." He pronounced it "Lee-June," Miami-style. They fell silent. The lights of the office across the street seemed artificially bright. The windows were curtained with white nylon net. Caine looked at his watch. Nearly ten.

"We got action!" Lavery hissed urgently.

A man came out of the Acme building. He could not see them. He went around back, and they heard a car start up. Lights sliced through the darkness. Genevevo's Daytona swung into the dead-end alley. They heard the *graaack* of the emergency brake. The driver got out, leaving the headlights on, and went back into the building. A few minutes later, the lights in the upstairs offices went out. The watchers heard voices, footsteps. The doors were opened, and they saw Young and Wurzel being frog-marched into the alley where the Daytona was parked. When they got into the beam of the headlights, the watchers could see blood on Young's face. Wurzel was slumped in the grip of the two men holding his arms.

Next, two men came out of the building carrying a body. One of them opened the driver's door of the Daytona and put the limp figure in the driving seat. It did not move.

"That's Genevevo!" Lavery hissed.

"I count nine of them, Pete," Caine said. The ASP held seven rounds. He knew Lavery was not armed. There probably wasn't a telephone nearer than six blocks away.

"We got to do some—"

The sound of a single pistol shot silenced him. One of the

Cubans had shot Genevevo through the forehead. Almost simultaneously, another shot was fired. Wurzel was slammed back against the wall of the building, then slid down it into a sitting sprawl, dead before he stopped moving. Young made a clumsy grab at the man with the gun. The man shot him, too hastily. The bullet tore through Young's throat, smacking him sideways off his feet, kicking and flopping like a gutshot squirrel. The assassin skipped back to avoid being spattered with blood.

"Jesus Christ!" Lavery muttered.

"Okay, let's go!" someone shouted. They ran out of the alley and into the parking lot. Car doors slammed; then two cars lurched out of the lot and turned on the deserted street. Their headlights swept over the prone bodies of Caine and Lavery, flat on their bellies in a patch of scrub.

"I got the lead car," Caine said, memorizing its license number, knowing Lavery would do the same with the second. Tail lights glowed briefly as the two cars braked on the corner of Le Jeune. Then they were gone. Cicadas burred again in the warm darkness.

"Come on," Caine said urgently. "We can't get ourselves tied into this, Pete."

"What about Wurzel and Young? What about Genevevo?"

"They're dead," Caine said harshly. "There's nothing we can do for them."

"And that's it? You just going to leave them there?"

"I'll call the police first chance I get," Caine said. "You get back to town and tell Tom Crandon exactly what happened. Tell him to get a make on those two cars. I'll contact him tomorrow. Got that?"

"Jesus fuckin' Christ," Lavery breathed. "You coldhearted bastard!"

Caine looked at Lavery for a moment. "Let's go," he said.

7

By the time Dade County's finest reached the scene of the killings—tipped off by an anonymous phone call—all three corpses had been stripped. The guns, of course, were gone. Wallets, credit cards, everything. The trunk of Genevevo's Daytona had been prized open, the spare wheel and the tools taken. The thieves had even taken the shoes off the dead men's feet. None of that surprised the prowl-car boys. There were street vultures in Miami that made the ones in the Everglades look like lovebirds.

The blues found Genevevo lying half in and half out of his car, and most of his brains on the rear window. Sprawled on the ground nearby was the body of another man. A third lay crumpled against the wall of the alley, between Acme Novelty and the Merritt Furniture Repository.

The two men were identified by their fingerprints as Leonard Wurzel and Robert Young, employees of a Miami company called International Security Systems. Each of them had been shot once: Wurzel through the upper chest just above the heart, and Young through the throat. The ME's report said that Wurzel would have died almost instantly, whereas Young might have lived two or three minutes after he was shot. Preliminary ballistics findings indicated that two weapons had been used: both .38s.

The physical evidence posited the following scenario: Genevevo had met the two security men in the alley, possibly to

48 ▪

consummate a drug sale—there were traces of cocaine on the carpet of the Daytona. A shoot-out had ensued in which Genevevo killed Wurzel and fatally wounded Young without being hit. Then somehow Young, bleeding like a stuck pig, had put a bullet through Genevevo's head at close range.

Thomas Crandon, who ran the Miami branch of the security firm, said his people had been on a simple surveillance case in Coral Gables. The client was a major credit company. He knew of no reason why his men should have met with Genevevo, who formed no part of their investigation. As for the shooting: it was against ISS policy for its personnel to carry firearms, although all were licensed to do so. He was shocked by what had happened, he said. It made no sense at all.

"No sense?" Frank Forsyth said, throwing the police dossier he'd "borrowed" on the floor in disgust. "Goddamnit, it sucks!"

Damned if he didn't sometimes wish he was a thousand miles away from Miami, away from his chief of station Donald Bensen, and most of all, away from the drug scene. For all the newspaper headlines, drugs were at the not very important end of Company business: the CIA was spending more on covert operations in Afghanistan than the entire Federal antidrug budget. So being at the not very important end of drug investigating did not carry a hell of a lot of clout at best, and if you were Frank Forsyth, even less.

He had been transferred to Miami in 1982, part of Shotgun Reagan's high-profile Operation Thunderbolt, "the most massive war on drugs ever seen." It had involved teaming Army, Naval and Air Force intelligence, Pentagon spy planes, the FBI, the DEA, and God alone knew who else. The thunderbolt had turned out to be a wet wick; far from wiping out the drug traffic, it seemed to have had the opposite effect. What had been a $30 billion industry in 1981 was now estimated to be turning over four times that much. Trying to stamp it out was like trying to put out hell with a bucket of spit. The men who controlled the drug rackets could buy the world and still have change. Whoever they couldn't bribe or buy outright, they simply ran right over. Which, Forsyth was certain, was what had happened to Tony Genevevo.

For the past year and a half, Genevevo had been working undercover, feeding information on Avranilosa's Cuban intelligence contacts and narcotics dealings through Forsyth to Domestic Operations in Washington. Forsyth had put up the proposition that the Fat Man was high enough in DGI's Cuban hierarchy to be worth trying to "double," and Tony had gone in undercover to send out enough information to make it possible. Somehow, God alone knew how, his cover had been blown, and now he was dead. And no matter what the police report said, Forsyth knew whose finger had been on the trigger.

Well, that was Pedro Avranilosa's mistake. When Forsyth had first come to Miami, embittered over what he still felt had been an unfair demotion, the only human being he found in the entire regional organization was Tony Genevevo—big, lanky Tony who'd buy him a drink, agree with him that Donald Bensen was full of what made the grass grow green, then take him off to some Cuban bordello and get him laid. He figured he owed Tony, and he planned to pay off.

He leaned over and picked up the report Mickey Garrity down at police headquarters had copied for him, found his place again, and read the rest. A check had been made on Crandon's story, of course, and it held up. ISS had been employed by a New York credit company to report on a number of Miami corporations which were being remiss in loan payments. The list of the companies involved provided no clues. Until somebody could prove otherwise, they were clean.

There was a missing factor someplace, Forsyth thought. Like a signpost in a fog: it was there but he just couldn't see it. Any way you examined the killings, they came out looking like an execution. And if it had been an execution, it had to be Avranilosa's people who had carried it out. He could see where they might kill Genevevo if somehow they found out he was a cop. So Question Number One was, how did they find out? And Question Number Two was, why ice the security men along with him?

Forsyth didn't do many things by the book, but this time he did. He handed the case over to the Sewer Squad, leaving that unsung Company department to tidy up the mess. They would liaise with the Miami police, take care of the funeral arrangements, tie up the loose ends. Anyone on the team killed in the line of duty was always decently taken care of. Meanwhile, he had things to do.

Forsyth knew his reputation as a maverick was not entirely unjustified. He preferred working outside the system because he knew how the system worked, and how it worked was inefficiently. The system was in the hands of people like his chief of station, who would trade ten men like Genevevo for a jacket commendation, and sell his grandmother to a Chilean whoremaster for an overseas posting. So although Genevevo's murder had set off one of the biggest police operations in Miami history, Forsyth wasn't optimistic about the possible results. If anyone had asked him, he'd have told them not to waste their time. The police could question every deadbeat in the sovereign state of Florida and they'd get no nearer to Tony's executioners than they were right now. Forsyth planned to kill his own snakes.

He admitted—to himself, no one else, and especially not his boss, Bensen—that he'd been worried about Genevevo. Tony had been "out" a long time, and latterly he hadn't been delivering the way he was supposed to. Forsyth had covered for him, wondering whether it was the right thing to do, but understanding better than most the pressures Genevevo was under.

There was a hell of a difference between how you lived on government pay and how you lived working for the Fat Man. Working for Avranilosa got you a fancy pad in Kendall, a white Mercedes convertible, a boat, a plane, and all the pussy you wanted to stroke. Working for Avranilosa got you reservations in fancy beachside restaurants where fawning maître d's greeted you by name and told you how happy they were to see you. It got harder and harder to remember you were a cop, dedicated to bringing all this down on the heads of the people you were sharing it with. The last time they'd talked, Forsyth remembered wondering: does he *want* to come out?

Can he?

Genevevo's assignment was simple: to catch the Fat Man with his feet in the snow, then turn him around. Threaten to take away the house in Bal Harbour, the lithe young Cuban waiters he liked to entertain there; promise him twelve to twenty in the black wing at Tallahassee; and he'd crack. With the Fat Man in their pockets, they might be able to infiltrate DGI operations in Miami and southeast Florida, roll up Avranilosa's drug interests, and maybe as a bonus get an inside line on what the Comrades were up to in other parts of the country.

That was the proposition before Genevevo was killed. Go on, say it, Forsyth told himself: shot in the head, executed, assassinated. That was what didn't make sense. Espionage agencies went to extreme lengths to avoid assassination. Killing the other side's men threw a monkey wrench into the machinery: the game wasn't played that way. Counterespionage was a *react* discipline. You watched your quarry, waited till he made an overt move; then you responded to it. That way you found out whether his move had been made to provoke yours, or not. When you knew that, you watched and waited to see what he would do next. According to what it was, you reacted again; and so on. Chess, played with live pawns.

And now dead ones, Forsyth thought.

Of course, he knew what Bensen would say: that irrespective of Genevevo's death, their aims remained the same—to find a way of compromising Avranilosa, and if he really was working for DGI, to turn him. He would consider Forsyth's personal involvement unwise and unprofessional, so Forsyth had no intention of letting Bensen know how he felt.

Before he did anything else, however, Forsyth needed to know whether he, too, had been blown. Unlikely as it was, he took all the routine precautions. He closed down his apartment in Coral Gables and checked into the Holiday Inn at the Civic Center under the name of Cecil Smith. He verified with the Sewer Squad that the house on South Lake Drive and Genevevo's car had been properly vacuumed. They hadn't found anything, but then they hadn't expected to. Their job was to make sure there was nothing there for anyone else to find.

After two days, during which the watchers in Coral Gables reported nil activity, he called them off. He had decided anyway to abandon that possibly compromised identity. In due course, the apartment would be put up for sale by a Company realty front, and the neighbors would be told of an unexpected transfer abroad. The Joe Roberts who had lived there briefly would soon be forgotten.

Next Forsyth checked with Bensen. Given the choice, he would rather have eaten glass, but he knew if he wanted to get back in harness, he had to have Bensen's clearance. He called the office on Brickell Avenue.

"What have you got in mind?" Bensen asked.

"Among other things, I want to check out this security firm."

"Haven't the police done that?"

"Not the way I'll do it," Forsyth said.

"You think there's something there?"

"I don't know where else to look."

"All right," Bensen said. "I'll get you operational clearance." He sounded reluctant. Maybe he thinks he's doing me a favor, Forsyth thought.

ISS was as good a place to start as any. He recalled the old Company saying: if God had expected you to know all the answers, he wouldn't have invented the head office. Smiling at the thought, he sat down to compile a shopping list. He used the same pay phone to dictate it to a coding clerk at Vanguard. Within an hour, it was being transmitted via the CIA's protected computer circuit to the office of the divisional director of the Domestic Operations Division on Pennsylvania Avenue in Washington, D.C.

8 Forsyth's signal was logged on the Domestic Operations computer at 11:04 and sent immediately to the office of the divisional director. A simultaneous printout at CIA headquarters on its wooded 125-acre site at Langley, eight miles from the capital, was taken by internal courier to the office of the area divisional controller. This procedure, in Langley as at the Pennsylvania Avenue building which housed the Domestic Operations Division, involved the negotiation of numerous gates guarded by Internal Security officers in bulletproof glass kiosks. At these gates, each courier's ID badge was carefully checked for the appropriate security clearances.

On receipt, Forsyth's requests were graded for priority and authorization; since they appeared mainly routine, they were rerouted from the office of the director to the coordinator of information, Stephen Greene. Greene was a suntanned man of fifty-nine with neat, unsmiling features and iron gray eyes which occasionally—but only occasionally—betrayed a faint hint of amusement. He did not drink anything stronger than tea. He smoked three cigarettes a day, no more, no less. He ran five miles every morning without fail.

Forsyth's signal was just one of many requiring his authorization that day. Immediately after he finished reading it, Greene picked up the direct phone link and spoke to his opposite number in Clandestine Services. CICS said he knew of no reason why the information should not be made available to Miami, whereupon Greene endorsed Forsyth's request for action and passed it to the Office of Communications in its IBM-designed underground bunker.

A copy was also sent to Intelligence Requirements Service, a division of the Directorate of Intelligence, asking for their input. By three that afternoon, the computers had correlated and printed out their information, ready for pretransmission coding prior to being sent to Forsyth in Florida. The dossier was then directed to the Pretransmission Coding Section, where it arrived finally on the desk of Paul Bogdanovich, the senior of three coding clerks in Office PTC/D/2857 on Level Four. Bogdanovich set to work immediately.

After first keying in the secret access codes which would protect the computer transmission, he began enciphering the dossier. It was a long and boring job, but all of Bogdanovich's work was boring if you cared to look at it that way. He did not. There was always the element of the unexpected in PTC. And always the strange, inexplicable satisfaction of watching the powerful computers turn page after page of secret text into something that might easily have been Martian.

The material he was handling today was of more than usual interest. It was generally understood that the CIA was not permitted to operate within the United States, although in fact, anyone with a knowledge of intelligence operations knew this was nonsense. A whole area division, Domestic Operations, conducted clandestine activities in the United States, not overseas. Exactly what those activities were was classified information; and because he knew this, Bogdanovich's interest was immediately aroused. He was further intrigued by Forsyth's request for a full personnel breakdown on a British-owned security company operating in Miami. A familiar thrill of nervous anticipation coursed through his body as it always did at times like these.

He worked steadily until he had completed coding all the documents. When this was done, he picked up the phone on his desk and dialed the office of the coordinator of information, which gave him clearance to transmit to Miami. As soon as the transmission was effected and acknowledged, the computer memory was to be cleared and the unenciphered originals returned to their various points of origin.

While the computer hummed and buzzed, transmitting direct to Miami, Bogdanovich prepared security folders with Alpha Black tabs denoting the security rating of the material they would contain. He then took the working papers he had used to encipher the dossier and pushed them into the shredder, watching impassively as they turned into paper spaghetti. Without haste or hesitation, he took the unenciphered dossier and slid it into his briefcase. Into the security folders he had earlier prepared, he now placed a set of completely unrelated documents. He placed the folder in his OUT tray for courier pickup and pressed the button which would summon the messenger. A few minutes later, the courier arrived, signed for the documents, and hurried away. Bogdanovich looked at the clock. His shift would be ending in an hour and twenty minutes.

He waited until Miami acknowledged that the transmission had been received and safely stored, then cleared the computer's memory. He continued working steadily until the bell that marked the end of the second of the day's three shifts rang, a frown of concentration on his face. He went through his end-of-shift routine carefully, as if it were for the first time. He put all his disks, papers, and codebooks into the safe behind his desk, spinning the dials of the combination lock. He checked that the disk slots in the computer were empty and the memory cleared. He then switched off the machine and locked it. Next he locked his desk. His two colleagues were doing the same thing.

"You wanna get a beer after work, Paul?" Marty Fielder asked him. Fielder was a tall, slat-thin man whose clothes always looked a size too big for him. He had worked in the same office as Bogdanovich for about six years. They usually played racquetball on the Thursdays when they weren't on night swing. The third clerk, Harry Tracy, was a relative newcomer. He wasn't much of a talker. He looked up with interest when Fielder issued his invitation, as though hoping it included him.

"Can't tonight, Marty," Bogdanovich said. He stretched his arms above his head, watching as Fielder and Tracy went through the same end-of-shift routine he had observed. He was tall, thin, and weedy and his complexion was bad. He looked like what he was, a man with a sedentary job who spent most of his time indoors and got nothing like enough exercise. "I'm taking Eva to dinner."

"You celebrating something?"

"Yeah," Bogdanovich grinned. "She gets paid today."

They swapped gossip while they waited for the security officer to come and check them out, as he did every half hour or so. Anyone who left classified material unsecured got a VC in his jacket. So did the person in the office designated to check the others. That was why Bogdanovich always worked so methodically. The last thing he wanted in his personal file was a violation chit.

When the security officer had finished his perfunctory inspection and cleared them to leave, Bogdanovich and Fielder rode up to ground level in the elevator.

"Where you eating?" Fielder asked.

"Going to try a French place on Twentieth, Le Provençal. I'm told it's good."

"I'm told it's expensive," Fielder said. "Maybe I oughta send Janie out to work, we could join you."

They passed out through the security gate, smiling at Charlie, the potbellied guard, who checked their passes. Bogdanovich said so long to his colleague and walked across the parking lot to the numbered slot where his Toyota Tercel was parked. He drove to the gate of the compound where he again showed his ID to a security guard. The man hardly looked at it. He was there to stop people getting in, not to stop people getting out.

Bogdanovich thanked him impassively and said good night, even though his shirt was wet with sweat as he drove out.

On his way home to Pimmit Hills, he stopped for gas at an Amoco station on Route 650. While the attendant filled the tank and checked the oil, Bogdanovich made a call from the pay phone alongside the cashier's desk. He paid cash for the gas and drove on home. He did not put the car away when he got there. Eva came out to meet him. She got home before he did when he was on this shift.

"Hi," he said, kissing her. "Had a good day?"

"Not bad," she said. "Old Appleby was being a pain as usual. Otherwise fine."

She was short, dark, and if not pretty, then vivacious enough so that people thought her attractive. She worked in a downtown ad agency. Bogdanovich put his arm around her waist, and they went indoors. Eva had opened a bottle of Chablis. They poured two glasses and clinked them: their evening ritual.

"Ah," he said. He took off his jacket and put it carefully on a hanger, which he then hung in the hall closet.

"I was looking at those garage doors, Paul," Eva said. "We're really going to have to do something about them."

"We?" He grinned, leaning back on the sofa.

"You," she said. "You never do anything around the place."

"Tomorrow," he said. "I'm taking you out tonight."

"I bought pot roast."

"Put it in the freezer. Tonight we dine deluxe."

"What's the occasion?"

"The anniversary of the invention of the corkscrew," he said. "I just feel like eating out, okay?"

"Okay," she said, smiling. "What time do you want to leave?"

"I've made a reservation for eight. I've got a couple of things to do. Work things. They won't take long. We'll leave around seven-thirty, okay?"

"Do I dress up?"

"Put on that pink suit," he said. "I like that."

"Where are we going?"

"That's for me to know," he grinned. "And you to find out."

He finished his wine and then went into the little study on the far side of the hall. He drew the blind and switched on the tungsten lamp standing at one side of the desk. From his briefcase he took out the dossier he had earlier encrypted and transmitted to Miami. Using a Minox ultracompact 35GT camera, he carefully photographed every page twice. When he was finished, he put the dossier back into his briefcase. Tomorrow, when he went to work, he would discover his silly "mistake"— an inadvertent substitution of one set of papers for another— and send the correct dossier across to IR, explaining that it had been locked in his safe all night. It wouldn't even cause a raised eyebrow: such things happened all the time.

He took the roll of film out of the Minox and put the camera away. Next he took a pack of Lark cigarettes from his breast pocket, emptied it out, and put the roll of film into the pack. Then he put back as many cigarettes as would comfortably fit, putting the rest into a cigarette box on the desk.

He went into the bedroom. Eva was drying her hair. He took off his clothes, showered, shaved, and got dressed. He decided to wear the dark blue lightweight mohair suit he'd bought at Wallachs on Fifth Avenue last time he was in New York. By the time he put on his jacket and tie, Eva was ready. She was wearing the pink Jaeger suit with a navy blue polka-dot blouse.

"Yum-yum," he said, rolling his eyes.

"Oh, you!" Eva said.

The restaurant was a large, split-level place with ceiling beams that radiated from a central point like the spokes of a great wheel. A collection of framed celebrity photographs and certificates from travel magazines flanked the doorway. The chill of the air-conditioning was like a blanket of cold. There were paintings on the walls of nymphs and shepherds.

They ate onion soup and steak *au poivre*. Bogdanovich ordered a bottle of Zinfandel. It was ten forty-five when he called for the check and almost exactly eleven when they left the restaurant.

"That was lovely," Eva said contentedly. "But I ate too much."

"You always say that," he said.

At that moment, a man came hurrying along, head down. He did not seem to see Bogdanovich, who held up his hands to fend the man off.

"Hey, watch it, Jack!" he snapped angrily.

"Sorry, pal," the man grunted. "Din see ya." He hurried away. Bogdanovich watched him go, feigning anger, then walked around the car and unlocked it.

"Are you all right?" Eva asked.

"Yes," he said. "Fine."

"Want me to drive?"

"It's all right," he said, and smiled to show her he was no longer angry. "Get in."

They drove past the Kennedy Center and across Roosevelt Bridge. He pushed a cassette into the player, and the gentle voice of Karen Carpenter filled the car. Eva smiled: they would make love when they got home, she decided.

She had absolutely no idea of what had happened outside the restaurant on Twentieth Street. In the brief moment they had been in contact, Bogdanovich had passed the Lark pack containing the film to the man who had jostled him. By now, he imagined, it would already be in the hands of Stepan Lykov, his case officer at the Russian embassy.

He smiled. Money in the bank, he thought, and put his hand on his wife's thigh. She put her hand on top of his and held it there. Karen Carpenter began to sing a rainbow.

During the three days following the killings, David Caine spoke to Tom Crandon only once. His first priority, as he saw it, was to establish a new cover. That wasn't something you could do overnight, or alone. After he had called the police from the phone booth on Le Jeune, Caine had gone directly to the River House. He had swapped cars with Lavery, who had taken the Porsche back to town and reported to Crandon. Next morning, Lavery had come back out to the River House in a cab to pick up his own car. At the same time, he dropped off the ISS PAPD—a people-and-places digest of the surveillance dossier on Genevevo—for Caine.

After five hours of fitful sleep, Caine picked up the dossier at the registration desk, checked out of the hotel, and got a ride in the hotel bus to the airport. From there he took a cab into town, telling the driver he wanted to go to the Omni International. The man's expression of terminal boredom changed to cupidity.

"You want I should take the expressway?" he said. "Drops you right down on Biscayne."

"Gosh," Caine said. "You know the way."

It was a cheap shot, and he regretted making it the moment the words left his lips. Everybody hustles; it was the American way, and only a jerk complained, right? He heard the man mutter something uncomplimentary under his breath. Ah, well, he thought, there goes another potentially rewarding relationship.

Ignoring the driver's surliness, he concentrated instead on the options he had left. There weren't too damned many.

First, it was logical to assume that Genevevo's case officer, Forsyth, would go after ISS like a coyote after a rabbit, the firm's Alpha Alpha Seven security clearance and friend-of-the-Company status notwithstanding. It would not take Forsyth long to establish that Wurzel and Young had been operating in Genevevo's backyard, and when he did, he was going to wonder why Tom Crandon had told the police the two agents were working on an unrelated case. Which meant the next priority was taking Crandon out of the line of fire before that happened. And Crandon wasn't going to like that one damned bit. Well, tough.

The Omni complex was a ten-acre sprawl of boutiques, shops, movie theaters, restaurants, tennis courts, swimming pools, and playgrounds, all topped off with a five-story atrium in the new God-how-do-they-do-that? style of construction which is to architects what Oscars are to movie stars.

Caine checked into the hotel and, for a daily rate not much less than the amount he had paid for the first car he ever owned, was given a room on the fourteenth floor. Everything in it was color-coordinated, modern, and pseudoluxurious. To Caine's eye, it had about as much personality as an egg carton. He picked up the telephone and called Memphis. The ISS specialist there was a lanky, slow-spoken Mississippian named Geoff Beale. Caine wasted no time in small talk.

"I'm at the Omni International in Miami. We've got problems here. Advise Arlington I'm off the air until further notice."

"You got it," Beale said. "Anything else?"

"I need a new set of clothes. Get over here as soon as you can."

"There's a flight around four," Beale said. "I'll be on it. What name are you using?"

"Philip Howard."

• 63

"Long stay or short?"

"Depends."

"Always admired decisive men," Beale said. "See you tonight."

Next Caine called Tom Crandon. He did not think he was taking too much of a chance, but even though he was fairly sure he hadn't been followed to the hotel, and knew Crandon would sweep the office phones hourly in case the Company was bugging them, he avoided using his name.

"I've changed my address," Caine said. "And I'm getting a new set of clothes from Memphis."

"Two smart moves. You're doing well." In the jargon, a new set of clothes was a legend, a completely new identity. "What do you want me to do?"

"Meet me at Rendezvous Two. Can you make noon plus one?" The phrase "plus one" meant tomorrow and not, as a listener might assume, 1 P.M.

"You got the digest okay?"

"Sure."

"Watch your ass."

"I'll do my best."

The rest of the day, Caine stayed in his room, going over the surveillance reports on Tony Genevevo until the print blurred before his eyes. He stood for a long time by the window, looking down at the streets below, where ordinary people were going about their everyday business, selling soap, buying clothes, drinking coffee, planning trips. He wondered whether any of them gave so much as a moment's thought to men like Tony Genevevo. Not hardly, as John Wayne used to say.

He had some lunch sent up, then returned to the dossier, studying it assiduously. There was nothing else he could do until Geoff Beale got in with the documents and accessories that would provide him with a new identity. Genevevo's range of contacts had been wide: it would be hell's own job checking them all out. But there was one name that kept recurring, and he made a note of it: Lynda Sanchez, an address in Kendall, manageress of La Paloma restaurant on Key Biscayne. Genevevo had been a frequent visitor at both places. Caine put the woman high on his list of people to see.

Shortly after seven, the registration desk called to say Geoff Beale had arrived. Caine told them to send the Mississippian right up. As soon as the door closed behind him, Beale got straight down to business.

"Got you everything you asked for," he said, lifting the small suitcase he had brought with him onto the bed. "Clothes, car, new ID. That's the good news."

"And the bad news?"

Beale tossed an envelope onto the writing table. Caine picked it up and opened it. Inside was a folded telex form addressed to the Memphis office. He read what it said.

CAINE: KEEP ME INFORMED YOUR LOCATION AT ALL TIMES. REPORT DIRECT TO ME BY LANDLINE ON UNLISTED NUMBERS MINIMUM TWICE DAILY NO EXCEPTIONS NO EXCUSES.

It was signed "Kingly."

"Boola-boola," Caine said. "You eaten, Geoff?"

"On the plane."

"Want a drink?"

"Why not?"

Beale collapsed into one of the armchairs like a shot heron, his long legs crossed. Caine got two miniature bottles of whiskey out of the minibar and poured the golden liquid into glasses.

"Here's lookin' at you, kid," Beale said. "You want to talk?"

Caine shrugged. "There isn't all that much to say. I'm still trying things on, to see if they fit. There's something about all this that gives me a bad feeling."

"Go on."

"The man Genevevo was working for, Pedro Avranilosa, is probably a Cuban agent of some kind. Let's suppose he found out somehow that Genevevo was a plant. He wouldn't be able to act independently, and I can't believe even DGI would be dumb enough to sanction the assassination of a Company agent. Even if they were dumb enough, why would they go after our people, too? It doesn't make any sense at all."

"Maybe our people saw something DGI didn't want them to see."

"That's possible. All their surveillance tapes and photographs were gone. Always supposing it was DGI who took them."

"Who else would want them?"

"Someone who wanted us to think DGI. Whoever really did the shooting."

"Someone like who?"

"I don't know. That whole business out there near the airport was set up to look as if Genevevo, Wurzel, and Young had a shoot-out. Why go to so much trouble if all you want to do is take them out of the picture?"

"Maybe DGI wanted it to look like a gang shooting because that way there'd be no heat from the Feds about Genevevo's death."

Caine shook his head exasperatedly. "There'd be heat from the Feds no matter which way it went down. There's an element missing, Geoff, and I can't get a handle on it."

"Maybe Crandon will come up with something."

"Maybe," Caine said.

Twelve hours later, he was still brooding about the slayings he had witnessed, trying to make sense of something that only made sense in a way he didn't choose to accept. Well, maybe Geoff Beale had been right, he thought. Maybe Tom Crandon would come up with something. He drew the drapes and looked out of the window. It was a bright sunny day. Surprise, surprise.

He went down to street level and picked up a copy of *Newsweek* at the newsstand. He dawdled for a while, watching people come and go. The people who had lifted Genevevo were Cuban, or Cuban-American. So were the men who had done the killings out near the airport. So were a lot of the people milling around the Omni complex. So what? A lot of them were fat; that didn't mean anything either. It was impossible to be certain no one was watching him. In the end, Caine said the hell with it and went into the coffee shop for breakfast.

At eleven-thirty, he went across to the elevators and rode up to the third floor. Nobody else got out with him. He walked down the stairs to the lobby and out into the street. Nobody took any notice of him. Nobody came after him. He flagged a cab and headed for the meet.

Long ago, he and Crandon had set up a series of prearranged meeting places they could refer to by number for maximum security. Rendezvous Two was the Sixteenth Street entrance to the Orange Bowl Stadium. He had been waiting only a couple of minutes when Crandon eased up to the sidewalk in a beaten-up, anonymous-looking LTD. Caine got in, and Crandon gunned the car into the traffic, driving north.

"Nice car," Caine said.

"Thought the Porsche might be a tad conspicuous," Crandon grinned.

"Where is it?"

"Pete Lavery's driving it around," Crandon grinned. "Trying to attract attention."

"You haven't got a tail?"

"Haven't seen anything. I took the usual precautions."

"Keep your eyes skinned," Caine said.

"Amen," Crandon said. "You see the paper?"

"I saw it," Caine said, tossing his copy of the morning paper onto the rear seat. The headline glared at him: POLICE STILL WITHOUT LEADS IN MYSTERY SHOOTINGS. "You heard from the boys in blue, of course?"

"They were banging on my door ten minutes after they got a make from the Bureau."

"What did you tell them?"

"Just what it says in the paper. Lennie and Butch were on a

simple surveillance job. They had no reason to know or meet with Genevevo.''

"How long will it stick?"

"A little while, as long as it's only local police asking. We really are doing some work for Mercantile and Industrial of New York." Crandon threaded the big car expertly through the traffic. "Where we going, by the way?"

"Anywhere they got Rolling Rock."

Caine knew his attempt at humor was strained and knew Crandon understood. Neither wanted to broach the subject they had to discuss. Crandon drove in silence for a while, then pulled into a shopping plaza off Seventeenth.

"You serious about the beer?"

"Coffee would be better."

"Mens sana in corpore sano."

"I wish I could speak French," Caine said.

They went into a deli and sat in a booth. A sour-faced waitress brought them menus they didn't need, then waited expectantly, hands on hips.

"Just coffee," Crandon said.

"That all?" she asked.

Crandon looked at her. "You wanna get me a caviar taco?" he asked.

"Anh," she said wearily. "A wiseass." She went away to get the coffee pot.

"Don't you ever take anything seriously?" Caine said.

"I think," Crandon replied. "Therefore, I ham."

"First Latin, now philosophy. I'm dazzled."

"All right," Crandon said. "I heard Lavery's version. Now you tell me about it."

Caine told him, pulling no punches, about the long vigil, the abrupt appearance of the men from the Acme building, and the brutal, unexpected murders.

"Bastards," he said, softly. "I want them, David."

"I know," Caine said. "But first we have to find out who they were."

"You know who they were!"

"Is that what I know, Tom? Or is it what I'm supposed to know?"

"What the hell does that mean?"

"It means, don't jump to conclusions."

"You saying it wasn't the Fat Man's people?"

"I'm saying don't jump. What about the cars?"

"I checked them. They were both stolen."

"What about the warehouse? Acme Novelty?"

"It's owned by something called the Diversified Entertainment Corporation. Which is a subsidiary of another company called Sunshine State Enterprises. Sunshine State is one of Saturnino Baca's fronts."

"Who he?"

"Local hero," Crandon said. "King of the shitheap."

In 1980, he told Caine, Fidel Castro had "permitted" about 125,000 people to emigrate to the United States, a compassionate gesture which relieved him not only of the unskilled, the uneducated, and the poor of his island, but also the scourings of his prisons, detention centers, hospitals, and asylums. In among the huddled masses yearning to breathe free who embarked at the Cuban port of Mariel was the biggest assortment of junkies, rapists, extortionists, pimps, and thieves ever to land on the shores of America.

In the makeshift camps set up for them beneath the highway ramps and overpasses of Miami, the Marielitos soon discovered that the only ticket out of the hell they were living in was one of the coveted green cards which entitled you to work in America. If you had a trade, no problem. If you were a professional man, likewise no problem. If you were neither, maybe you could buy a card from somebody who was. If you had no profession, no trade, and no money, then maybe you got a knife or a gun, you killed someone who fulfilled all the legitimate requirements, and you took his place.

By the time anybody realized that Saturnino Baca was not a poor but honest union leader from the Havana electric company, he had a stranglehold on the South Beach area, he had his papers, and he had protection. Soon his reach extended to cover most of Miami south of Calle Ocho. His organization was so tight it was almost impossible to infiltrate. The supply of Cuban-Americans willing to try it tended to diminish in direct proportion to the number of times TV newscasts showed police fishing another bound, battered, bloated body out of some swampy canal.

"You think Baca had anything to do with this?" Crandon asked.

"Suppose those Cubans weren't DGI. Suppose they were Baca's people," Caine said thoughtfully. "Suppose he was watching Genevevo—and us—all the time."

"Not his style," Crandon said emphatically. "Baca isn't the subtle type. His people go in for chain saws."

"That's not a reason, Tom, that's a prejudice."

"Why would Baca want to kill our people? Or even Genevevo, come to that? It was Avranilosa he was after, not Baca."

"But if he busted Avranilosa, wouldn't he be busting Baca at the same time? If Baca is the head drugs honcho in South Miami . . ."

"The word on the street is that Baca's hold is slipping badly," Crandon said. "The Colombians are slowly but surely taking over the trade, driving the Cubans out. Or killing them off. They're not too damned particular."

"I still think Baca's a better bet than DGI. I can't believe Cuban intelligence ordered this done. They don't want to make those kind of waves. It doesn't make sense."

"We'll crack it," Crandon said. "Don't worry."

"No," Caine said flatly. "Not 'we.' You're out of this, Tom."

70 •

"The hell you say!"

"That's right, the hell I say."

They glared at each other across the table. The waitress came back and put two mugs on the table. She sloshed coffee into them and went away. Her performance made them grin in spite of their own tension.

"All right," Crandon said. "All right. Tell me why."

"It's not going to take Domestic Operations long to make a connection between ISS and Genevevo, Tom," Caine said. "When they do, I want you elsewhere. Like maybe Melbourne, Australia."

"It won't make any difference whether I'm around or not. Those guys don't take 'I don't know' for an answer, David."

"I just want to stall them as long as possible. That means putting you out of harm's way for a while."

"David, I want to be in on this. I want—"

"Sorry, Tom," Caine said flatly. "You're off the case, and that's final. Come on, let's get out of here."

Crandon paid the check and left seven pennies on the table as a tip. Caine smiled. Tom fought small wars with just as much enthusiasm as big ones. He felt a surge of affection for the rangy Miamian. There was no one he would have liked better at his side in the days ahead, but it was just not possible.

"I'm giving you twenty-four hours to git outa town, kid," he said, doing his best John Wayne voice.

"Hey, Jimmy Stewart, right?" Crandon said. He got into the car and started the engine. Caine lifted a hand in salute, and Crandon touched his finger to his forehead in farewell. He looked over his shoulder to check the oncoming traffic.

Automatically following Crandon's glance, Caine half saw a blue Chrysler Fifth Avenue accelerating past the LTD, and he hurled himself backward as a staccato burst of bullets blazed from its open window. He heard screams, the whine of ricocheting slugs, glass smashing. He landed in a heap, sending a display of fruit outside a grocery scattering all over the sidewalk.

He scrambled to his feet. An elderly man sat with his back against the wall, his shirt stained with blood, a look of surprise on his face. Tom Crandon was slumped over the wheel of the LTD. The windshield was spattered with blood. There was no sign of the blue Chrysler. A burly, red-faced man came out of the store, gesticulating. Caine turned sharply away so that the man could not see his face and walked briskly up the street.

"Hey!" someone shouted. "Hey, you!"

Caine kept walking, not hurrying. The voices died as he put distance between himself and the scene of the shooting. There was a K-Mart at the next corner, its parking lot half full. He found a shopping cart, then walked with it between the rows of cars. In the third row, he spotted a Ford Tempo with the keys in the ignition. Swiftly checking that no one was nearby, he got into the car and started it up. Fifteen minutes later, he abandoned it near Highland Park and walked back to the Omni International. By the time he got there, he had stopped shivering.

10

"Atletchnay," Drosdow said in Russian. Excellent.

Everything had gone well. With Avranilosa as his front, it had been easy to get Baca to take the bait he had offered. Baca was stupid and greedy, perhaps even stupider and greedier than the Fat Man. Drosdow liked working with such people. There were no nuances: you gave them money and they ate shit.

He smiled at the thought. It was not a sympathetic smile; Frederic Drosdow was not a sympathetic character. His brilliant blue eyes were hard and unforgiving, his mouth an uncompromising slash in a square, swarthy, pockmarked face. Saturnino Baca believed him to be Turkish: in fact, Drosdow had been born in the Zeravshan valley near Bukhara, in Uzbekistan, USSR. It was on Russian orders that Avranilosa's Cuban masters had instructed the Fat Man to present Drosdow to Saturnino Baca as a big-time supplier from Bogotá.

Drosdow had opened up the contact with ten kilos of hashish, the very finest Afghanistan, flown in direct from Moscow to Bogotá in the diplomatic bag and brought over by an airline pilot working for DGI. Once the connection was made, the bona-fides established, Baca asked for more. Drosdow got it for him, and then offered cocaine. Baca went after it like a shark after chum. Cocaine was the smart-money drug. Everyone wanted it, from ghetto kids sticking their money through the door slots of rock houses to the superrich of Miami Beach, who served it along with caviar at their flashy parties.

Drosdow's first shipment of cocaine had a street value of about $3.5 million. It came in by courier this time, two human "mules" each of whom had more than a hundred plastic sachets of cocaine in their stomachs. The next, much bigger shipment came in by air, landed on an airstrip up around Loxahatchee. Then, finally, last night, the payoff shipment Drosdow had been working up to: $60 million worth, brought in on a schooner and landed without incident at Lower Matecumbe Key.

He would be glad to get out of Miami. He had not much liked Bogotá, but Miami was even worse. How could people live in a place where alligators crawled out of the canals and ate their pets? The downtown streets were as sleazy as the ones in Havana, but without the Cuban city's character. As for the Cubans, they were irresponsible, unreliable, lazy, and corrupt. Apart from their gilded, garish plaster saints, the only thing they believed in was money. They were only good at one thing: they hated, with a fine impartiality, anyone and anything not Cuban.

My kalutsky, he thought. It was an old Russian phrase that meant "it's nothing to do with me." The fate of men like Baca and Avranilosa was of no consequence. They deserved neither loyalty nor sympathy; they were mercenaries, to be used, like a Kleenex, then thrown away.

He turned north on Collins and drove steadily, up through Haulover Beach Park Golf Course and the glitzy resort developments at Sunny Isles. At Interama, he made a left, cruising the mile or so it took him to reach U.S. 1. Billboards exhorted him to visit the ancient Spanish monastery of St. Bernard and its gardens. A quarter of a mile north on 1, he turned off into East Greynolds Park. A road ran down to the edge of Maule Lake, with a turning loop at the end. There were picnic tables and barbecue stands beneath the trees. The place was deserted. Drosdow checked his watch: four minutes to three.

At two minutes to three, a Cutlass coasted down the road and pulled up alongside his Mercedes. The man who got out was a short, barrel-chested man with cropped hair. He wore a rumpled lightweight suit and heavy leather brogues. He rapped on the window of the Mercedes and Drosdow opened it.

"Miami is pleasant at this time of year," the stranger said in Russian.

"I prefer Washington myself," Drosdow replied, completing the recognition code. "How are you, Comrade Lykov?"

"Good, fine, excellent," the stranger beamed, getting into the Mercedes. His full name was Stepan Ivanovich Lykov, and he was a counselor at the Russian embassy in Washington. This rank, which placed him fifth in seniority under the ambassador, was of course only a cover: Lykov was a GRU officer with special responsibility for "illegals"—Soviet spies working in the United States as businessmen rather than as members of the diplomatic establishment.

"What news have you for me?" Drosdow said.

"Good news, Comrade Major. Moscow advises us that Smert Ptyetsa will be ready to fly on schedule. They are anxious to hear your report. Has everything gone to plan?"

"Everything," Drosdow said.

Baca and his people had rented a vacation house on Lower Matecumbe Key, south of Miami, which had a dock big enough to accommodate the schooner bringing in the cocaine. The schooner was a local boat, with a sailing pattern familiar to the customs agents. For a fee of $1 million in cash, her skipper had agreed to pick up some goods—nobody said what, nobody needed to—from a cargo boat off Bimini. She slid in without incident an hour after dark, and by ten o'clock she was unloaded and on her way to Boca Raton, her home port. Long before she got there, Baca's chemists had done their alkaloid tests and pronounced themselves satisfied, and the cocaine had been transferred to three U-Haul trucks and driven north to Miami.

Neither Drosdow nor Baca was at Matecumbe: they waited

together at the Indies Inn on Duck Key, and when Avranilosa called to say the shipment was cleared, the payoff was made: $60 million, packed into cartons like so much waste paper. Which, in a way, it was, Drosdow thought.

"So the properties have been purchased?"

"I'll be finalizing that today," Drosdow said. "What about the girl?"

"She will be waiting for you at the Holiday Inn in Key Largo when you arrive. Her name is Katja Renis."

"What are the paroles?"

"The first line of *Anna Karenina*."

Drosdow nodded. "And the clerk? Bogdanovich?"

"He has been programmed. He will leave Washington the day after tomorrow. As you instructed. What about Avranilosa?"

"Leave him to the CIA."

"You're serious?"

"I've filled him full of disinformation. It will be no use if it doesn't get to them."

"As you wish," Lykov said. "I'll talk to Havana. They'll withdraw their support. That should do it."

"The poor fat bastard," Drosdow said unsympathetically. Avranilosa had been living like a prince for a long time. The man would have no grounds for complaint. In this business, nothing came with a guarantee.

He had been honest with Avranilosa about only one thing: the name of the game he was playing. It was *chaos*. He was sowing disinformation like a man planting corn, and in his wake he would leave chaos.

"You're going straight back to Washington?" he asked Lykov.

"I'll go to the airport from here."

"Then I'll be on my way. Good luck, comrade. Honor the work!"

"Honor the work!" Lykov echoed. He got out of the Mercedes and into the rented Cutlass. He raised a hand as he drove away. Drosdow did not return the compliment. His mind was already busy on what he must do next.

In due course, he had no doubt, Avranilosa would divulge what he had been programmed to reveal. As for Baca, fuck him. Sooner or later, the CIA would establish that he had executed their man Genevevo, and when they did, arrangements would be made for something unpleasant to happen to the Cuban: his limousine sideswiped by a truck on a freeway, an inexplicable gas leak at his home. While the security agencies went baying down the false trail he had laid for them to follow, Drosdow would be proceeding with the second phase of his plan, financed by the sale of the drugs in Miami. That was the sole reason for everything which had happened so far: money.

Drosdow grinned.

They'll make an American of me yet, he thought.

PART TWO

AIM

11 "I want you to walk away from it, David," Kingly said. His voice sounded tinny; was he recording what they were saying? "You know the rules."

"Go tell Tom Crandon the rules."

"Don't get truculent with me," Kingly snapped. "If you were dead, I'd be saying the same thing to him. And you know it."

He was right, of course. The organization's first priority was to protect its carefully constructed cover. Knowing he was right didn't make it any easier.

"I've got a new set of clothes. Nobody even knows I'm on the ground."

"You can't be sure of that," Kingly said. "And even if you could, my answer would be the same."

"What about Domestic Operations?" Caine said. "What happens when they find out we were watching Genevevo?"

"I've anticipated that," Kingly said smugly. "We're going to let it leak to Sam that Tom Crandon was working free-lance for our Customs and Excise people, acting on a tip that Genevevo might have been involved in running drugs to London. Of course, we'll assure them we had no idea he was working undercover—how could we?"

"It's pretty thin. You think they'll buy it?"

"The indications are they will," Kingly said. "Domestic Operations is already embarrassed—the last thing they want is to be visible on the mainland. So they're not going to make too many waves. If the matter is raised, our answer will be that Crandon was acting on his own initiative, and that was why we didn't know about the surveillance setup. Either way, our interest in Genevevo is terminated.''

''And what about whoever killed my people? Is our interest in them terminated, too?''

''I know how you feel, David, but—''

''One thing is certain, Miles,'' Caine said. ''You do not know how I feel.''

He wasn't yet altogether sure how he did feel. The shock of the assassination had ebbed, leaving a numb, undirected anger. Tom Crandon had been that rare thing in Caine's solitary life, a friend. Long-term relationships and the clandestine world tended to be mutually exclusive. You were taught not even to believe someone who said he was going to fetch the milk until he came back with the bottle in his hand. That was why so many agents were divorced. Or drunks. Or both.

''Even if you stayed down there, what could you hope to achieve?''

''I don't know. I've got the people-and-places digest. I want to follow up on a few things.'' Caine heard the space-opera sounds of relays bleeping and pinging on the long-distance line as Kingly pondered.

''You're a stubborn bugger sometimes, David,'' Kingly said. Caine didn't argue. ''All right. I'll give you another seventy-two hours. If you come up with anything, we'll review the situation. If not, you walk away. Fair enough?''

''Fair enough,'' Caine said.

''I'll patch you through to McClelland,'' Kingly said. ''Give him your contact numbers and legend.''

And lots of luck, kid, Caine thought as the connection closed. Well, that was Kingly's style. No use expecting a snake to tap-dance. After a few moments, Dick McClelland came on the line. Caine gave him the information he needed and hung up.

He tried to put himself into Forsyth's shoes. The Company's first priority was still Avranilosa: they would leave investigation of the murders to the FBI and the local police. If he stayed on the street and moved fast, he might be able to beat the CIA's man Forsyth to the punch. Forsyth had to go by the book: he would be hampered by the bureaucratic restraints he had to work with.

Caine's first task was to change his appearance. He darkened his hair with Clairol and put on heavy horn-rimmed glasses with plain lenses. He exchanged his gray Hart, Schaffner & Marx lightweight for a pale blue Dacron sport jacket, plaid slacks, a dark blue open-necked shirt, and Thom McAn loafers. He packed his own things into a Samsonite two-suiter and checked out of the hotel, paying cash.

The dark blue Chevrolet Impala was parked where Beale had said it would be. It looked clean inside and out. The tires had plenty of tread on them, and the muffler was in good shape. He lifted the hood and checked the engine over. The wiring was tidy and the hoses looked all right. There were no oil leaks on the crankcase. He got in, started the engine: it ran without hunting. The odometer showed seventy-something thousand miles.

He drove out of the parking lot and south through Shenandoah, where he picked up the South Dixie Highway, a continuous wilderness of billboards and neon signs, sprawling shopping plazas and clusters of stores, restaurants, laundromats, garages, clothing stores, repair shops, ice-cream parlors, and greasy spoons.

It was hard to believe that this area had once been a tropical paradise where panthers lived among the mangroves, where ospreys and pelicans soared over manatees basking in the shallows of uninhabited keys. Now the ospreys nested in TV aerials, the pelicans scavenged in the wake of tourist boats, and the manatees were all but gone.

Their world had been taken over by the realtors, the tourists, and the retirees. Because of them, every vacant stretch of sand was a potential gold mine. Real-estate signs advertised "residential communities" called Citrus this or Pine that, each with its own exclusive golf course—ten thousand dollars a year to join and another three to play. Over on the Gulf side, island houses were selling for seven million. Man was inexorably destroying all the beautiful things that had attracted him to this lovely land in the first place. Nobody seemed to give much of a shit.

Caine grinned at himself in the driving mirror. He was beginning to sound like Travis McGee. Next thing he knew, his long-lost daughter was going to turn up and tell him what a schmuck he was.

He drove automatically, going through in his mind what he had read in the dossier about Lynda Sanchez. First-generation Cuban-American—her parents had come over in the same wave as Avranilosa—she had worked as an auxiliary nurse at Jackson Memorial, where she met Jim Sanchez, an intern, whom she married in 1969. Sanchez had been killed near Danang in August 1972, just a few days before the last American ground troops left Vietnam. His widow found work in a restaurant in Key Biscayne and became its manageress on the retirement of its owner in 1980. She had been running it, very successfully, ever since.

The Dadeland Shopping Mall loomed on his right, rows of parked cars behind it glittering in the sunshine. Lynda Sanchez lived on SW Eighty-eighth Street, about a half mile past the mall. The building was a cream-colored, U-shaped block with a Spanish tile roof. A sign over the door said EL PALACIO APARTMENTS.

He went into the lobby. A middle-aged black man sat behind

a desk facing the doors. He laid down his newspaper and got heavily to his feet, hitching up his belt.

"Whatever you sellin', we don' want none," he said.

"I'd like to see Mrs. Sanchez," Caine said, giving him a winning smile.

"Miz Sanchez ain't seein' nobody."

So much for the smile, Caine thought. "Tell her it's in connection with Tony Genevevo."

"*Sir,*" the man said with long-suffering patience, "I jus' got through tellin' you, Miz Sanchez ain't seein'—"

"Humor me," Caine said. "Tell her I'm here. Philip Howard, Alliance Interstate Mutual Insurance Corporation." He handed the man one of the business cards Beale had given him as part of his new identity. The super took the card reluctantly, then went back to the desk, where he punched a button on his phone and waited.

"Oh, hi, Miz Sanchez. Got a guy here name Howard from the Alliance Interstate Mutual Insurance Corporation wantsa see you? Yeah, that's right, A-lliance. Yessum, I *tole* him that. He say it's about Mr. Genevevo? Ahuh. Oh? Okay, if you say so." He put down the phone and looked up. "Miz Sanchez wants a word with you."

Caine picked up the telephone. "Hello, Mrs. Sanchez. This is Philip Howard. I apologize for the intrusion. I'm making inquiries into the death of Anthony Genevevo?"

"What do you want to know?"

"I'd rather not discuss it on the telephone, Mrs. Sanchez. This is a confidential matter."

He heard her sigh. "Very well," she said. "Let me speak to the super."

Caine handed the phone back to the black man, who listened and nodded. He put the phone on the cradle and looked up at Caine.

"She say you to go on up. Second floor, apartment 220."

Caine took the carpeted stairs two at a time and walked down the mirrored corridor. Through the windows he could see the area enclosed by the wings of the building. Three women lay on loungers around the pool. The nearest of them was a slim brunette with a model's figure and a thousand-dollar tan. She was reading Kierkegaard. What ever happened to dumb blondes? Caine wondered.

He knocked on the door of 220. It opened six inches. Caine held his card where Lynda Sanchez could see it. He heard her release the chain and the door swung open.

"Mr. Howard?" she said. "Come in, please."

She was not tall—few women of Cuban descent were—but she was unusually slender and carried herself well, giving an impression of height. She had on a linen-and-cotton-blend white suit, with random horizontal stripes on the jacket and matching vertical ones on the skirt. She had dark, liquid eyes and a good figure. Her hair was black and long, and looked as if it was naturally waved. Her fingernails were well kept, and she wore a minimum of makeup.

"You say you're investigating Tony Genevevo's death, Mr. Howard?" she asked. "Surely, the police have done that already? I've told them all I know."

"We prefer to conduct our own investigations. Particularly when there is such a great deal of money involved."

"Tony had a big insurance policy? He never mentioned anything like that to me."

"You were very close?"

He caught her reaction and made a deprecatory gesture. "Forgive me, but we insurance investigators do sometimes have to ask personal questions. To find out, you know, what kind of man we were dealing with."

"You want to know what kind of man Tony Genevevo was?" she said. "I'll tell you. He was a bastard."

"You surprise me, Mrs. Sanchez," Caine said. "The local papers are making him out to be something of a hero."

"He may well have been," she said. "He was still a bastard."

"Why do you say that?"

She looked at the telephone, and he knew what she was thinking. He took a card out of his pocket and gave it to her.

"That's the number of my Washington office if you want to call them," he said. The number on the card was a hand-on phone somewhere in Annandale. If she rang it, she would be patched through to Dick McClelland, Caine's "supervisor." She looked at the card and then at Caine. It seemed like a long moment.

"I'm sure that won't be necessary," she said. "Please, sit down. What about something to drink?"

"Coffee would be good."

She went into the kitchen and Caine looked around. To the right, an archway led into a dining area with a walnut table and ladder-back chairs. The furniture looked comfortable and lived-with; a brown, leather-covered three-seater sofa, two vast armchairs in dark brown Dralon, off-white shag pile carpeting, wall lights. Two bedrooms, Caine decided.

It was a very American-looking apartment. None of the usual Cuban touches, the Lazaro or Carita de Cobre shrine with flowers and food, or the photographs of family still "on the island." On one wall hung a large framed print of a Renoir painting: it looked like the garden of the rue Cortot. On the opposite wall was a bookcase, books piled into it in haphazard stacks. In one corner stood a Toshiba portable TV and a Panasonic hi-fi stack with a pile of records alongside it.

Lynda Sanchez came back with the coffee and caught the direction of his gaze. "Show tunes," she said. "I collect everything. Like a squirrel."

"You get to a lot of shows?"

"Tony and I used to fly up to New York. See everything, bam-bam-bam."

"I thought you said—?"

"That he was a bastard? Maybe I'm being too rough on him. I don't know. I've had a lot of time to think this past couple of days. About Tony. And myself. About our relationship."

"And?"

"I've come to the unpleasant conclusion that he didn't give a damn about me, Mr. Howard. He was just using me to get what he wanted."

"That sounds pretty cold-blooded."

"Yes," she said, looking fiercely out of the window. "It does, doesn't it?"

He let her fight with that until she felt she had it under control. He admired the way she did it without tears. If what she said was truly how she felt, her ego must be badly dented.

"I shouldn't have said what I did," she said, turning to face Caine. "Tony was a good man. Maybe I . . . expected more than he had to give."

"How did you meet him?"

"I run a restaurant on Key Biscayne, La Paloma. He came in with some people I knew. They introduced us."

"How long ago was that?"

"Two years, maybe a little longer."

"Did you know what he did for a living?"

"Not then, not at first. He told me he worked for the government. Something to do with the State Department."

"And later?"

"Later . . . he hinted. Never came right out with what he actually did. He said to forget he'd ever told me he worked for the government. If anyone ever asked."

"That was when he went undercover."

"I guess so. It's easy to understand in retrospect."

"You went on . . . seeing each other?"

"He was . . . square. Going out with him was like going on a date with a college kid. All very formal. We held hands. He would bring me home and kiss me good night, then he'd leave."

"It's none of my business, Mrs. Sanchez—"

"No, I'm trying to see it clearly," she said. "I thought, maybe he's just shy. Now I wonder whether . . . whether he really didn't care for me at all. Just . . . used me."

"How do you mean?"

"He said I could be very helpful to him in what he did. If I could keep my eyes and ears open."

"In what way?"

"Before I answer any more questions, I want to ask you something, Mr. Howard," Lynda Sanchez said. "Who are you? Who sent you here? Another of those faceless government agencies who tell you they prefer not to show identification?"

"I told you, I'm—"

"Mr. Howard, you're no more an insurance investigator than I am. You ask all the wrong questions."

Caine shrugged ruefully. When he did not speak, Lynda Sanchez's lips became a determined line.

"I guess I'd like to see some real ID," she told him. "Or I call the police right now."

"I'm a secret agent," Caine said.

She laughed out loud in astonishment. "You expect me to believe that?"

"It's true."

"You sound . . . what is it, British?"

"The two men who were killed with Genevevo were working for me," he replied, evading the question. "I'm trying to find out who killed them."

"The papers said—"

"Forget what the papers said, Mrs. Sanchez. They were all murdered, in cold blood."

"Then why—?"

"Why didn't all those quietly spoken gentlemen in the light-weight suits who came to see you after Genevevo was killed, and told you not to talk to anyone about him, mention the fact that he had been murdered? It's called the need-to-know principle, Mrs. Sanchez. Someone somewhere decided you didn't need to know."

"They couldn't . . . would they do that?"

"They most certainly would."

"And what about you?"

"I'm telling you the truth. You can believe it or not, as you please. If you tell me to get out of here, I'll go. I have no authority, no jurisdiction in this country. In fact, I would be deported at once if anyone knew what I just told you."

"Then why did you tell me?" she asked very quietly.

"Because I want you to trust me, and I don't know any other way to convince you that you can."

"Trust you?" she said. "Can I trust any of you?"

"It's up to you."

She shook her head very slightly, as if to rid herself of her own disbelief. When she spoke, her voice was little more than a whisper. "What is it you want to know?"

"What did Genevevo ask you to do?"

"He wanted information about my customers."

"And you obliged?"

"I told him to go straight to hell."

"That must have made his morning."

90 ·

"He said he admired me for saying that, but what he was asking me was important. He said there were Cubans, gangsters, giving the rest of us Cubans a bad name. He said it was his job to stop them, but he needed help. I tell you, I was glad to do it."

"Why?"

"My parents came over here in 'sixty-one, Mr. Howard. They had no money, no place to live. My father had been an electrical engineer in Cuba. Here he couldn't get a job. He pushed a broom in a factory eight hours a day, then worked another six hours in a car wash. My mother cleaned house for rich American ladies, waited on tables. They didn't complain, they didn't ask for handouts. They worked and worked because they wanted us kids to have a better life than they had. And where we lived, we'd see them, those other Cubans, letting gangsters use their houses for drug deals, making more money in a day than my father made in a month. And we knew what people said: those Cubans, they're no good, any of them. They're all into drugs, they ought to be run out of the country, they ought to be sent back where they came from. And I thought of how hard my mother and father worked, and . . . I don't know how else to say it to you. I wanted to do a good thing for them. For America."

"Genevevo must have known what he was asking you to do could be dangerous."

"Not so dangerous," she smiled. "Cuban men are very, you know, macho. A woman, bringing them food, they don't even see her."

"How did it work? Did Genevevo tell you who he wanted you to eavesdrop on?"

"He'd telephone, ask me who was in the restaurant. I'd tell him this man, that one. He'd say, 'See what you can get for me.'"

"Like what?"

"Oh, who they saw, who they came in with, who they talked to."

"Do you know why?"

"It was something to do with the man he was working for, a man called Pedro Avranilosa."

"I'm afraid the name doesn't mean anything to me," Caine told her.

"He claims to be a realtor. Tony said the real estate was just a front, that Avranilosa's real business was drugs."

"How do you mean?"

"He's a middleman, a fixer. Tony said he brings together interested parties—the people selling drugs and the ones who want to buy them."

"This Avranilosa—he came to your restaurant a lot?"

"Two, sometimes three times a week."

"And you told Genevevo who he met, what he talked about."

"That's right." She hesitated. "I . . . it wasn't the way I've made it sound. I was . . . I cared about Tony. What he was doing was brave. And dangerous. If by doing what he asked, I made it a little less dangerous, I was . . . I wanted to do it."

"Have you any idea why he was killed, Mrs. Sanchez?"

"No," she said, shaking her head. "It was . . . what the police told me, what it said in the papers, I couldn't believe it. I saw him the night before it happened. He was the same as always, you know, relaxed, buying drinks."

"He didn't seem tense or anything?"

"Not till I told him about Avranilosa meeting these men at the restaurant. I could always tell when he was excited. He'd talk staccato, words-all-strung-together-like-that, you know? I got the impression something important was breaking."

"What exactly did you tell him?"

"Avranilosa had met two men. One of them was from South America. Obviously, I didn't get all the details, but I heard enough to know they were talking about buying a property."

"Did you get their names, Mrs. Sanchez?"

"Yes. The one who said he was from South America was called Drosdow, and the other man's name was Percival."

"First name or surname?"

"I'm not sure."

"What was so special about them?"

"I don't know. I gathered Drosdow had a lot of money, I mean really a lot, and was looking for a place to live."

"In Florida?"

"I suppose so. But that wasn't what interested Tony. It was what I told him about Key Largo."

"Key Largo?"

"I overheard Drosdow telling Avranilosa the sparrow was waiting in Key Largo. It was such nonsense it stuck in my mind. But when I told Tony, he got very excited."

"Excited?"

"No, that's not the right word. Tony wasn't the excitable type. But . . . elated. He said I'd cracked it for him. He said everything was coming together."

"Are you sure that's what the man said, a sparrow?"

"No, wait a minute, not a sparrow. A swallow. He was going to Key Largo to see a swallow. I remember, Tony asked me the same thing."

"What did Genevevo do then?"

"He couldn't wait to get out of there, like someone lit a fire under him."

No wonder, Caine thought. Genevevo would have known the jargon, and concluded, like Caine, that if Drosdow was going to meet a swallow—a female operative used to sexually entrap a targeted male—then Drosdow and Avranilosa were engaged in setting up a honey trap.

"This man Drosdow," Caine said. "Can you tell me anything about him? Where he stayed, what he looked like?"

"Not much," she said. "He was well built, not tall. Good

clothes, imported, I'd say. About fifty. Dark brown hair, very blue eyes, swarthy, pockmarked skin."

"When you first mentioned him, you said he *said* he was from South America. As if you weren't convinced."

"Exactly," she said.

"What kind of accent did he have?"

"I don't know. But he was no more Spanish than . . . than you are."

"What about the other man, Percival?"

"Sixtyish. Tall, thin, stooped. Old-fashioned businessman look about him. I gathered he was some sort of realtor."

"Local?"

"I don't know. But if I had to guess, I'd say no."

"Tell me, was there anyone else Genevevo showed particular interest in? Anyone Avranilosa saw a lot of?"

She gave him a wry grin, and he interpreted it correctly. "The button-down boys asked you the same thing, I take it?"

"Yes."

"And what did you tell them?"

"I told them the one Avranilosa saw the most of was Saturnino Baca. Tony said he was the boss of all the rackets in South Miami."

"Do you know what his special interest in Baca was?"

"Nothing you could use in a courtroom, I guess. But I gathered there was some kind of deal going on between Avranilosa and Baca. Maybe drugs, maybe something else. Baca is into a lot of things: numbers, loan-sharking, women."

"Talking about women, did Avranilosa bring any to the restaurant?"

"Women?" She laughed. "Avranilosa isn't interested in women."

"How do you know?"

"I hear the waiters talking. That's what they say."

"I think he and Baca murdered Tony Genevevo and my people, Mrs. Sanchez. I don't know why. But I want to find out, and I need all the help I can get to do it. Will you help me?''

Lynda Sanchez stubbed out the cigarette she had lit and looked directly at Caine. ''There is a certain kind of Cuban that my people are not proud of, Mr. Howard. The ones who make a lot of money, usually dirty money, and then forget who they are and where they came from. They exploit their own kind worse than the worst kind of American, they spit on anyone who believes in hard work, a decent life. Avranilosa is one of those. Baca is another. If helping you will rid us of them and their kind, then yes, I will help you any way I can.''

He wondered whether what she was saying was genuine, or whether it was an act put on especially for his benefit. Her attachment to Genevevo seemed genuine enough, but there was no way of being sure about it. That was the trouble with this business: you ended up despising yourself because you were so far gone you could no longer trust anyone. Lynda Sanchez was a very attractive woman. It would not be difficult to get to like her. For a moment, he felt the ache of self-imposed loneliness.

''I'd better be going, Mrs. Sanchez,'' he said. ''There are a few more people I've got to see.''

''I wish you'd stop calling me Mrs. Sanchez,'' she said. ''You make me feel a hundred and four years old.''

''I'd hate to do that.''

''You said your name was Philip? Would you like to give me a ride as far as the mall, Philip? I've got some shopping to do. I can walk back.''

''I'd be glad to wait.''

''No, I want to dawdle,'' she smiled. He waited while she took out the coffee cups and got her pocketbook and a shopping bag. They walked out through the lobby, and Caine blew the man at the desk a kiss. The super raised a rigid digit. They got into the car, and Caine moved the Impala into the slow-moving traffic, checking the mirror. As far as he could see, no one was tailing him. He drove around into the parking lot of the Dadeland Mall. Lynda Sanchez got out of the car and stood by the open door, smiling.

"Well," she said. "I seem to have done a lot of talking."

"You've been very helpful, Lynda," Caine said. "It would be even more helpful if you didn't tell anyone I'd been to see you."

She said nothing for a moment. Then she nodded.

"Thank you," Caine smiled. "Will it be okay if I call you?"

"I haven't heard that one for a long time," she said, and for the first time he saw mischief dancing in the dark eyes.

"I'm old-fashioned."

"Music by Kern, lyrics by Mercer," she said. "You are one of the good guys, aren't you, Philip? You are going to catch the men who killed Tony?"

"Yes," he said. "If I can."

She smiled her brilliant smile again. In the context, it was heartbreaking. She looked at him for what seemed like a long while, then shook her head slightly, as if to banish a dark thought.

"I can't think of one good reason for trusting you," she said. "But for some strange reason, I do. For the time being."

"Thank you."

"I'm in the book," she said. "Call me."

She walked away. He watched her go, knowing she was aware of his scrutiny. She had a good figure. Nothing noisy, but everything in the right places. Caine sighed. If he had been doing any other job than the one he was doing, he might have been tempted to take her up on that invitation. As it was . . . Next life, maybe.

13

Just one more, Forsyth thought.

He eyed the bottle of Johnny Walker Black Label judiciously: old Johnny had taken a beating tonight. One more smack over the head would just about finish him off.

He sloshed the whiskey into his glass and stared moodily at the newspaper on the table in front of him. The headline mocked him: GANGLAND LINKS SEEN IN DOWNTOWN SLAYING

"Goddamnit!" Forsyth said, banging the empty glass down on the table. He had just returned from an interview with Bensen, who worked out of a front called the American Agency for International Development in a forty-story steel-and-glass block on Brickell Avenue. Forsyth had gone there expecting Bensen to tell him to give maximum precedence to finding out who had killed Tony Genevevo.

Fat chance.

"Crandon's death was inexpedient, Frank, but it's not our brief to go out on the streets looking for whoever killed him," Bensen said primly. "Leave it alone."

Inexpedient, for Christ's sake! First Genevevo and the two ISS men. Now somebody had burp-gunned Thomas Crandon in broad daylight on a city street and Bensen called it inexpedient!

The Miami police had come up with zilch: a dozen Ingram shells on the street, the testimony of an old man who'd taken a ricochet in the upper arm, and that of a few shocked bystanders who were seeing more every time they retold their story. The sum of it was that the shooting had been done by two, four, or five men, who were either Cuban, Puerto Rican, black, or white, and driving a late-model blue, or black, or purple Buick. Or maybe it was a Chrysler, or a Dodge. Or a goddamn flying saucer, Forsyth thought disgustedly, tossing the paper on the floor.

"You don't attach any special significance to the murder of Crandon, then?" he'd asked Bensen.

"Look, Frank, there are two, three hundred murders in Metro-Dade every year, half of them drug-related. We can't waste any more time on this. You've got to see the bigger picture."

"The bigger picture."

Bensen's head came up. Like all insecure men, he read criticism into irony and was constantly on the alert for the imagined slight. He was a short man, thickset and balding, with rimless glasses that imparted a moonlike impassivity to his face. He was what Forsyth privately termed a breakdancer—impressive to look at, but when their act was finished, they hadn't produced a damned thing. There were a lot of them in the Company. Careful, reticent, petty men who never took risks and snapped up every break. College boys, success-oriented, upwardly mobile, with the morals of the Great White.

"You've got a reputation as a maverick, Frank," Bensen said. "You've got to play with the team, or I'll take you off it. Make up your mind."

"I'll stay," Forsyth said, perhaps a shade too quickly. He saw the little glint of triumph in Bensen's eyes and cursed himself. You never let a man like Bensen think you wanted something; that gave him the sadistic pleasure of making you sweat for it.

"You've read the option papers?"

"I'm not altogether in agreement with them. I'd still like to know why those ISS people were watching Tony."

"Frank, Frank," Bensen said, grindingly patient. "You saw the memo from Langley. They were free-lancing for the British Customs people."

"That's not what Crandon said."

"You didn't expect he'd be telling the truth, did you?"

No, of course not, Forsyth thought. Nobody told the truth. Everything, including the truth, was a lie. You could always draw two sets of vastly different conclusions from the same set of facts. Which was why he mistrusted Bensen's option papers and the analysts who prepared them. Analysts were to his line of work what lady detective story writers were to homicide cops.

"Let me ask you something," he said. "How did the British Customs, or whoever the hell it is, latch on to Genevevo?"

"He gave one of their people some information."

"Bullshit. I was his case officer, Donald. He met any British agents, I'd have known."

"You admitted yourself there was a possibility Tony was off the leash, Frank," Bensen pointed out. "If you'd lost him, he wouldn't have told you anything."

"I hadn't lost him!" Forsyth snapped, feeling his own anger rise. Bensen knew all the cheap shots. "But if Tony had gone over the line, there'd have been even less reason for him to talk to some British narc."

"Well," Bensen said. He always said that when he had no argument but didn't want to be left with nothing to say. After a while, it just got tiresome. What am I fighting him for? Forsyth asked himself. Nobody cares but me.

"Just tell me one thing, Donald," Forsyth said. "On a scale of one to a hundred, how big is this?"

"I don't measure things that way," Bensen said, prim as an old maid. "And neither should you. Avranilosa is part of a bigger picture we're putting together. That's why I want you to give it all you've got."

Give it all you've got? Did anyone still say things like that for real? Yes, Forsyth thought. In his fifteen years with the Company, he'd met a lot of men like Bensen. They all seemed to think all they had to do was latch on to some inspiring phrase to quote you, and you'd go out and die for them.

Asshole, he thought, still angry over the interview. He knew what Bensen's "bigger picture" was. Avranilosa, a junk peddler with less to recommend him to humanity than a bubonic rat, would provide a means by which Domestic Ops could infiltrate Cuban intelligence operations in the Miami area. Instead of frying the bastard's ass for his part in the death of Genevevo, they'd kiss it. They'd make him a government employee and pay him more money in one lump than Forsyth could earn in five years. They'd give him anything he wanted, including a pension.

He opened another bottle of Scotch and poured a good one. He wished he could get really drunk; he never did. It was as if he had some sort of built-in mechanism that prevented it from happening, although he often drank more than he should. Kidneys probably look like the sole of a running shoe, he thought.

Again he wished he was a thousand miles away from Miami, away from Bensen, away from acting for Domestic Ops in a scenario that nobody seemed to care shit about. The only thing that kept him from calling it a day and sending in his papers was the fact that Tony Genevevo's murderer was still at large. Somehow or other, he was going to find that turkey.

It was a cinch nobody else was going to: the death of one undercover operative was to the head office what a pinprick might have been to a dinosaur. They had bigger things on their minds: SIGINT and ELINT, destabilization in Nicaragua, troop movements in El Salvador, Afghanistan, Iran. Nuclear submarine bases at Severomorsk, political assassination in Lebanon, multimillion-dollar covert operations in Kampuchea and Korea and Chile. Street killings were a local matter: let the head of station handle it.

So Forsyth was stuck with Bensen, who seemed to care even

less about Genevevo than the head office did. All Bensen wanted was to bring Avranilosa across, a nice little coup, one more commendation on his way to that overseas posting with virtually unlimited expenses and the chance to buy a duty-free Mercedes.

Screw him. Screw them all.

They could take their option papers and jam them where the sun never shone. Tony Genevevo had found out something that got him killed, and Crandon's security company was tied into it. Whatever it was, Forsyth promised himself, he was going to find out, then level the score. He didn't know how, yet. But he'd do it. Meantime, Bensen wanted Avranilosa turned. Forsyth grinned. He'd turn the fat bastard, all right.

Inside fucking out.

14 The Holiday Inn of Key Largo was at Mile Marker 100, on the western side of U.S. 1, about a mile south of the entrance to the John Pennekamp State Park. Drosdow sighted the familiar sign with relief. The highway south from Miami was as ugly a road as he had ever traveled, and he had traveled some pretty ugly ones. To drive it was to be ceaselessly affronted by signs, hoardings, and poster come-ons, mile upon mind-numbing mile of them. Eat at Beefsteak Charlie's, Burger King, McDonalds, Wendy's, Hamburger Heaven, Leon's Bar-B-Que, Taco John's. Visit Tropical Dreams, Lion Country Safari, Planet Ocean, Parrot Jungle, Metrozoo, the Serpentarium, Monkey Jungle, Mossosukee Indian Village, Fairchild Tropical Garden, Six Flags Atlantis, Flipper's Key West, Orchid Jungle, Coral Castle. Stay at Holiday Inn, Best Western, Ramada Inn, Flamingo Inn, Howard Johnson's, TraveLodge, Quality Inn, Marriott, Hilton, Hyatt. Rent from Quality, Budget, Avis, Hertz, Econo-Car, Olin, Alamo. Fly Delta, TWA, Eastern, Air Florida, American, United, Air Jamaica, Pan Am. Smoke Marlboro, Kent, More, Salem, Lark, Winston, Chesterfield. Drink Budweiser, Miller's, Michelob, Old Granddad, Jack Daniel's, Canadian Club, Smirnoff. Burritos, Tacos, Hot Dogs, Gator Burgers, Eats To Go. Ice Cold Drinks, Airboat Rides, Boat Rentals, Bike Rentals, Shells, Fishing Tackle, Guns, on and on, endless, unavoidable.

When he turned into the parking lot in front of the Holiday

Inn, Drosdow was surprised to see a battered old boat on a huge trailer in front of the hotel. The boat looked spuriously old, like a fake antique. On its bow was the name *African Queen*. A sign on the towing truck announced that this was the original boat used in the movie of the same name.

Americans, he thought: they turn the sites of actual history into parking lots but lovingly preserve artefacts from old movies. He got out of his car and walked around the boat, remembering the scene where Humphrey Bogart got the leeches all over him and Katharine Hepburn rubbed salt on them to get them off. His memory told him that the boat had been sunk at the end of the film, ramming the German cruiser. Maybe they had two, he decided.

He went into the lobby. The registration desk was on his right. On the left, a doorway led into the restaurant. The Bogart theme was continued: Casablanca Room, and so on. Probably nobody in America had ever heard of Key Largo till they used the name as a movie title, he thought. He asked for a room facing the pool, and the girl at the desk drew him a sketch to show him how to park his car in back. Nobody offered to help him with his luggage.

"Did Miss Jones check in yet?" he asked. "Miss Mary Jones?"

The girl checked the register. "She's in 115, Mr. Smith," she said. "Three doors along from you."

Drosdow nodded and went back out to his car. He drove around the back of the hotel. The parking lot was enclosed by a chain link wire fence. A sign offered rides in a glass-bottomed boat. Loud rock music blatted from a radio somewhere nearby. He parked the Mercedes close to the building, so that it would be in shadow in the morning, and carried his two-suiter to the room. It was like every Holiday Inn he had ever been in, phony but comfortable, ugly without being offensive, with carved wooden headboards on the beds and huge lamps on the bedside tables that gave off just too little light to read by.

An armchair and a round glass-topped table stood between the air-conditioning unit beneath the window and the twin queen-sized beds. In the bathroom, a white paper strip across the toilet seat advised him that it had been sanitized for his protection. So Americans still believed you could get clap off lavatory seats.

He opened his case and took out the bottle of Glenfiddich he'd bought at the liquor store in South Miami on the way down. He got the ice bucket from the bathroom and padded around the building to the machine, filled the bucket, and went back to his room. Kids were screeching in and out of the pool. Water streamed across the pathway where the jungly plants were being hosed. Drosdow locked his door and poured himself a large drink. He put ice into the glass, although he knew that was no way to treat a good single malt. To hell with it. He needed a cold drink, and he had no intention of drinking the piss Americans drank under the delusion it was beer.

He looked at his watch. Five o'clock. He picked up the phone and dialed 115. A woman's voice answered, low-pitched, relaxed.

"Happy families are all alike," he said.

"Every unhappy family is unhappy in its own way," she replied, completing the opening sentence of *Anna Karenina*. "I've been expecting you. What room are you in?"

"One-oh-nine," he said. "Join me for a drink?"

"Give me a couple of minutes."

While he waited, Drosdow reviewed in his mind what he knew about Katja Renis. Born in Prague, she was the second of the three daughters of Hanna and Karl Malinkov. Her father was a lecturer at the University of Prague, where Katja had graduated in 1966. Fluent in Czech, Russian, French, German, and English, she had no trouble in obtaining a job as an assistant news editor with FSZS, the Czech Federal News and Information Service. Very soon thereafter, she became the mistress of Leszek Cubr, head of the Second Department of the StB—

Státní Tajná Bezpečnost, the State Security Agency of the Interior Ministry. In 1973, after intensive training which included attendance at the assassination school, a former monastery on the banks of the Vltava in the Prague suburb of Vyšehrad, she and her "husband," Vaslav Renis, chosen by Cubr to accompany her, had made their way to the United States posing as anti-Communist refugees. A year after their arrival, they "separated," and Katja moved to Washington. Before long, she obtained employment as an executive assistant at the School of Foreign Service at Georgetown University. This placed her ideally for making contacts in the intelligence world—her boss was a former CIA White House briefing coordinator—as directed by her case officer, Arkady Shuvarov.

Shuvarov had protested bitterly when Katja was selected to work as Drosdow's swallow, claiming she was far too valuable to waste on one operation. His protests were overruled. The GRU *rezident* in Washington reminded him of Colonel General Ivashutin's dictum that the neutralization of the American satellite was to be effected at all costs: nothing took precedence over Undertaking Open Window.

Drosdow got up and opened the door when she knocked. He smiled and she came in. She was everything he had hoped for: tall, blond, beautiful, with a good figure and that unmistakable Continental style that American women strive for but never achieve. She had blue eyes, a full mouth, elegant hands and ankles. Her skin was lightly tanned, with a scattering of freckles across the bridge of her nose. She wore a white linen suit, white shoes, and a dark blue open-necked silk blouse. Yes, he thought, perfect: a centerfold with a brain.

"Sit down," he said. "Do you want some whiskey?"

"Thank you, no."

"You have been informed about your assignment?"

"Only that it is a sanctification."

"A very important one. Perhaps the most important one we have ever undertaken."

"Then I am honored to have been selected."

"You come highly recommended. Not too highly, I hope. I do not tolerate failure."

"I understand," she said. "Who is the subject?"

"His name is Butler Mitchell. He is a deputy chief of what is known inside the National Security Agency as the S Organization. Its full name is the Office of Communications Security, COMSEC for short."

COMSEC, he told her, provided the methods and equipment which protected the entire range of American intelligence communications: command, control, voice, data, teletype, and telemetry among them. It also prescribed the way these systems were used, from the scrambler phone in the presidential limousine to the banks of chattering crypto machines on the sixth floor of the State Department, and anywhere in between.

"Mitchell is directly responsible for the security of an NSA computer network known as Platform," Drosdow said. "It is the host environment for fifty-two separate computer systems all around the world, including the British GCHQ complex at Cheltenham. Our intention is to penetrate it."

He took a folder out of his case and opened it, taking out an assortment of photographs, some of them Polaroids, others black-and-white eight-by-tens. Many of them had been taken with a very long telephoto lens. They showed a house, vacation photos, a man and a woman standing in front of two cars. The man in the pictures was dark-haired, in his middle forties, with the husky shoulders of a football player. Katja Renis went through them in silence.

"This is his house?"

"And his wife. Study the pictures thoroughly. Then go through the dossier. A great deal of effort has gone into its compilation."

"Later," she said. "Tell me something about the man. His personality."

"He is forty-six," Drosdow said. "Born in Plymouth,

Massachussetts, eldest of three brothers. An old family, originating in the South. They are what the British call snobs. They boast a great-grandmother who was a French aristocrat, one of those who fled the slave insurrection in Santo Domingo in 1794 and settled in Georgia. They put great value on such nonsense and consider themselves a cut above the common herd. The parents virtually bankrupted themselves sending their children to the right schools. Mitchell, for instance, went to MIT and was recruited there. His wife's name is Catherine. He married her against his parent's wishes: they thought her a social inferior.''

"For a people who pride themselves on being a classless society, Americans are very class-conscious.''

"That is because most of them are hypocrites. Now, the wife: Cathie, as she is known, works part-time in an office in Laurel, Maryland, near Fort Meade. She plays tennis at her country club most weekends, spends all her money on clothes she doesn't need. Typical American bourgeois mentality. The marriage is a sham, of course, as many of them are. There is no evidence that she sleeps around, but he has a reputation as a womanizer. He's not very imaginative on that front, but then, people who work with computers rarely are.''

"Likes; dislikes?''

"He likes people to think he's rich. He dresses well. As you see, he drives an expensive car, a Dodge 600 Turbo convertible. He takes a vacation trip two or three times a year, alone. Picks someone up, has a fling. He's a bad gambler, given to plunging. He lost a lot of money in Atlantic City last month: more than he could really afford.''

"He sounds like a very unhappy man.''

"That's precisely what makes him your meat,'' Drosdow said. "Not only is he dissatisfied with his personal life, he is unhappy at work. He has been twice passed over for promotion and believes it is because of his wife. She's one of those women who drink too much at parties and get maudlin. As a security officer himself, Mitchell knows his superiors must view her lapses with some unease. The more he cheats on her, the unhappier she becomes. The unhappier she is, the more she makes a fool of herself. He hates her for that.''

''How long will we have?''

''The timing of every phase of this undertaking has been minutely planned. So far, it is exactly on schedule. The financing has been effected, the properties purchased, the decoys set running. Now we need Mitchell in the bag, and sooner rather than later. Red Center has scheduled the launch of our bird for October third, four months from now. We must effect our brute-force attack at the end of September.''

''I understand,'' she said. ''Don't worry.''

''You sound very confident,'' Drosdow said.

She smiled a feline smile, tossing her well-modeled head so that the long blond hair swung away from her face. ''I am,'' she said silkily. ''I'm very, very good.''

Drosdow smiled, too. He kicked off his shoes and loosened his tie.

''All right,'' he said. ''Show me.''

15

Somebody once described a CIA man as a cross between a Boy Scout and a mugger. There was enough truth in the description to make Forsyth grin as he made his preparations. He did not discuss his plans with Bensen or anyone else.

It was at times like this that being an old hand paid off: you knew how to cut any corner that needed cutting. Forsyth had been around since the days when filing cabinets were made of wood and you had to make a reservation if you wanted to call overseas. There might be more than one or two people in the Company who'd spit if you mentioned his name to them; but there were plenty of others who owed him.

One of them was J.G. "Jack" Dempsey in M&S. Management and Services was where you went if you needed manpower, money, transportation, untraceable weapons or cars, and Dempsey was the area controller. On his desk was a sign that said TELL ME YOU WANT IT YESTERDAY—I HAVEN'T HAD A GOOD LAUGH ALL WEEK.

He asked Dempsey for a motor-driven Canon A1 with a 70-210mm zoom lens and a dozen rolls of XP1 black-and-white film. XP1 could be up- or down-rated in the camera, which made it the ideal any-light film.

"Don't log this, Jack," he told Dempsey. "I'm on a private shoot."

"Frank, you know the rules," Dempsey protested. He was a

tall man with a long jaw, dark auburn hair that had thinned at the crown, and wide brown eyes which surveyed the world with benevolent amusement. Like Forsyth, Dempsey had been a Company man pretty much all his working life.

"Damned right, I know the rules," Forsyth said. "If you log this, I've got to give you a case number, and I don't have one. Jack. Trust me. I'll get it all back to you, don't worry."

"'Don't worry', he says," Dempsey said. But he was grinning.

"Now, about wheels. Something anonymous, Jack."

He decided on a panel truck, and Dempsey came up with a theatrically filthy GMC Safari with enough onboard equipment hidden inside to follow a fish up a river. Forsyth signed it out and hit the street. When he came back in, three days later, he had almost two hundred shots of the fat man going about his business.

He checked in the camera and took the elevator down to Archives. He fed his ID into a slot for a computer scan, and after a few moments the unmarked door opened with a metallic clack. Beyond it was a desk at which he signed the log. He filled out a requisition form and took it across to the Issue counter, where a clerk gave him a call unit with the number 38-F Dymo-taped to it. While he waited, Forsyth got a cup of coffee from the dispenser.

After about ten minutes, the call unit gave its discreet signal and he went back to the Issue counter and picked up the files he had requested. It took him most of the afternoon, but when he was done, he had a stack of perhaps twenty black-and-white photographs set aside. He went back to the Issue clerk and told him which photographs he wanted to sign out.

"Okay, you've got to fill out an ATRD," the clerk said. "Five copies, press hard. Signature, authorization code, and service number."

"I know, I know," Forsyth growled impatiently. The man looked at him the way Issue clerks always do. Forsyth filled in the authorization to remove documents, then took the tie-flap envelope containing the prints up to the fifth floor, where he knocked on Jack Dempsey's door.

"Frank, not again," Dempsey said, alarmed. "What are you after now?"

"Relax," Forsyth said. "This is Ongoing Situation time. I just need some speciality work, Jack. These are from Archives. Sign the chit, will you?"

Dempsey signed the back copy of the release chit and put it into a cylindrical container with a red *R* on top. He fed the container into a slot beside his desk. The machine gave a thud as compressed air sped the container to Archives, verification that the photographs had reached their intended destination. The top copy would remain with Dempsey until the photographs were returned.

Dempsey opened the envelope and riffled through the photographs. "Nasty-looking bunch of mothers," he observed. "Who are they, Frank?"

"Various kinds of Miami sewer life," Forsyth said. He laid twelve rolls of XP1 on Dempsey's desk. "I've got a couple of hundred shots of a man named Avranilosa on these," he said. "I want him married into as many of these pictures as possible."

"You've indicated where?"

"On the back of each picture."

"Some of these shots are blurred, Frank," Dempsey remarked. "It won't be easy."

"Use Maximum Entropy," Forsyth said.

"Know it all, don't you?"

"My mama didn't raise no fools." Forsyth grinned. Maximum Entropy was a mathematical principle invented by two Cambridge scientists named Skilling and Gull. Fed into a computer, the algorithm could turn an out-of-focus blur into a sharp and recognizable picture. Dempsey's technicians could strip the picture of Avranilosa in, then defocus the result to restore the telephoto blur.

"What are you up to, Frank?" Dempsey asked suspiciously. "Who is this Avranilosa guy, anyway?"

"Don't ask," Forsyth said. "Can you get me these fast, Jack?"

"Couple of days. That okay?"

"It'll have to do. Lose it on another case, will you? Don't bill it to me."

"Frank—"

"I know, I know. Just this once, Jack. Okay?"

Dempsey shook his head like a vexed uncle. "One of these days, Frank . . ."

"You're a pal, Jack. Hey, what's green and smells?"

"I'll buy it."

"Kermit's ass," Forsyth said.

Three days later, on a bright sunny morning with a sky the color of bleached denim, Forsyth drove out to Bal Harbour. He pulled the big Olds to a stop in front of the pole barrier at the gatehouse and wound down the window as the guard came out. The man had on a white pith helmet and an all-white uniform with blue epaulettes. He had a beer belly and a gun that looked big enough to blow a hole in a battleship.

"The agency I work for prefers not to show ID," Forsyth said to the man. "If you insist, however, I will do so."

The guard's eyes widened. He was an ex-policeman, and he knew the formula. "CIA?" he said. "What can I do for you?"

"What's your name?"

"Reilly, sir. John F. Reilly."

"That your cruiser over there, John?"

"Yessir."

"Let's you and me get in it, then, and you can give me a ride up to the Avranilosa house."

"Uh . . . sir, I can't—"

"What, John?"

"I'm supposed to call the house first."

"You know anything about Pedro Avranilosa, John? You know where his money comes from?"

"Look, whoever you are, it's not my responsibility, right? You take it up with Armorgard Security. They send me here, I do my job. And my job is to call all residents before admitting visitors."

"Today, you forget," Forsyth said, getting out of the car. "Come on, let's move it."

They got into the cruiser, a white Ford Mustang with a dome light and a blue stripe along the body. Reilly drove slowly through the estate, easing the car over the ramps. The air smelled of flowers and wet grass. And money, Forsyth thought as they rolled to a stop outside the gates of Avranilosa's house. He squinched down in back as the CCTV cameras swung in their watching arc. Reilly picked up the phone, waited, and said what Forsyth had told him to say.

"John Reilly here. Got a special-delivery package."

There was a short wait, long enough for the camera to scan the car, and Reilly standing in the sunshine. Then the ornate gates swung back. Reilly drove up to the parking area and stopped by a covered walkway that led up to the house. He was sweating badly.

"Get lost," Forsyth advised him. He got out of the car and walked up the ramp. Ahead of him, a young Chinese wearing a white coat and black trousers came out of the door.

"What you want?" he said. "How you get in here?"

"Where's your boss?"

"You leave, now!" the Oriental said.

"Drop the Charlie Chan act, kid, and take me to your leader," Forsyth said. The manservant moved in front of him, hands at his side, face impassive. Forsyth took a step, and the houseman immediately fell into a karate fighting stance, a sibilant hiss coming from his lips. Forsyth grinned and flipped back his jacket.

"What I have here is a Model 92 SB-C Beretta," he said conversationally. "It fires thirteen 9mm Parabellum slugs at a muzzle velocity of three hundred and ninety meters a second. Call it eight thousand five hundred miles an hour. What I want you to do is think about one of those bullets hitting your head."

The manservant looked at the gun and then up into Forsyth's eyes. He shrugged and put his hands down.

"I never was any good at that karate shit, anyway," he said. "He's out on the tennis court."

"Who else is around?"

"Chauffeur's day off. Two maids in the house. Bodyguard is with the Boss. That's it."

"Very good," Forsyth said. "Let's go surprise him."

The manservant led him through a patio commanding a splendid view across Biscayne Bay. The lawns were like green carpeting. The water in the pool was pellucid. A Hatteras 36 Convertible swayed at its mooring. The wages of sin, Forsyth thought: luxury.

He kept the Beretta in his hand as he followed the servant to the raised tennis court. He heard the familiar *blop!* of racquet hitting ball, and then, as they turned the corner, he saw Avranilosa. The Fat Man was alone on the court, returning balls fired at him by an electric tennis-ball cannon. A young Cuban with a skeletal face sat slumped in a canvas chair off to one side, torpid in the heat. Avranilosa swung angrily around when he saw them.

"What the—?" he snapped. "Lee, I told you never—"

"He's got a gun," Lee said laconically. The bodyguard snapped upright, his hand moving for the gun in its shoulder holster. Forsyth let him see the Beretta and he froze. Avranilosa looked left and right, edgy-eyed, like an animal hunting a hole.

"Stay put, Fat Man," Forsyth said. "Don't make me nervous, now."

"How the hell did you get in here?"

"Free fall," Forsyth said. He gestured at the bodyguard,

come here. "Take the gun out of the holster with your left hand, finger and thumb. That's it. Drop it on the ground, then step away from it."

The pistol hit the lush grass almost soundlessly. The Cuban took two steps backward, hands at his sides. His dark eyes glittered with anger.

"Face down on the ground," Forsyth said. "You, too, Confucius." The bodyguard and the servant stretched out prone, face down. Forsyth went across and picked up the Cuban's gun. It was a .357 Combat Magnum Smith & Wesson with a two-and-a-half-inch barrel. He threw it into the swimming pool.

"I know you," Avranilosa said. "I know you from someplace."

"The name is Forsyth. Is that any help?"

The Cuban's eyelids dropped, hooding his eyes. He put his tennis racquet down and wrapped a white cotton towel around his neck.

"What happens now?" he said.

"You and I are going to talk, Fat Man."

"I doubt we got anything to talk about."

"We'll see. You boys stay right there, hear me?" He gestured with the pistol toward the patio, where there was a white garden table shaded by a multicolored sunshade. "Let us cross over the river and rest in the shade of the trees," he said.

"What?"

"Never mind, Fat Man. Lead the way."

He sat in one of the chairs where he could keep an eye on the two men still lying prone on the lawn. Avranilosa sat on his left.

"You know who I am?" Forsyth said.

"I know," Avranilosa said. "What you want with me?"

"I want to talk to you about Nino Baca, Pedro," Forsyth asked. "You do know him, don't you?"

"I know who he is."

"Do business together?"

"I don't know what you're talking about."

"Let me put it into words of one syllable for you," Forsyth said. "Co-caine."

"I don't deal in drugs. My business is real estate. I'm a legitimate businessman, and you can't—"

Forsyth held up a hand. "Cut the bullshit, Pedro. You're talking to a pro."

Avranilosa started to say something but stopped when Forsyth thrust the fat folder of photographs into his hands.

"Look what I brought you," Forsyth said. The Cuban slid the eight-by-tens out of the envelope and shuffled through them, frowning. When he looked up, the anger in his eyes was burning bright.

"What is this?" he said.

"We call it 'compelled accommodation' these days," Forsyth said cheerfully. "It used to be called a frame-up."

"You out of your mind?" Avranilosa said angrily. "You think you can walk in here and pull a stunt like this?"

"Ask yourself a question," Forsyth suggested. "Ask yourself what I'm going to do with these pictures."

"You can set fire to them and jam them up your ass for all I care!"

"I tell you, Pedro, I admire you," Forsyth said. "I admire any man that can make jokes while he's looking death in the face."

Avranilosa frowned. "Just what the fuck are you talking about, Forsyth?" The veneer of sophisticated wealth was slipping a little. Forsyth smiled benevolently. It was like bringing in a sailfish: you had to know when to reel in, when to give it slack.

"You haven't put it together yet, have you?" he said. "I thought you were smart, Pedro."

Avranilosa's eyes narrowed to slits. "You think you can get away with this?" he hissed. "I make one call, you dead, man!

Hear me? You fucking dead!'' He slapped the table hard to emphasize his threat.

Forsyth made a little sound of annoyance and brought the butt of the Beretta down heavily on Avranilosa's hand. The Fat Man screeched with pain. Forsyth saw the bodyguard's hands curl tensely, but he didn't move. Smart cookie.

"I warned you, Pedro," Forsyth said. "This isn't a TV movie. You fuck with me, you're gonna get hurt."

"Looka my hand!" Avranilosa wailed, his voice halfway between a sob and a shout. "Look what you done to my hand!"

"I came here to get some information, pally," Forsyth said unsympathetically. "And you are going to give it to me. If you want me to beat the shit out of you first, say the word."

"I don't talk to you!" Avranilosa whined, nursing his hand beneath his arm and rocking from side to side. "I don't tell you fucking nothing!"

"You still haven't got it through your thick skull, have you, you tub of lard?" Forsyth said, putting all the contempt he could muster into his voice. "You tell me what I want to know, you do like I say, or Nino Baca gets a complete set of these pictures. And you wind up in a canal in Hialeah with your dick in your mouth."

"He wouldn't believe this!" the Cuban panted, his face slick with sweat. "Those pictures are fakes, and you know it!"

"Sure I know it," Forsyth said equably. "But your friend Baca doesn't. What you think he's gonna say when he sees this one, Pedro? That's you talking to Raoul Ramirez, deputy director of DGI. Or what about this one in the boat? You're shaking hands with Paco Ortiz—remember him? He went down for twenty years at Tallahassee a couple of months ago for smuggling coke. Didn't he try to muscle in on Baca's territory in South Miami? What you think Nino-baby would say if he saw this, Fat Man, or this one of you coming out of the Ministry of the Interior building in Havana?"

"I wasn't in any of those places! I've never seen Paco Ortiz in my life."

"All you got to do now is get Baca to believe you," Forsyth said. "What you think he'll do when he finds out he's been doing La Dirección's dirty work for them?"

Avranilosa did not reply, although if he could have killed Forsyth without moving, Forsyth would have dropped dead on the spot. The silence lengthened. Forsyth was in no hurry. The hook was in and set. He could see the sweat beading on the Cuban's upper lip. A big jet roared somewhere up high. Bees hummed in the flower borders. A blackbird landed on the lawn, saw them, and flew away.

"I can't talk to you," Avranilosa mumbled. "They would kill me for that just as easy."

"This is really a nice place you've got here, Pedro."

"You don't realize what you're asking."

"Pretty view," Forsyth said as if he hadn't heard the Cuban speak.

"You asking me to double, *hombre*," Avranilosa said. "I couldn't do it. I just wouldn't be able to cut it."

"It's not as if you had a choice," Forsyth said, turning to face him. "Is it?"

Avranilosa sighed; his shoulders slumped. "You hurt my hand real bad, you know that?"

"Tell me about Tony Genevevo," Forsyth said. "And the others."

"Listen, I'm not talking to you till I get some guarantees. I don't even know for sure who the hell you are."

"You know who I am, Fat Man. You know who I work for, just like I know who you work for. As for guarantees, I guarantee you I will shoot that bodyguard of yours right up the ass if he doesn't stop twitching."

"Raoul!" Avranilosa said sharply.

"That's better, Raoul," Forsyth said agreeably. "Now, about Genevevo. Baca wasted him, right?"

"You know, why you asking?"

"What was in it for him?"

"You got any idea what it's like on the street right now, fucking Colombians taking over everything in sight? Nino had a big deal going down, he couldn't take any chances. Genevevo knew everything we were doing."

"Too simple," Forsyth said. "Lay it out for me. Right from the beginning. How did you get onto Genevevo? Why were the security people taken out? Whose idea was it to dress it up like that? What was the payoff? Let me tell you what I'm thinking, Fat Man. I'm thinking that all this stinks of smokescreen. Am I right? Was the whole thing pulled to cover something completely different, something put up by your friends in Havana?"

Avranilosa fell silent again, his only reply a shrug of the shoulders. Time to give the fish a few fathoms of line, Forsyth decided: there wasn't much more fight in him. He let the silence lengthen again, watching a sailboat on the bay, gulls soaring effortlessly above its wake.

"Tell you what I really want to know, Pedro," Forsyth said, choosing his moment. "Did Genevevo find out what DGI was up to? Was that why you conned Baca into killing him?"

The Fat Man stared past him out across the blue water. After what seemed like a very long time, he sighed.

"You ever heard of a man named Frederic Drosdow?" he said

16

Eastern Airlines Flight EA 173 from Baltimore touched down at Miami International dead on time, a few minutes after 11 A.M. As it was the only such flight of the day, the plane was full, and there was a twenty-minute wait before Butler Mitchell got his luggage and headed for the cab rank. After a few minutes, the dispatcher signaled him to a Courtesy cab, and Mitchell told the driver to take him to the Hilton Fontainebleau at Miami Beach. Not for a moment did it occur to him that he was being watched.

At the hotel, he let the system wash over him. That was the great thing about luxury hotels: everywhere you went, there were doormen, bellmen, reception staff, and maids, smiling brightly, waiting to cater to your slightest whim. He always traveled with a wad of singles ready: everyone who lent a hand—and there was always someone ready to lend a hand—got a dollar. It wasn't big tipping by Miami Beach standards, but he knew that if you tipped frequently, word soon got around, even in a place as big as the Fontainebleau.

As soon as he was unpacked, he phoned down to the Oceanfront Spa and told them he'd like a massage. He put on a white Ralph Lauren polo shirt, a pair of white Dacron slacks, white toweling socks and a pair of Adidas Oregon running shoes. Then he went down to the main gallery of the hotel, feeling the familiar excitement of anticipation.

He always came to the Fontainebleau: the place had class.

Fourteen million dollars' worth, to be precise. That was what they'd spent refurbishing what had always been the most astonishing of all the "flabbergast" hotels on the beach. Soft lights, candelabra, real paintings on the walls. Class: the Fontainebleau had it in spades. Eighteen acres of tropical gardens, twelve hundred feet of private beach, a half-acre swimming pool, its own eighteen-hole golf course, three Jacuzzis, a bowling alley, six bars, a nightclub. In the Main Gallery restaurant, with its plants and antiques and statues, you could get the best prime rib in Florida. And in the Poodle Lounge, the best tail.

Mitchell went down to the restaurant in the tropically landscaped pool area. A calypso band beneath a thatched hut was playing a song about a little girl in Kingston Town. The maître d' showed him to a table beneath an umbrella.

"Welcome to Under the Trees, sir," he said. "Enjoy your meal."

The sun was hot and strong, a wonderful change from the gusty winds and rain of Baltimore. The jungly smell of irrigated plants mingled with those of good food, suntan oil, perfume, perspiration, the sea. Mitchell felt good, relaxed. He had been glad to get away from Cathie, from her constant catalog of dissatisfactions and her watery smile and the pathetic way she kept trying to get him to make love to her. He banished the picture of his wife from his mind: he had come to Miami for fun, not to think about Cathie.

The waitress came and took his order: two eggs over easy, Canadian bacon, hash browns, white toast, coffee. He leaned back in his chair, watching the lissome bodies of the young women around the pool with a fond, unfocused lust.

Six tables away, Drosdow watched the American and smiled. It looked as if this might be easier than he had thought.

That evening, relaxed after a whirlpool bath and a massage, Butler Mitchell patted some Aramis aftershave on his cheeks, looked at his watch, and then at his reflection in the bathroom mirror. Not bad, he thought. He had good shoulders, a deep chest, a flat belly. He was particularly careful about that. In his opinion, nothing turned a woman off faster than a fat gut.

He put on a Sea Island cotton shirt with monogrammed French cuffs, fastening them with chunky gold cuff links. He selected a dark blue silk Countess Mara tie with a narrow white diagonal stripe, and then put on the Palm Beach suit he'd bought for this trip. He slipped on his tasseled Gucci loafers, picked up a pack of Winston 100s, his loose change, his wallet, and his room key, and went out of the room.

He went straight down to the Poodle Lounge, which was on the same level as the starkly art-deco Steak House. The sounds of music, laughter, and conversation washed toward him like surf as he went in. He walked over to the bar. The bartender, a tubby, balding man wearing a white jacket, wore a lapel nameplate.

"Hi, George," Mitchell said, putting a twenty on the bar. "Let me have a large whiskey sour. Make that very sour, okay?"

"You got it," the bartender said, crashing a glass into the chipped ice. When the drink came, Mitchell left his change on the Leatherette bar in front of him. Glass in hand, he swiveled around on his stool to look the place over. Most of the tables were occupied by formally dressed couples, or foursomes. Formally dressed for Miami, anyway. The trio was playing an up-tempo version of "My Funny Valentine" for the dozen or so couples dancing in the center of the room. Older couples sat together, not saying anything to each other. Younger women, obviously vacationers, sat together in pairs. A blond woman with a sunburn met Mitchell's gaze and held it. She wore a pale blue V-necked sleeveless dress. Her hair was cut short, Kim Novak style. Mitchell smiled at her and then looked away. There was no rush. He ordered another drink and invited George the bartender to join him. George drew a Coke from the mixer and took a five-dollar bill from the pile on the bar.

"Pretty quiet, tonight," Mitchell observed.

"Early yet," George said, industriously polishing a glass. "Another half an hour, the place'll be jammed. You just get in today?"

"Right."

"Seen you before, though, ain't I?"

"I get down three, four times a year."

"Thought I knew your face. You get so you remember the regulars."

The man sitting next to Mitchell slid off his stool to leave, and Mitchell glanced at the newcomer taking his place. He was a swarthy, middle-aged man of medium height, with brilliant blue eyes and a pockmarked face. He wore a dark blue lightweight suit, a white shirt, and a neat tie. He ordered Glenfiddich on the rocks. Catching Mitchell's eye, he smiled sheepishly.

"Shouldn't do that to good whiskey," he said apologetically.

"Diff'rent strokes for diff'rent folks," Mitchell said.

"You on vacation?"

"Just taking a few days' break," Mitchell said.

"Where you from?"

"Near Baltimore," Mitchell said, half turning away. He didn't want to get tied up with some talkative traveling salesman or conventioneer.

"That's a coincidence," the man said. He had a faint regional accent that Mitchell couldn't place. Hell, he thought, half of the population of America had some sort of accent you couldn't place.

"You live in Baltimore?"

"I've got a place in Easton."

"Very nice," Mitchell said. Easton was in the heart of what they called the Maryland Tidewater, full of tradition and old money. "You on vacation, too?"

"Business and pleasure trip," the man said. "My daughter's down here with me. I'm in computer software. My own company, FD Associates."

"Can't say I've heard of it."

"We're small, but growing. Eight million turnover this year. It'll go to ten next year. The 'FD' stands for Fred Drosdow. That's me. What did you say your first name was?"

"Butler. But most people call me Mitch." Mitchell said reluctantly. The blond girl with the great haircut gave him another long look. If he was going to make a move on her, it had better be soon, Mitchell decided.

"Let me get you another of those," Drosdow said. "George, give us the same again here."

"No, don't do that," Mitchell said hastily. "Thanks all the same, Fred. I'm meeting someone. Don't want to be squiffed when they get here."

It was at that moment that she walked in. She was about five feet eight, maybe a hundred and twenty pounds. Blond hair framed a heart-shaped face with violet-colored eyes and a sprinkling of freckles across the bridge of a slightly retroussé nose. She wore a white Halston day dress and Ferragamo sandals. To Mitchell's astonishment, she came directly toward him, smiling. Just as he thought she was about to speak to him, he realized she was looking at the man sitting next to him.

"I thought I'd find you here," she said, shaking a finger at Drosdow mock-reprovingly. "Can't take my eyes off you for a second, can I?"

"There you are, Kate," Drosdow said. "I was just talking to this gentleman here while I waited for you."

"How do you do, Mr.—?"

"Mitchell," he blurted, shaking the soft, slender, cool hand. "Butler Mitchell. But everyone calls me Mitch. May I offer you a drink, Miss Drosdow?"

"I think . . . not," she said, looking around. "I prefer somewhere a little . . . quieter."

She happened to be looking right into Mitchell's eyes as she spoke, and for a moment he thought there was a message behind

124 •

the words. She was still looking at him, the indigo eyes guileless. No, he told himself. He was imagining it. Still . . .

"Have you any plans for dinner?" he heard himself saying, astonished by his own temerity.

Drosdow looked at him, surprised. "I thought you said you were meeting some friends?" he said. "Anyway, we can't. Already got a date. Some other time, maybe."

"You're staying here?"

"Penthouse," Drosdow said. "We'd better be going, Kate."

"You will give us a rain check, won't you . . . Mitch?" the girl said, touching the back of Mitchell's hand as Drosdow turned to leave. It seemed to him that there was something in the contact, a hint of a promise that made his heart bump suddenly. Their eyes met again. He had not been mistaken: there was frank invitation there now.

"Of course," he mumbled, hoping his voice didn't sound as thick as it felt in his throat. He watched Kate Drosdow as she followed her father out of the room. She made the other women in the place look dowdy. Class, Mitchell thought, you can always spot it. She had been wearing an emerald ring that must have been worth every cent of five thou. He finished his drink. The blond woman was still sitting alone. She met his glance and smiled.

Much later, as she squirmed and moaned beneath his thrusting body, he tried to imagine that the blond woman was Kate Drosdow. It was no use; he began to loathe her ten seconds after he climaxed. Her name was Martha Cobbett, a divorcée from Boston. As she got dressed, she asked him if he could loan her a hundred, you know, until her alimony came through. He gave her a fifty to get rid of her, then took a long, punishing shower to wash the bitch smell off him before he went to sleep.

Next morning he called the penthouse. Drosdow answered, and they arranged to meet for brunch in the Gallery. Mitchell made a reservation, then showered and shaved, putting on a pale lilac Yves St. Laurent shirt and a white Calvin Klein suit. He got to the restaurant ten minutes early and asked for the wine list. He knew only a little about champagne, so he played safe by ordering Dom Perignon. He told the sommelier to bring it right away and open it. He was sipping his first glass, looking out over the tropical gardens and the rock grotto at the ocean, when Drosdow and his daughter came in.

Kate Drosdow was wearing a lemon-yellow Bill Blass shift that bared creamy shoulders and elegant, lightly-tanned arms. The shift was gathered loosely at the waist by a thin gold chain. She wore no jewelry other than a tiny white gold Rolex Cellini watch. She looked cool and very self-possessed.

"Champagne!" she said. "How lovely!"

"Dom Perignon, too," Drosdow observed. He had on a dark blue Corbin blazer and pale gray slacks, a white shirt open at the neck to reveal a heavy gold chain. "You must be doing well, Mr. Mitchell. What line of business are you in?"

"I work for the government," Mitchell said, giving the standard nonspecific answer. "Just another civil servant."

"You must be a very well paid one if you can afford Dom Perignon in a place like this," Drosdow said. "What do they charge for that here?"

"I'm afraid I didn't look," Mitchell said, hoping it sounded as casual as he wanted it to.

"Oh, Fred, stop being crass!" Kate said fondly. "Just ignore him, Mr. Mitchell. It was a lovely thought."

"Most people call me Mitch," he said.

"What's your first name?"

"My mother called me after a character in a book," Mitchell said. "*Gone With the Wind*. She said we had some vague family connection with the woman who wrote it."

"I saw that movie," Drosdow said. "What was the man's name?"

"Clark Gable," Mitchell said. "He played the part of Rhett Butler."

"I remember," Kate said. "He was quite a man." She looked into Mitchell's eyes as she spoke, and yet again, he felt there was more coming at him than the words alone.

"Well, young fellow, are you ready to eat?" Drosdow said.

"Thanks for the 'young fellow.'" Mitchell smiled. "It's very flattering, but a bit inaccurate, I'm afraid. I'm forty-six."

"You don't look it," Kate said. They went across to the buffet. Mitchell was pleased to see she wasn't one of those women who make a production out of what they can and cannot eat. It was one of the things about Cathie that gave him such a pain. Kate Drosdow selected herself a healthy meal.

"How old is your father?" he asked as they walked back to their table.

"He's . . . fifty-five. Fifty-six this year. But don't tell him I told you."

"So how come he called me 'young fellow'?"

She laughed. "Anyone younger than him is a young fellow to my father."

"Are you his only daughter?"

"That's right."

"How come a beautiful woman like you isn't married?"

"Well, thank you, Mitch. As a matter of fact, I was married once. A long time ago. I prefer my freedom."

"Me too," he said.

During the meal, he discovered that they had a lot in common. They agreed that Hawaii was ruined, Acapulco, too. They argued over which of the Caribbean islands was best and whether the clams were better at Faidley's or Obrycki's. The talk turned to films, then books, then TV. They seemed fascinated by Mitchell's opinions. Drosdow ordered another bottle of champagne. People turned their heads when the cork popped. Mitchell feigned indifference. He felt witty and worldly. The problems he had left behind him in Maryland seemed a million miles away.

". . . If you ask me, Sondheim hasn't written anything to

compare for sheer theatrical daring with *Pacific Overtures*," he said, pouring the last of the champagne. "There were magnificent things in *Sweeney Todd,* of course, notably that marvelous moment right at the end when Todd slams the door. But—"

"Mitch, I could sit here all day listening to you," Drosdow said. "But I've got to run. One of my people flew in from Rio especially to see me. He's got to fly back tomorrow, so I've got no choice. You'll forgive me?"

"Don't give it a thought," Mitchell said, waving a lordly hand. "Let's do this again real soon."

"Good idea," Drosdow said. "Kate, you coming?"

"I'm in good hands, Fred," she said, smiling at Mitchell. "You run along."

When he was gone, she turned to Mitchell and smiled conspiratorially. "I bet I know what you're thinking," she said.

"What?" he said, startled, thinking, *If you knew.*

"You're thinking, 'Oh, God, I'm stuck with this damned woman for the afternoon.' Well, you're not, so don't worry about it. I'm used to Fred dashing off and leaving me on my own."

"I can't think of anyone I'd rather be stuck with, as you put it," Mitchell said with what he felt was clumsy gallantry.

"The man's a charmer!" she said, amazed. "It must be the champagne."

"You're very beautiful," he said. The smile on her face did not change, but again he thought he saw something in her eyes and decided to believe it was encouragement. "And I can think of nothing I'd like more than to be with you . . . as often as possible."

He said it in a way that left her no room to doubt what he meant. He saw her expression change: impatience, annoyance, what? She looked away from him and then back again, and now the smile was gone.

"I think I'd better leave," she said coolly. She rose, and

Mitchell stood, too, awkwardly uncertain. "Thanks for brunch."

"Please," he begged. "It came out wrong. I meant—"

"Good-bye, Mr. Mitchell," she said. He watched the soft, flowing movements of her thighs and body as she walked away, and he thought *shit!* Kate Drosdow wasn't some housewife from Oshkosh looking for a quickie to round out her Florida package tour. She was wealthy, sophisticated, and intelligent, and he had gone at her like a drunken marine in a Kobe whorehouse. *Jerk,* he told himself.

He called for the check. It was well over a hundred dollars. Like all rich men, Drosdow hadn't given a thought to the second bottle of champagne he'd ordered. Mitchell's dismay lasted only a few moments. Look at it as an investment, he told himself. So he'd been a jerk; that was no reason to go on being one. Anything in life worth having cost money. You had to go for it.

He went down to the florist in the shopping gallery and ordered two dozen long-stemmed roses for delivery to Kate Drosdow. He stared at the card for a long time trying to decide what to write. Finally, he wrote four words: *"Let me try again."* After much thought, he added another: *"Please."* Then he went back to his room and stayed there, smoking his way through a pack of cigarettes and staring sightlessly at the daytime soaps on TV. Shortly after five, the telephone rang. He pounced on it.

"Thank you for the flowers," her soft voice said. "They're lovely."

"They ought to be ashamed to be in the same room as you," he said. "Kate? Are you still there?"

"I'm here."

"I just . . . I apologize. But I'm not sorry for what I said. I meant every word of it. I want to—"

"Don't waste it on the telephone," she said, and he thought she sounded as if she was smiling.

"Just say where," he said, "and when."

"Fred's here, but he's got to go out again," she said. "Why don't you come up for a drink? Later we can go out to dinner."

"Ten minutes," he said, and hung up. *"Later,"* she'd said. He shaved carefully, cleaned his teeth, and changed his clothes from the skin out. When he was ready, he looked in the mirror, a smile of triumph on his face. It would have vanished in an instant had he been able to overhear what was being said in the penthouse suite on the crescent-shaped top floor of the hotel.

"He's coming up," Katja Renis said to Drosdow.

"You think he's hooked?"

She smiled contemptuously. "He's hooked," she said.

17 Once he accepted what had happened to him, Avranilosa became positively anxious to talk. That happened sometimes: you turned someone, and the information spilled out of him like a pan boiling over, as if the telling itself were an act both of confession and contrition. That was the good news.

The bad news was that, as usual, Forsyth's boss had gone for the glory. Avranilosa wasn't a very big fish, but Bensen acted as if they'd turned the chief of the KGB, firing off a series of memoranda to Washington to make it perfectly clear that if anyone deserved credit for rolling up the Cuban espionage operation, that someone was good old Donald Bensen.

Forsyth wasn't as worried about who got a gold star as he was about the fact that Bensen's memos would bring all sorts of I-teams down from the head office to interrogate the Fat Man. Which meant he had to get what he wanted before they arrived. To his furious surprise, Bensen told him he was keeping Avranilosa under wraps until the dredgers arrived.

"Domestic Operations Division wants first interrogation privileges," he announced. Forsyth shook his head in disbelief.

"What about us? Aren't we acting for Domestic Ops?"

"They're sending specialists to debrief this man, Frank."

"We don't need specialists. We don't need anybody!" he said angrily. "This honey trap thing is our baby, Donald. It's on our patch. It's my privilege, for Christ's sake, not Langley's!''

"You'll get your chance, Frank," Bensen said. "Lighten up.''

"What the hell kind of talk is that?" Forsyth said savagely. "If it means what I think it means—'take it easy'—I'm not in the mood. I want first turn with the Fat Man, Donald. Goddamnit, I'm the one who brought him across.''

"I remember," Bensen said waspishly. "And if I were to forget, I'm sure you'd remind me. But you'll have to wait, Frank. A lot of people—"

"Let *them* wait!''

"You want me to tell Langley they'll have to get in line because one of my field agents wants priority?" Bensen said sweetly, twisting the knife of emphasis on Forsyth's rank. "You'll just have to be patient a little longer.''

"Look, you've read my preliminary report," Forsyth said. "From what Avranilosa told me, it looks as if we've probably had Cuban—and for 'Cuban' you can read 'Russian'—military intelligence working right under our noses, and we didn't know a damned thing about it.''

"I'm aware of that," Bensen said tartly. He did not need reminding: some sharp words had been spoken when he talked to the head of Domestic Ops at Langley. "All sorts of other people are interested now, Frank. Whether you like it or not.''

"Donald, let me have Avranilosa for a few hours, and I can wrap this thing up for you," Forsyth said. "Just a few hours.''

He watched Bensen carefully, saw the flicker of opportunism in the evasive eyes. He knew how the man's mind worked. To trash a Russian operation on home ground, on top of turning Avranilosa—it was too sweet for someone as greedy for kudos as Bensen to resist. Come on, Donnie baby, he thought: go for it.

"Well," Bensen said, pursing his lips and steepling his fingers. "I don't know, Frank. How many men would it take?''

"Just a couple," Forsyth said. "I'll handle that. But I need the Fat Man, Donald."

"Well . . ." Bensen deliberated. "Where do you plan to talk to him?"

"How about the Sonesta Beach Hotel on Key Biscayne? To-morrow morning, ten-thirty."

Bensen drew in his breath sharply. "Tricky, Frank," he said. "We'd be putting him in harm's way if he was on the street. I don't think that would be at all wise."

"I want some psychological distance, Donald. I don't want to talk to him in the interrogation suite."

"How long would you need? There's a team flying down from NSA. DEA are asking for him, too. And—"

"I'll have him back before you know he's been out."

"I'm not sure—"

"Who is?" Forsyth said.

The Sonesta Beach Hotel looked like a pre-Columbian Mexican temple would have looked if the Mayans had known about prestressed concrete. It was about the last place on earth anyone would have chosen for an intelligence debriefing, which was why Forsyth selected it. The moment you walked into the place, you became as anonymous as the plants. He took a luxury double on the fifth floor. The room had a king-size bed with a coverlet that matched the drapes, a table, some chairs, a couch upholstered in white plastic. A balcony overlooked the beach. Some kids were sailing a catamaran on the ocean; its multi-colored sails had the name of the hotel stenciled on them.

Two IS officers brought Avranilosa in. He looked tired, older. He was wearing a rumpled seersucker suit, a white cotton/poly shirt, and scuffed loafers. He looked at Forsyth and then, without much interest, at the two men by the window.

"The tall one is Mike, the other one is Harry," Forsyth said. Harry Lloyd was forty-five, balding, short, and overweight. His clothes looked as if they'd been bought at a K-Mart. Balfour was tall, thin, and studious-looking. He wore a dark blue mohair suit, a white shirt, and a dark tie. He had the air of a small-town high-school teacher.

Avranilosa sat down and waited; he had become used to waiting. He was happy to have a change of scenery, to be in a room with real furniture, with a window with a view. Outwardly, he appeared calm, but it was a pretense: inside him fear seethed. He had been a fool. Suppose they weren't going to give him a pension and a new identity, as he'd thought? Suppose they were going to put him back on the street and use him as a double agent? He would spend the rest of his life walking on eggshells.

"How've you been, Pedro?" Forsyth asked. "They looking after you okay?"

"Oh, yeah, great," Avranilosa said heavily.

He was being kept in a safe house in Kendall. He never knew where he was or whether it was day or night. Food came at irregular intervals; he ate it automatically, as if it were a chore. He slept in an air-conditioned room which had no windows. Two doors: one that was always locked, except when the bland-faced orderly brought in his meals; the other leading into a second, equally anonymous room with a table and four chairs. There were no windows there either. No clock, no calendar, nothing.

Forsyth began very slowly, asking innocuous questions that were easy to answer. He knew the secret was to make Avranilosa relax and lose his fear. They talked about what would happen after all the debriefings were over; Forsyth assured the Fat Man he'd see to it personally that they didn't put him back on the street. He understood him. He respected his views. They talked about the island, sports, anything. Avranilosa relaxed. His uneasiness began to abate.

"I guess I got to start talking to you guys, right?" he said.

"Sooner or later," Forsyth said.

"Where you want me to begin?"

"Anyplace you like."

Avranilosa began by describing how Havana had financed his real-estate operation so that he could provide cover residences in Miami for DGI agents. He laundered money which was used to fund the political campaigns of agents DGI wished to infiltrate into local government and law-enforcement agencies. He was supplied with narcotics connections in order to establish a relationship with Saturnino Baca, so that DGI could infiltrate the man's organization and monitor his activities.

"So DGI knew Baca was finding it harder to make good connections in Colombia," Forsyth said.

"I told you. Them Indians, they won't deal with nobody but each other."

"And when your friend Drosdow came along, it must have been like answered prayers—a reliable source for big shipments of top-quality cocaine."

"Answered prayers is right."

"Listen, Pedro," Forsyth told him. "What we're here for today is, I want you to tell Harry and Mike about your friend Frederic Drosdow."

"Jesus, I already spent hours telling you about him," the Fat Man said wearily. "Don't you ever quit, Forsyth?"

"'Winners never quit. Quitters never win,'" Forsyth quoted sententiously. "Old American saying."

"Old American bullshit," Avranilosa said irritably. "Why don't you guys just listen to the tapes I made for Forsyth here?"

"Drosdow, Pedro. Start at the beginning."

"Okay, okay. I got word from Havana, make contact with this guy Drosdow, staying at the Omni. Give him anything he asks for, *carta blanca*. I asked a few questions, but he wasn't giving anything away. They tell me his name, Drosdow, they say he's Turkish. Well, he's dark-skinned, he could be anything, but Turkish he isn't. So I figure he must be KGB; they usually are. Later I decided he might just be GRU. Whatever he was, he had a lot of juice, man. Havana couldn't do enough for him. So he tells me he's from Colombia, he's got a connection down there for cocaine. My job is to be his guarantor, he wants to do business only with Nino Baca. I ask him why, he says I don't need to know.''

"Didn't you wonder what it was all about?"

"Of course I wondered. I couldn't figure it out. I thought, What's DGI doing, why are we helping Moscow to run snow? Then I thought maybe he's doing it on the side, you know what I'm saying? Making a few bucks after hours, you know how they go for hard currency. Then I find out this guy was talking sixty million dollars worth, man. And the best. I mean, the *very* best.''

"He told you he bought it in Colombia?"

"That's what he said.''

"Who was he dealing with?" Balfour asked, polishing his glasses like a fussy old maid. "You got any names for us?"

Avranilosa shrugged. "He never told me any more than he had to. Same as you people, right?"

"You're cute," Lloyd said. "How'd you like a smack in the mouth?"

"Let's try some on you," Balfour interrupted. "How about Ocampo? No? What about Pablo Escobar? Alberto Prieto?"

"Prieto's all washed up, man," Avranilosa sneered. "Don't you guys know that?"

"Who, then?"

"Jesus, how many times have I got to repeat this? I don't know, man. You want me to guess, I'd say it was Fabio Ochoa. Drosdow once said something about seeing a corrida while he was down there. Ochoa's son Jorge thinks he's some kind of bullfighter. They fly toreros in from Mexico, Spain even, just so he can show off.''

"You think it's worth checking out Medellín, Frank?" Lloyd said.

"Suppose you go down to Medellín, what you think you gonna find out, man?" Avranilosa said patiently, as if explaining a complex mechanism to a child. "This isn't some tourist you're dealing with here. You think he went down there and told them his real name, asked for a copy of *Pravda*, maybe? Shit, you can't be that dumb."

"All right, let's move on. You made the intro, Drosdow checked out, Baca made the deal. They brought the coke in on a schooner," Forsyth said. "You were at Lower Matecumbe Key when it came in. What was the name of the boat?"

"I never even looked," Avranilosa said flatly. "They told me, keep the hell away from the dock, I kept the hell away from the dock. I'm gonna get my throat cut just to look at a *boat*?"

"They moved the stuff in three trucks. Where did it go?"

"First, to Little Havana to be cut and packed. Then it was shipped north, like I said. They send it up in limos driven by women dressed as nuns. They make drops in New York, Washington, Atlantic City."

"Names, names," Lloyd said impatiently. "What about some names, Pedro?"

"I know nothing about that side of it," Avranilosa said, shaking his head. "I've never even been in Baca's warehouse."

"You said Baca paid Drosdow off at the Indies Inn. Sixty million in cash?"

"If you want to be picky, it was actually sixty-one million," Avranilosa said. "But yes, the payoff was in cash."

"Trusting soul, your man Drosdow," Harry remarked. "What was to stop Baca feeding him to the sharks?"

"They were doing *business*, man!" the Cuban said wearily. "Why would Baca want to ice a good supplier?"

"Then Drosdow went to Key Largo."

"That's what he said. To pick up the woman."

"Ah," Balfour said. "Tell us about her."

Avranilosa repeated it all: that he had never seen the girl, that her name was Katja, that she was to meet Drosdow at the Holiday Inn on Largo. That was it.

"He tell you how he planned to use her?"

"Not in so many words. But I knew this, I heard that, it wasn't too hard to figure out. The plan was to compromise some CIA guy, name of Bogdanovich or something. Drosdow had a contact in Washington who knew Bogdanovich, a guy name Crane. He gets Bogdanovich to come to Miami, where he introduces him to the girl. She takes him to Marco Island. You know how it goes."

"What else do you know about this Crane?"

"Only what I told you. What Drosdow said."

"We ran Bogdanovich through the computers till steam came out, Pedro," Forsyth said. "And we came up zilch. Bogdanovich doesn't know anybody named Crane, or any imaginable variant of the name."

"What do you want me to say?" Avranilosa said. "I'm telling you what I heard. I'm not swearing that it's true. That bastard Drosdow lied to everyone else, why wouldn't he lie to me?"

"Something else, Pedro," Lloyd said. "Apart from the fact that Bogdanovich is clean enough to squeak, he's a nobody. If your friend Drosdow is GRU, as you seem to think, why would he be going to so much trouble to recruit a lousy coding clerk?"

Avranilosa shrugged. "You think he'd tell me?"

"Let's go over it again," Balfour said in his pedantic way. "You're talking to Drosdow. He's telling you about the man in Washington. What were his exact words?"

"He said he didn't want to spring the trap in Washington. Not enough psychological distance, he said. Fortunately, Bogdanovich is very friendly with this guy Crane who works for British intelligence in Washington. What Bogdanovich doesn't know is that Crane is a sleeper GRU turned in Germany years ago."

"You're sure he said Washington?" Forsyth insisted. "He actually said that?"

Avranilosa frowned. "No," he said slowly. "Now you mention it, he just said the guy was a friend of Bogdanovich's. I assumed if he was, it would be in Washington."

"Could the name you heard have been Caine?" Forsyth asked. "C-a-i-n-e?"

"Just as easy." The Cuban shrugged. "I told you, I'm not sure, man."

"Drosdow didn't by any chance mention Louisville, Kentucky?"

Avranilosa shook his head. "No," he said decisively. "I'd have remembered that."

There was no doubt in Forsyth's mind that Avranilosa was telling them the truth. Put a polygraph on him and you wouldn't get a flicker. Which wasn't the same as saying that what he was telling them was *true*. He was telling them what Drosdow had told him, or allowed him to know. And there lay the anomaly: if Drosdow had been feeding Avranilosa disinformation, that would suggest Drosdow knew what was going to happen to the Fat Man.

And there was no way he could have known that.

Was there?

"Who's Caine?" Harry Lloyd asked.

"Just a thought," Forsyth muttered. The security firm which had been watching Genevevo had been working for British Customs and Excise—they said. The dossier he had requested from Langley had shown that their senior man in the southeastern United States was called David Caine. The two names weren't all that dissimilar. It might be worth running a check on the off chance.

Forsyth decided to try the long shot. He went across to the phone and put in a call to Jack Dempsey. Speaking quietly, so the others would not hear, he told Dempsey what he wanted and asked him to get it on the mainframe as soon as he could. Then he turned back to Avranilosa.

"Okay, Pedro," Lloyd was saying. "Exactly where on Marco Island is this house they're using?"

"I don't *know,* man!" Avranilosa shouted irascibly. "How many times I got to say it, I don't *know*! Go put it through you fucking computer!"

"Tell you what," Mike Balfour said, standing up to stretch his arms above his head and yawn cavernously. "We're reason able men. Let's go over it again. But this time we concentrate on Drosdow, right?"

"How many more times you gonna make me go through this?" Avranilosa complained. "My throat's like a chemica toilet!"

"You want something?" Forsyth said. "Coffee, tea?"

"How about a piña colada?"

"Sure," Forsyth said. He dialed room service and told them to send up drinks. Meanwhile, Harry Lloyd was telling Avranilosa he might as well get started.

"What you tryna do, man?" the Cuban complained. "You tryna break my brain?"

"Don't tempt me," Lloyd said.

"It's just as wearing for us, Pedro," Balfour smiled, taking the sting away from his partner's retort. "But you might jus have forgotten something, some unimportant detail that wil help us crack this. You never know."

They went over it all again. The drinks came and were consumed. Another hour went by, and then another. They kept or at the Cuban until they could think of nothing else to ask him. until they felt confident there was nothing more he could tell them.

"Okay, Pedro, relax," Forsyth said. "Take it easy."

"Listen, man, I need another drink," Avranilosa said.

"Not worth bothering now, Pedro. Time for you to go back where you came from."

140 ▪

"You guys are all fucking heart, you know that?" Avranilosa said disgustedly. "I break my ass for you here, what? Two, three hours, what do I get? One lousy piña colada."

"Tell you what," Lloyd said brightly. "We'll lie awake tonight and feel bad about it."

Forsyth went across to the telephone and called Internal Security. Then he hung up and dialed another number.

"Forsyth," he said. "We're through with the Fat Man. IS is on its way now. No, nothing new. Yes, Marco Island. We're flying out there in about an hour. Yes, Lloyd and Balfour. Uh-huh. Uh-huh. Did you talk to the local police, Donald? Who? Is that like Byron the poet? Lieutenant Tom Byron, Collier County Sheriff's Office. Got it. No, I can find it. Okay, good."

He hung up. Lloyd and Balfour were watching him expectantly.

"We're in business!" Forsyth said. "The local police did the legwork for us. They've located the house on Marco Island. They're keeping an eye on the place till we get there."

After about half an hour the IS escort arrived to take Avranilosa back to the safe house. Forsyth patted the Cuban on the shoulder as he went out the door. "Stay out of trouble, *amigo*," he said.

"Thanks a lot," Avranilosa said. "What happens to me now, Forsyth?"

"A lot of people want to talk to you, Pedro. You're going to be kept busy for a long time."

"I mean, when all this is over? What then?"

"You'll get a new name, money, a new place to live. You'll be okay."

"You better be right, man. If Nino Baca or DGI ever get a line on me, I'm alligator food."

"Any alligator tried to eat you would puke," Forsyth said. "Go on, get him out of here!"

The security men led Avranilosa out into the corridor and down to the rear entrance in the freight elevator. All the way back to Miami, the Fat Man kept thinking about Forsyth. And Baca. And Drosdow. And how nice it would be if they all killed each other.

18

After two days of kicking his heels at the Willard waiting for the telephone call summoning him to Arlington, Caine's nerves were stretched thin. He knew Miles well enough to know he was being punished, not so much for his actual insubordination—if you wanted to call it that—as for flouting Kingly's direct order. He went through the usual check-in procedure and proceeded to Kingly's office. Betty Torre waved him in, avoiding his eyes.

The office looked just the same. So did Kingly. He was wearing another of his Tom Gilbey suits, with a pale blue silk shirt that looked like Turnbull & Asser. This time the tie was Stowe.

"Sit down," he said. His manner was stiff with disapproval. He put the papers he had been working on into a drawer and leaned back in his chair.

"I've read your report," he said. "Interesting."

"That's one way of describing it," Caine replied.

"You believe this Sanchez woman?"

"No reason not to."

"You followed up on what she told you?"

"It's all in the report."

"You were supposed to check in twice a day. No excuses. You did not do so."

"Miles, you knew where I was."

"*Au contraire*, dear boy, I knew no such damned thing. And I am not best pleased with your conduct."

"I made what seemed like a sensible decision. I'm sorry if it was wrong."

"You didn't really think you were going to find this Drosdow in Key Largo, did you?"

"I thought it was worth checking out."

"So you spent three days sitting by the pool of a Holiday Inn without feeling it necessary to tell anyone where you were."

Caine did not speak. Kingly's attitude would have been quite different if he had located Drosdow; but he hadn't, and now it was time to pay the piper. Nothing he said would make any difference now anyway.

Kingly folded his hands and unfolded them again. "There's no easy way of saying this. I imagine you know why I called you in, David. I'm taking you out of the field."

"Damn it, Miles, I—"

"No arguments, please," Kingly said sharply. "You're lucky I'm not sending you for a face job."

Caine shrugged. It was *de rigueur* for consultants whose face had become the property of the opposition to be sent to Los Angeles for plastic surgery. At least he was being spared that.

"Who will you put on this?"

"We'll see," Kingly said, evading the question. He took a batch of computer printouts from the drawer of his desk and plunked them in front of Caine.

"I want you to look at something before you go," he said. There was a strange, expectant look in his eyes.

"What's this?" Caine asked.

"Your friend Forsyth turned Avranilosa. He's singing like a nightingale."

"I don't believe it."

"It's all in the summary. Take it away and read it."

Caine looked at the printout. It was an ISS summary of a Domestic Ops interrogation transcript, security code BLACK-ALP, dated three days earlier.

144 •

"How the hell did you get hold of this?" he asked. Kingly gave his noncommittal, ask-me-no-questions smile.

"Maybe I got it off the Comrades," he said playfully.

"Then you'd have to tell me how they got it."

"All right, then, suppose I told you that the Joint Intelligence Chiefs got DI6 to request Langley's cooperation in an ongoing Customs and Excise investigation into cocaine smuggling out of Miami, and asked for anything they had on a man named Avranilosa. On a quid pro quo basis, of course."

"Is that what happened?"

"It could be. Or it could be that I've got my own man inside Domestic Operations. Or that I put a squad of computer hackers on to it and they broke into the Domestic Ops mainframe."

"That I'd find easier to believe."

"Take your pick. My point is that you don't need to know where I got it from," he said coldly. "Just read it and tell me what your conclusions are."

"Yes," Caine said. "Sir."

He was still trying to figure out how Forsyth could have turned the Cuban so quickly. He must have gotten him between a rock and a very hard place, and Caine wondered what it had been. He realized Kingly was sitting back in his chair, steepled fingers touching his lips, as though he was expecting to be asked something. Caine could not imagine what it was.

"I'll use the visitor desk," he said.

"Yes, do," Kingly said remotely.

An hour later, Caine put down the ITS, a frown of concentration creasing his brow. He went through it slowly in his mind, to fix it there once and for all. Frederic Drosdow, probably a GRU officer, had arranged to sell $61 million worth of cocaine to Saturnino Baca through Pedro Avranilosa, not realizing the latter was under surveillance by Genevevo. The Cubans got a tip-off that Genevevo was an undercover agent (from whom? Caine wondered), and DGI surveillance not only confirmed it but revealed the presence on the ground of ISS. Somehow Avranilosa had persuaded Baca that whatever Genevevo knew, ISS knew, too. The only way he could protect the drug deal was by killing Genevevo and at the same time neutralizing ISS.

With Genevevo and the ISS operatives out of the way, the drug sale was finalized, and now Drosdow was using the proceeds to finance a honey trap operation on Marco Island, near Naples, Florida. The target was a senior coding clerk in CIA Communications, Paul Bogdanovich. Simple, except for the questions it raised. Like what possible reason could Russian military intelligence have for setting up so sophisticated an operation to suborn a low-level paper pusher? And what was Drosdow doing with the rest of the money?

Caine went back along the corridor to Kingly's office. Betty Torre waved him in.

"He's been waiting for you," she said. Caine frowned; that wasn't Kingly's style at all.

"You've read the ITS, then?" Kingly said. "What's your reaction?"

"Puzzlement," Caine said. Kingly was watching him very closely. He wondered why. Was there something about this he hadn't been told?

"Because?"

"They're going to an awful lot of trouble for a low-echelon coding clerk."

"They're not particular," Kingly said.

"The Comrades never spend a dollar when a dime will do," Caine retorted. "Do you think Avranilosa could be lying?"

"Hardly likely," Kingly said. "They'll have dredged him pretty comprehensively."

No doubt of that, Caine thought. The Russians had no monopoly on ruthlessness. The CIA would squeeze Avranilosa like a lemon, and then some more, and then some more. When they were through, they would know everything he knew about everyone he knew. Especially Saturnino Baca. The Company

146 •

didn't like having its operatives killed by the opposition, especially on American soil. Sooner, rather than later, Baca would be involved in what the Punishment Squad at Langley called, with typical gravedigger humor, a "Pan Am," from the airline's initials PAA, Prearranged Accident.

"There's an element missing somewhere," he said to Kingly. "Whatever Drosdow is up to, there's more to it than a honey trap in Florida."

"We'll be keeping it under review," Kingly said. "Is that all?"

"What do you mean, all?"

"Was there anything else in the ITS you want to discuss?"

Caine frowned. "No."

"Very well," Kingly said. "Where are you going to take your gardening leave?"

"I'll leave it to you," Caine said. "Gardening leave" was civil service argot for "suspension time." "London, perhaps?"

"See what we can do," Kingly said.

"I'll need to pick up some things in Louisville," Caine said. "I can take the four o'clock plane."

"Good," Kingly said. "Call McClelland when you're ready to travel. I'll be in touch as soon as you can be reestablished." He did not get up or offer to shake hands. Caine swallowed his frustration and went out, squeezing Betty Torre's shoulder as he passed. She gave him one of those instant on-off smiles. He decided to call in and see Dick McClelland, who had just returned from a courier trip to London. He beamed as Caine came through the door.

"Hello, old son, how are you?" he said, getting up to shake hands. "I hear you had a bit of poor luck in Miami. Tea and sympathy?"

"Coffee would be better."

McClelland waved him to a chair and glanced over at his duty officer. Dave Hedges, a small, neat man, caught his chief's look, smiled, and went out, closing the door softly behind him.

"Damned good chap, that," McClelland said.

"How was London?"

"Full of grockles," he grumbled, using his pejorative word for tourists. "Tubes are worse than bloody cattle trains, especially the ones from Heathrow. Harrods is full of people screaming 'Take my money, take my money, give me anything but take my money!'"

"Any news?"

"Didn't Miles tell you? Curzon Street House is vibrating like a bloody Chinese gong, old lad. They lost Viktor."

"What?"

"Disappeared without a trace, two months ago. Red faces all round. Nobody can figure it out."

Caine recalled Kingly telling him about Viktor, the colonel in the GRU's Second Directorate who had defected the preceding year. Viktor was the one who had named Jamison, the KGB mole at Curzon Street House, and precipitated the investigation of Genevevo.

"DI5's been sitting on it for two months?"

"I gather they thought he'd been lifted by his own people. They're leaning more now toward the idea that he's done a runner. Tony Duff is absolutely livid. They'd only had him six months. Nowhere near finished with him. Lots of other agencies waiting in line. I rather gather relations between DI5 and Langley have become somewhat strained."

Caine recalled that the Americans had been asking for their turn with Viktor. Was that why he had decided to disappear?

"What's the consensus?" he asked.

"There isn't one. If he ran, where did he run to, and why? If he was lifted, why hasn't there been a circus?"

When a defector was taken back by his own people he usually reappeared in Russia very soon thereafter, most often at a press conference stage-managed by the KGB. Before the world's press, he would protest at the outrageous methods of the British secret service, which had lured him to a hotel, drugged him,

148 •

flown him to London, and forced him to write propanganda lies for the state-controlled newspapers. He would go on to reveal just enough real names and addresses in London to ensure that his story got front-page treatment all around the world.

For a couple of days, the "spy scandal" would give the leader of the opposition a club with which to belabor the prime minister, while the names of Blunt, Philby, Burgess, and Maclean were once again exhumed from their dishonorable graves. Then everything would go quiet. The defector would disappear from public view, and the Soviet news agency, Tass, would report a "breakdown" caused by the treatment he had received in England. No one would ever hear of him again. His usefulness over, he would be disposed of as dispassionately as a paper cup. That was what Five had expected to happen in the case of Viktor, McClelland said, but it had not.

"What have we got on him, Dick?" Caine asked.

"Full dossier," McClelland said. "He's Most Wanted, old chap. Alpha Apple Red."

"Is it on the box?"

"I can whistle it up for you if you like."

"Do that for me, Dick."

McClelland swiveled his chair around and switched on his PC. When the access-code request appeared, he muttered something vivid under his breath, checked his log, and punched in the required sixteen digits. An index appeared on the screen. He rolled it over until he found what he was looking for.

"Access Viktor 5-8-7-4-3-1-9-4," he chanted as he tapped the keys, "6-9-9-6-4-0-0-5."

He leaned back and waited while the computer whirred softly. Then lines of text began to zip across the screen. He got up out of his chair and gave Caine a stagy bow.

"Ta-daaaaaah!" he said.

Caine slipped into the chair and frowned at the monitor. The index to the dossier was formidably comprehensive. Biographies came in sections: ADK, all details known; APD, all personal details; AKA, all known associates; AAP, all available photographs; ATC, all telephone contacts made. Caine keyed in the letters ADK and waited. The lines filled the screen. He stared at them in utter disbelief.

It was Guchkov.

. . . and every window in the front of the house blew in simultaneously, a shattering crash that was the echo of a harder, louder explosion outside. He ran out screaming his wife's name. The Opel was lying upside down in the middle of the front garden, burst apart and burning furiously . . .

Andrei Ilyich Guchkov. He would be fifty-three now. When Caine had crossed swords with him in Berlin, more than ten years earlier, he had only been a captain. Caine read the dossier, although he already knew much of what was in it. Born in Uzbekistan, fourth son in a family of eight, a graduate of the Lenin Military-Political Academy, Guchkov had found his way into GRU after distinguishing himself as an Army officer during the Hungarian uprising of 1956. Since then, he had seen service in Prague, Hanoi, Belfast, and Berlin. In 1961, he had married Irina, daughter of his former Army group artillery commander. There were no children. He spoke fluent English, French, and German, which accounted for his being in the Second Directorate. There followed a complete listing of all the man's preferences: food, drink, sex; even the brand of cigarettes he smoked and the make of the clothes he had been wearing.

Andrei Guchkov, a defector?

Caine went methodically through the rest of the dossier, making notes on a small pad beside the monitor. Apart from Jamison, Guchkov's gifts to DI5 had included a bag of diplomats at embassies in Paris, Brussels, The Hague, and London, all of whom had been given their walking papers. The rest were a curious mixture: seven servicemen at the Composite Signals Organization Station in Hong Kong who were selling secrets, and other agents in sensitive locations around the United Kingdom. A senior collection officer at the Morwenstow listening post near Bude, Cornwall; a supervisor of traffic at the Foreign and Commonwealth Office—DI6—transmitting station near Aylesbury. Guchkov also named as a KGB plant an analyst working in the Palmer Street office of GCHQ in London, as well as a cipher officer in the three-story computer annex at Century House, DI6's headquarters building on Westminster Bridge Road.

A motley bunch, Caine thought. Highly placed defectors usually produced bigger rabbits out of their hats than these. Guchkov might easily have been expected to name GRU operatives at all his earlier stations, not to mention the United States, but he had notably failed to do so.

Next Caine checked the debriefing schedule. It was much as he'd originally thought: Saltdean, the out-station at Vauxhall Bridge Road—he wondered whether they'd had the clock fixed yet; it had been stopped at nine-thirty for as long as anyone could remember—the Old Felbridge Hotel at East Grinstead, then safe houses in Sheen Court, Richmond, and finally Redcliffe Square in Earl's Court. A whole series of intelligence officers had interviewed him, notably Colonel Peter Harland, head of K-7, and his deputy, Lieutenant Colonel David Gill. Considering how long they'd had him, they had got a lot less out of Guchkov than Caine would have expected.

Caine keyed in another three-letter code and watched as a sequence of photographs of Guchkov appeared on the screen. Many of them were surveillance shots, taken without the man's knowledge. One or two were studio pictures, probably taken at Curzon by A-2, the photographic section. He looked much the same: a little jowlier, a few more lines around the eyes, but that was all. It was still the same unforgettable face, the one Caine had seen in his nightmares for the last ten years, the face of the man who had killed his wife.

He kept his mounting excitement under control. The worst exercise your mind could get was jumping to conclusions. But if . . . if he was right. . . ?

Dick McClelland came back into the room.

"Well, genius?" the big man said.

"They did him proud, didn't they?" Caine said. "Two passports, one British, one American. Both false names, of course. And forty thousand pounds sterling. He could be anywhere in the world."

"And probably is." McClelland grinned. "More coffee?"

"A phone."

McClelland tossed a Sanyo cordless across the desk, and Caine dialed Delta to make his reservation to Louisville. As he passed the phone back, McClelland asked him if he wanted a lift to the airport.

"It'll give us a chance to talk," he said.

He drove a red Subaru, a honcho wagon with big tires and four-wheel drive on demand. Caine had once asked him why he needed such a vehicle; McClelland said he'd always wanted a car that would climb trees.

They came down through Fort Myer Heights. The Iwo Jima memorial slid past on the right, the gentle green wooded slopes of Arlington National Cemetery behind it.

"I never drive past here without wondering how many of the men buried in there ever really knew what they were dying for," he said. "Like Tom Crandon, or Lennie Wurzel, or Butch Young. Christ, David, we work in a shitty business."

"They knew, Dick," Caine said. "We all do."

"I suppose so," he said. He was silent for a while, the silence of someone who is working up to say something unpleasant.

"How do you get on with Kingly?" he asked eventually.

"It's not a love affair," Caine said.

"Does he trust you?"

"That's a strange question, Dick."

"He wanted to know why you had asked for the file on Viktor. As a matter of interest, why did you want to see it?"

"I've got something going around in my brain, Dick. There's something about that whole Miami business . . ."

"Would it help to talk it through?" McClelland said. "I can park the heap. You've got forty minutes till flight time."

"It's too damned nebulous to put into words," Caine said. "Forget it. I'm probably just being an old woman."

"You're sure there's nothing you want to tell me?"

Caine nodded, frowning at the way the question had been phrased. McClelland pulled to a stop behind a tan Buick Park Avenue parked in front of the Delta bay, two Army officers standing beside it. Caine got out, and McClelland came around the car as though to shake hands. As he did, Caine saw the two Army officers start toward them. Alarm bells rang in his mind as McClelland grabbed his arm and tried to hustle him toward the Buick.

"Get in the car," McClelland gritted, "you bloody traitor!"

Caine reacted without hesitation. Half turning, he drew his Nova stun gun, jammed it against McClelland's sternum, and pulled the trigger. McClelland's knees buckled and he lurched away, falling heavily. A woman screamed. The two Army officers stopped dead in their tracks, confusion on their faces.

"Heart attack!" Caine shouted. "I'll get a doctor!"

He ran into the terminal, heart pounding wildly. As soon as he was inside, he slowed to a brisk walk. Nothing drew attention more quickly than a running man. He saw that there were crowds up around the car-rental desks and the baggage claim area below Gates 1 to 8. Holding the stun gun ready in his hand, he went out through the doors to the cab rank. He looked around warily. Nobody came toward him. Nobody shouted. He signaled a Barwood cab.

"Dulles," he snapped. "Fast!"

"You want I should go nort or sout?" the driver asked. He was a squat, bald-headed man. The license shield on the dash gave his name as Zbigniew Bojak. "I go nort we gonna hitta rushow traffic. Ya wan I should try Washenton Boulvar?"

"Just get this heap out of here!" Caine snapped, leaning well back in the seat. "Move it, for Christ's sake!"

"Ah, shit," Bojak said resignedly, "another nut."

The cab lurched into motion. As they went by the Delta gateway, Caine saw the two officers standing beside the Buick, watching the entrance. One, a tall, cadaverous-looking individual with patches of gray hair, wore the insignia of a colonel. The second, a major, was shorter, with blond hair cut very close at the back and sides. There was no sign of McClelland.

Caine stowed the stun gun, blessing the day he had bought it. No larger than an electric razor, it worked by shooting an electrical discharge which interrupted messages from the brain to the muscular system, causing severe disorientation in the victim lasting between ten and fifteen seconds. It was otherwise quite harmless. Caine had picked it up in Austin, where it was manufactured. Some Texas police forces used it to pacify arrestees.

Zbigniew Bojak tooled up the George Washington Memorial Parkway, past the waterfowl sanctuary and the Marriott Twin Bridges Motel into a maze of feeder roads and overpasses. The great squat hulk of the Pentagon loomed on the right as he cursed his way through the clotted traffic on the Shirley Memorial Highway. He circled around the upper perimeter of the cemetery to Arlington Boulevard and headed toward Falls Church. Caine hardly noticed. All he could hear, repeating itself in his mind like the nonstop tolling of a bell, was the name Dick McClelland had called him: *traitor*.

Why?

He was still asking himself the same question—and a lot of others—when they reached Dulles Airport. The cab driver's voice broke into his reverie.

"Take the lower drive," Caine said. "I'm meeting someone."

He had never had any intention of flying anywhere. His dossier would already be on the wire from Langley, or Fort Meade, or wherever the military types had come from. His name would be on a high-priority list in a national surveillance trawl within hours. He paid off the cab and went to a pay phone. He took off his Omega chronometer, set the stopwatch to zero, and dialed ISS. It took them forty-two seconds to put him through to Kingly. He knew why, of course.

"Where are you?" Kingly said without preamble.

"I'm timing this, Miles," Caine told him. "Don't bother putting a trace on me."

"You're on a landline, of course."

"Naturally. Would you like to tell me what the hell is going on?"

"You tell me, David."

"McClelland called me a traitor."

"That was . . . ill-considered," Kingly said. His voice was placatory, even paternal. "We just want to talk to you. Something that needs clarifying."

Caine checked the watch: one minute. He couldn't talk much longer. "Why did McClelland have military waiting for me at National? Who were they, Miles?"

"I can't discuss this on an open line," Kingly said. "Tell me where you are and we'll come and get you."

"Damned right you would."

"Don't be foolish, David," Kingly said, no trace any longer of friendliness in his voice. "You can't run away from this. You've nowhere to hide. There's nowhere you can go that we can't find you."

"He called me a traitor, Miles," Caine persisted. "Why?"

"I told you we can't discuss it on the telephone."

"Has it got anything to do with the Drosdow case?"

"What makes you think that?"

Caine looked at the stopwatch: ninety seconds. He had another thirty seconds.

"Who said it, Miles? Who told you I was a traitor?"

"Are you telling me that you are?"

"Don't be so fucking dense!" Caine snapped.

"No point losing your temper," Kingly said. "Think about it, David. Be sensible. Come in, and we can sort this whole thing out."

"Which whole thing?" Caine shouted. "For God's sake, Miles, tell me what I'm supposed to have done?"

"Of course I'll tell you. As soon as you come in. We can't do it any other way. You know that."

Caine looked at his watch and hung up. He had nothing more to say to Kingly anyway. He strapped on the Omega and walked over to the car-rental desks. With any luck at all, he would be able to put a few hundred miles between himself and Washington before they traced his reservation.

19

Drosdow hummed unmusically to an easy-listening program on WBAL as he pointed the Mercedes 380SEL across the Severn River bridge en route to Easton. It was a bright blue day. Sailboats leaned away from the breeze off Annapolis. His meeting in Baltimore with Lykov had been highly satisfying: how many men had single-handedly effected a payment of over fifty million dollars in cash to GRU funds? The Soviet trading organization Amtorg would be able to buy a lot of hi-tech equipment with that kind of money.

"An Order of Lenin at least," Lykov had beamed, "when you get back to Moscow, my friend."

I'm expecting more than that when all this is over, comrade, Drosdow said to himself as he recalled Lykov's words. He reviewed his plans in his mind as he drove. Red Center was ready to move. And so was he.

Mitchell had been putty in Katja's experienced hands: he had never seen a man so sexually infatuated. The man hardly ever went home anymore: he spent every moment he was not working—he had long since boasted to Kate about where he worked and what he did there—either with her at the house in Easton or on the town in Baltimore. They had gone away together for a weekend in New York, and now another in Atlantic City. It was time now to move Mitchell along to the next stage, which was why Drosdow was looking forward to getting back.

As for the rest of the plan, in spite of what the American

security services no doubt by now believed, there was no honey trap on Marco Island. There *was* a house there, bought and paid for out of the cocaine deal, an eighty-thousand-dollar unit on Alamo Court with a nice view across Roberts Bay. He had set it all up, no expense spared: a powerboat moored at its berth, gassed up and ready to go, with fishing tackle and scuba gear on board. Bogdanovich could take his choice of pleasures: he could swim, surfboard, scuba dive, fish, play tennis or golf at the Marco Island Club on Nassau Road, sail, hunt shells, spot birds or, if the outdoor life was not to his taste, simply sit on the patio nursing a long, cold drink from the well-stocked refrigerator and watch the pelicans making wide circles over the emerald water.

Bogdanovich should be there by now, he thought. Through his Washington case officer, Stepan Lykov, the American had been instructed to apply for leave, fly to Miami, stay overnight at the Marriott, then proceed in a rented car to Marco Island. On arrival, he was to go to a designated phone booth in the Island Plaza Shopping Center, and from it call a number he had been given, telling whoever answered that Pimmit—his code name— was in place. After that, he was told, he could enjoy himself until he received further instructions.

Drosdow smiled. The whole thing was nonsense, of course. The number Bogdanovich called would be linked to a tape recorder. The fact that "Pimmit" was "in place" would mean nothing to anyone, except possibly the CIA, and Bogdanovich's vacation would be short-lived. Lykov had confirmed that Avranilosa had dropped out of sight. An unexpected business trip, they were saying at his Miami office. Yes, and Drosdow knew what the business was. The Fat Man had "made new friends," so by now the wheels were probably turning quite fast. Unless the Americans were even more stupid than he had imagined, Bogdanovich would already be under intensive surveillance.

It was common knowledge that every member of the intelligence community with access to secret materials was occasionally put under spot surveillance for a couple of days. Bogdanovich was no exception; but Lykov had run him so skillfully that Bogdanovich had never encountered any problems. Once surveillance became intensive, however, as it was about to, Bogdanovich would be finished. Drosdow had left a trail a blind deaf-mute could follow. What happened to Bogdanovich was of no importance whatsoever: the man was expendable, his involvement merely another factor in Drosdow's chaos.

Outside Queenstown, he turned south, following U.S. 50 for another dozen miles past imposing mansions with magnificent landscaped gardens that stretched down to the shining bay. Just past the airport, he turned onto the Easton Parkway, then filtered left into Washington Street. When he got to the center of town, he stopped at Trader's Pharmacy to make a brief call.

"Is everything ready?" he said when Katja answered.

"He's here."

"I'll be there in twenty minutes."

He got back into the Mercedes and drove through Easton, queen of the Maryland Tidewater, with its early Colonial architecture and manicured streets. Sometimes it was hard to come to terms with just how wealthy some Americans were. They were like overgrown children, with wardrobes full of clothes they could never wear out, more shoes than they could use in a second lifetime. The men spent most of their adult lives making money, and with it they roamed the world, buying without pleasure or need.

South of town, he turned onto Route 333 to Oxford. It was pretty countryside, a neat pattern of spreading rivers and streams, large farms and fine homes. In some ways, it reminded him of the Zeravshan valley in Uzbekistan, and he sighed. He hadn't been home for a long, long time. He turned off 333 onto a private road that led to an ornate gate between two massive stone pillars surmounted by griffins. He identified himself by means of the intercom unit set into one of the stone gateposts, and after a few moments the gates swung ponderously back. He drove on a paved driveway through a stretch of woods which opened up into pastures and parkland running down to the water's edge.

Before him lay Highfield, spacious and serene. The gracious old house stood on an inlet looking out over the Tred Avon River, almost a mile wide at this point. Built by the grandson of a Marylander from Calvert County who settled in Washington in 1798, Highfield was an imposing estate in an area where the word imposing was not a superlative.

Constructed of fieldstone and wood, the house was surrounded by spacious living porches at the ground level and several large screened porches above; their steeply pitched roofs and wide, overhanging eaves made them a cool retreat on humid summer nights. The estate included a superintendent's cottage, stables, garages, two barns, greenhouses, and other outbuildings. There were six servants: a cook, two maids, a manservant, a groom, and a chauffeur—all, of course, supplied by GRU.

Four million dollars and worth every cent, he thought as he looked about him. The lawn and formal terraced gardens covered some five acres. There were two tennis courts and an Olympic-sized swimming pool. From now on, Drosdow thought as he got out of the car, all honey traps would be measured against this, the real one.

He heard music and the sound of voices beside the pool. He walked around the house and through the garden. Kate was swimming; Butler Mitchell sat on the apron of the pool, his legs dangling in the water. He looked up as Drosdow's feet crunched on the gravel.

"Fred, hello!" he said, getting up to shake hands. "Good to see you, good to see you."

"You, too, Mitch," Drosdow said, watching Kate. She had on a one-piece Anne Cole swimsuit with diagonal violet and black stripes, cut high at the hip and low at the back. Her skin was beautifully tanned.

"Come on in!" she called. "Wash the city away!"

"Later, maybe." Drosdow smiled. He looked at Mitchell, who was watching Kate with adoring eyes. No question of it, the girl was as good as she had claimed to be. Mitchell caught Drosdow's look and gave him a sheepish grin.

"How was Atlantic City?" Drosdow asked.

"Windy," Kate said, climbing out of the pool and vigorously toweling herself dry.

"Where did you stay?"

"The Boardwalk Regency," Mitchell said. "They know me there."

"You enjoyed yourselves?"

Mitchell hesitated. "Go on, tell him," Kate said.

"I lost," Mitchell said reluctantly. "A bundle."

Drosdow shook his head. "You're a sucker for punishment, Mitch," he said. "How much?"

"Not enough to break the bank," Mitchell said, forcing the laugh. "More than I intended, though."

"Well, you know what they say: you've got to lay it down to pick it up."

"He was ahead fifteen thousand at one point," Kate said.

"Some people like liquor. Some like fast cars. With me, it's the tables," Mitchell said. "I can't resist them."

"Never mind, it's only money," Kate said. "We had a lovely time, and that's all that matters, isn't it, darling?"

"Absolutely," Mitchell said, a shade too enthusiastically. Watching the man carefully, Drosdow saw the hint of a wince that had followed Kate's carefully aimed shaft of disregard for the American's losses. Mitchell was overspending wildly to impress them. Correction: to impress Kate, who succeeded in remaining utterly unimpressed.

"So how was Washington?" Mitchell said, changing the subject. "Business good?"

"Just the opposite," Drosdow said gloomily. "The software business is in hell's own shape at the moment."

"Hell, I thought it was booming," Mitchell said. "I was reading about some guy named McGovern in Boston who—"

"That was some time ago, Mitch. And anyway, computer publishing isn't software. I'll bet even IDG is hurting at the moment."

"If you two are going to talk business, I'll go on up to the house and change," Kate said. "Come on up for a drink in a little while."

She kissed Mitchell on the top of his head and walked up to the house. She moved like a well-oiled machine, and Mitchell's eyes never left her until she was out of sight. Drosdow was reminded of a phrase he had heard Saturnino Baca use to describe one of his men who'd been on a three-day binge with a woman in Miami: *pussy-whipped*. It fitted Mitchell perfectly.

"You listening to me, Mitch?"

"Sorry." Mitchell grinned, blushing. "What were you saying?"

"Software," Drosdow said. "Remember? There are a lot of people in Silicon Valley who thought they had a license to print money and have found out the hard way that they don't. I'm not planning to join them. I'm going to get me some of that government contract business."

"Smart move," Mitchell said. "That's where the big bucks are."

"Trouble is, Mitch, I don't know where to start."

"There's a facility at the Pentagon that advises—"

"I don't care to stand in line, Mitch," Drosdow interposed. "You ought to know that's not my style. What I need is some introductions. Get to know the right people."

"Easier said than done, Fred."

"I was wondering . . . Kate told me you work at the National Security Agency. Couldn't you get me in?"

Mitchell shook his head. "You'd have to go through channels, like everyone else."

162 ·

"You can't help me at all? Even though, in the long run, it's for Kate, too?"

"Fred, you know there's nothing I wouldn't do for Kate. Or for you. You've been more like an older brother to me than . . ."

"What were you going to say—father-in-law?"

"I'm sorry, Fred. Rules are rules, especially at the NSA."

"That is some place you work at, Mitch," Drosdow said, noting how Mitchell had avoided the topic of marriage. He was still maintaining the pretense that he was a divorcé. It would make things that much easier when Drosdow began to turn the screws. "The National Security Agency. It's enormous. I drove by it a few days ago. It's like a small town. How many people work out there, anyway?"

"Thirty-five, forty thousand, I believe."

"Is that big nine-story block the headquarters building?"

"At the moment. There are plans for a new one."

"Which department deals with buying equipment?"

"It's called I&L—Installations and Logic."

"That's not the division you work in."

"We call them 'offices' at the NSA, Fred. The one I work for is called the Office of Communications Security, COMSEC for short."

"What about this other one, I&L? Who's the head guy there?"

Mitchell shook his head, uncomfortable yet determined. "I'm not permitted to discuss other agency personnel, Fred. I'm sorry."

"It's all right, it's all right." Drosdow grinned. "You and your goddamn secrets. Look, just tell me this: if I want to see someone over there to try to sell them something, what do I do?"

"You call Fort Meade and ask for the OHP—that's the Office of the Head of Procurement, which is part of I&L. You request an appointment with a procurement officer. Then—"

"That could take weeks!" Drosdow said, feigning dismay.

"Sorry. That's the way it works, Fred."

"Mitch, listen to me, I'm in a bind," Drosdow said. "I can't wait weeks. I need turnover, and I need it now. Isn't there any way you could help me out? From what Kate told me, I figured you had some clout over there."

"I do," Mitchell said, nettled.

"Well, then, for Christ's sake, give me something, anything," Drosdow said. This was a critical moment in their relationship. He was acting the supplicant while watching Mitchell very closely. "You want to see me go to the wall?"

"Fred . . ." Mitchell said uncomfortably. "It's not that easy."

Drosdow felt a small glow of elation. The absence of refusal was the beginning of agreement, the first breakthrough. The next step was to test the man.

"Listen, isn't there some kind of organizational chart I could borrow?" he asked. "Something that lists all the heads of departments . . . sorry, offices."

"There is, but it's restricted," Mitchell said.

"What does that mean?"

"Documents have different security classifications. An organizational chart is restricted, but not classified."

"In other words, it's not secret."

"I can see you're like most civilians, Fred. You don't understand how the system works. Everything is secret. But some things are more secret than others."

Bravo, Drosdow thought dryly. He's described the espionage business in one sentence. In spite of himself, he was tense. Getting Mitchell to this stage had taken a lot of careful maneuvering. They had to establish the man's motivations, what he would accept, what he would balk at. A loan "to tide him over" after a disastrous session at the Miami tables? No problem: it was implicit that Mitchell would pay it back "as soon as he got himself straightened out." A loan was not a gift, even if there was no term, no talk of interest, not even an IOU. In the world of espionage, this technique was known as expanding the area of conscience. It enabled Mitchell to accept and rationalize Drosdow's largesse without its becoming a constant burden.

"Well, never mind," Drosdow said, putting disappointment into his tone. "It was just a thought."

"I feel badly about this, Fred," Mitchell said. "I'd really like to help you out, but . . ." He shrugged. "You know how it is."

"Listen, Mitch, forget it," Drosdow said, as if to move away from the subject. "I've embarrassed you. I never should have asked."

He let the silence lengthen. Mitchell was staring at the water in the pool as if hypnotized by the dancing lights on its surface.

"How long would you need it for?" he said so quietly that Drosdow almost missed the words. Christ, he thought, he's mine! Easy, now, easy.

"An hour, half an hour, even. But Mitch, I can't ask you—"

"Hell," Mitchell said. "I guess I could do that much for an old friend."

And that was it. Drosdow felt the sweat trickling down inside his shirt. The threshold was crossed, the new relationship established. Drosdow let all the air out of his lungs and then took a long, deep breath. He felt good.

"I won't forget this, Mitch," he said, putting a hand on Mitchell's shoulder. "It could be a lifesaver."

"Hell, I haven't done anything yet," Mitchell replied, forcing a grin. He was just realizing what he had agreed to. It was the natural, the inevitable reaction: Drosdow had seen it a hundred times. But if the manipulator had done his work well, there could be no going back. He stood up and clapped Mitchell on the back.

"Come on up to the house," he said jovially, "and I'll buy you a drink."

"I could use one," Mitchell said.

Kate was waiting for them in the drawing room, a bottle of Veuve Clicquot and three Waterford glasses beside her on a low table.

"I thought you men would probably have sore throats after all that business talk," she smiled. "So I opened a bottle of medicine." She looked at Drosdow as she poured the champagne. His eyes told her what she wanted to know. A smile touched her lips.

"Bubbly?" Mitchell said. "What are we celebrating?"

"Success," Drosdow told him, smiling broadly.

"I'll drink to that," Mitchell said. They all laughed.

20 A thousand miles and four stolen cars later, Caine pulled to a stop outside the La Paloma restaurant on East Drive in Key Biscayne. It was a long, low building with stone facings; the sign showed a dove with an olive branch in its beak. It was a prime location: directly opposite lay the Key Colony Golf Course. He stood outside for a moment, wondering whether to go through with this. Then he shrugged. He didn't have a hell of a lot of choice.

It was dark and cool inside. He paused on the threshold while his eyes adjusted. He was in a small foyer with stuccoed walls on which hung a bullfight poster and a Spanish guitar. Through an archway on the left, he could see into the restaurant. It was empty at this time of the afternoon. He went through the archway and saw that there was a well-stocked bar on the right. Lynda Sanchez was behind the bar. She looked up as he came in.

"Remember me?" he said.

She regarded him levelly, as if she was uncertain what to say next. She was wearing a sleeveless cream linen dress, buttoned down the front. She looked very cool and very beautiful.

"Yes," she said. "I remember you. What do you want?"

"I need your help, Lynda."

"I think not," she said firmly. Her voice was cool, distant. "The last time I saw you, you said—"

"Then was then," she replied. "Now is now. I had some . . . visitors after you left."

"Ah," he said. "Not police, I assume."

"Definitely not police. Nice business suits, like the ones who came to see me after Tony Genevevo was killed. Very quiet-spoken, very precise. They said they were from a government agency which prefers not to show identification."

"When was this?"

"A week ago. Exactly."

"Go on."

"They wanted to know if I'd had anyone come around asking questions about Tony."

"What did you tell them?"

"At first, I said no."

"But they already knew I had."

"How did you know that?"

"I didn't know it. It just figured."

"They described you. Perfectly. They asked me to tell them what you were wearing, what you said, anything I could remember."

"And?"

"I told them. I said your name was Philip Howard and that you told me you were an insurance investigator."

"They, of course, told you I was not."

"They said you were an agent of a foreign power."

"What did you say to that?"

"I told them you told me you were some kind of secret agent."

"I bet that perked up their interest."

"One of them got on the phone. He talked to somebody long-distance and reported what I'd told them. They stayed a long while. They said they weren't supposed to say anything, but they thought I ought to know that everything you'd told me was a lie."

"Not everything, Lynda," Caine said.

"They said I should call them immediately if you contacted me again."

"Are you going to?"

"I should. You did lie to me."

"Only about my name. Everything else I told you is true."

"What is your name, anyway?"

"Didn't your visitors tell you?"

"They didn't tell me anything. They said it was a matter of national security and that I shouldn't discuss it with anyone under any circumstances."

"But you told them about Genevevo and Avranilosa. And Frederic Drosdow."

"Yes."

"Was one of them called Forsyth?"

"They never gave their names. Who is Forsyth?"

"He was Tony Genevevo's case officer."

"What?"

"The man he reported to."

"And you? You still haven't told me who you are."

"My real name is Caine. David Caine."

"Like the movie star Caine?"

"That's the only similarity."

She shook her head. "I don't think I believe any of you."

"I understand that. I know it's difficult. But what I told you when I came to your house is true. I really am trying to find the man who had Tony Genevevo killed."

"That's not what they said. They said you're wanted for questioning."

"As of four days ago, I am. That's why I came here. You're the only one who can help me do what I set out to do."

"Why should I believe you? Give me one good reason."

"Because you want the man who had Tony Genevevo killed punished."

"I do. But why do you?"

"I told you: the men who were killed at the same time as

• 169

Genevevo were working for me. For my company. We had Genevevo under surveillance.''

"Your company."

"We operate as a company."

"Who is we?"

"I think you're better off not knowing that, Lynda."

"Why did your . . . company have Tony under surveillance?"

"He was suspected of being involved in espionage."

"Tony? I don't believe it!"

"You don't have to. It isn't true. But it was made to look as if he was by the man who had him killed. Do you remember Frederic Drosdow?"

"Of course."

"He's the man."

"Drosdow had Tony killed? Why?"

"It's a long story. Are you going to help me?"

"You mean you won't tell me if I don't."

"That's right."

"Why me?"

"That day at your apartment, when I first talked to you—I left there feeling sure I could trust you."

"You, trust me? The question we ought to be discussing is, can I trust you?"

"What am I going to say—no?"

She was silent for a moment, her dark eyes thoughtful. "You really had me convinced, you know that?"

"Lynda, what I told you is true."

"If you're what you claim to be, why do you need my help?"

"I'm out in the cold, Lynda. You know what that means?"

"Only from spy books."

"I've been fitted up. Framed, if you like. My own organization is after me as well as the CIA. The only way I can clear my name is to find Drosdow, and to do that, I need you."

"Why not just turn yourself in?"

"Because whoever fitted me up is working for the opposition himself. I wouldn't get to Washington. An accident, killed while trying to escape. There are all sorts of ways to shut me down."

She shivered. "I don't know that I want to get involved in your world, Caine. Or with you."

"Yes," he said, turning away. "You're probably right. I won't bother you anymore."

"Wait a minute," Lynda said. "Just wait a damned minute. I didn't say I wouldn't help you. I said I shouldn't."

"Then you will?"

"Supposing I say yes. What happens then?"

"You come with me to Marco Island. Help me to find Drosdow."

"Let me get this straight," she said, leaning on the bar. "You want me to drop everything, come with you to Marco Island for some unspecified time, looking for this Drosdow. You don't know where he is, and you don't know what you're going to do if you find him. And I've got to take it all on trust. Is that about right?"

Caine grinned ruefully. "It's worse than that. I want you to pay for it."

"Pay for it? What does that mean?"

"That's why I need you, Lynda. I've been able to get this far only because nobody knew where I was going or when I'd be there. But I can't get away with that on Marco Island. I need someone to front for me, someone to rent cars and book rooms and ask questions. Someone legitimate. You."

"You don't want much," she said. "Just tell me one more thing. What have I done to deserve all this?"

"You said something when I first met you. It stuck in my mind. You said you wanted to do something good for America."

"I remember."

"That's why I'm asking you, Lynda."

She was silent for a while. Then she nodded. "I've got a feeling I'm going to regret this," she said. She opened a drawer, took out a bunch of keys, and put them on the bar in front of him.

"You know where I live," she said. "Go and get cleaned up, wait for me. I can't get away from here much before midnight."

"Midnight sounds fine," Caine said.

"Caine?"

"Yes?"

She held her nose. "Buy a clean shirt," she said.

From the moment he had driven away from Dulles, Caine knew he could take absolutely no chances. The Company probably had him tabbed as their best possible lead to Drosdow. Finding him would be given maximum precedence. This would include blanket surveillance by the NSA, which would immediately cut off his access to credit, his possessions, his friends and acquaintances. His name and a number of other key words would go into the computers scanning hundreds of thousands of telephone calls per hour looking for him. Any credit-card transaction, any reservation made via a computer system, any traffic violation, any bank withdrawal, any payment by check, any of the routine things millions of people do every day could be picked up in the surveillance trawl and lead them straight to him.

At Manassas he had scouted around till he found a car-parts dealer, where he bought a slide-hammer—the car thief's favorite tool—and a selection of switch assemblies. In a hardware store, he picked up a small screwdriver and a log-splitting wedge and took a couple of yards of nylon packing-case tape from a pile of junk in back of the store. Then he drove to the station parking lot where he abandoned the rental car and broke into a red Buick Somerset with Virginia plates. Stealing a car

172 •

was almost ridiculously easy: car thieves never stopped seeing the joke of carmakers putting a set of locks costing less than fifty dollars on a forty-thousand dollar vehicle. He used the wedge to prize the door open enough to slide in the packing-case tape and lift the locks. Two smacks from the slide-hammer took out the ignition lock, and one turn of the screwdriver started the car. He looked around. There was no one in sight. Commuter stations were always a good place to steal from: the theft would not be discovered until six or even later that evening, by which time he would be long gone.

He had run out of gas in Emporia, just short of the North Carolina line. He left the Buick on the street, took a Renault Encore he found parked in a blind alley—all he had to do was get in, whip out the starting switch, and substitute one of the assemblies he'd bought in Manassas—and headed south again. At Fayetteville he paid thirty dollars cash for a motel room and slept six hours.

When he got up, he walked over to a shopping mall and hung around until he spotted a likely pigeon, a middle-aged man in a yellow cotton polo shirt and gray gaberdine slacks, pushing a shopping cart while his wife shopped. A collision, profuse apologies, and Caine was on his way out of the market with the man's wallet in his pocket. He was in luck: as well as a Master-Card, and Diner's Club and Mobil gas cards, it contained $104 in cash. With any luck, they'd last him long enough.

He crossed the Georgia line and turned off onto Route 21, parking the hot little Renault from Emporia at Savannah Municipal Airport. There he selected a feisty-looking Honda Accord SEi, opened it up, and drove it away. That was the way the pros worked it: enter the short-term parking facility in a clapped-out wreck, dump it, and drive out in the new car of their choice, using the ticket they picked up on the way in.

He made a wide swing around Jacksonville, taking no chances on using its network of toll bridges: there were too many cops on toll bridges. Then it was due south on U.S. 95 to

Saint Augustine, where he made a night stop and ditched the Honda in "exchange" for a new-looking Toyota Cressida with Flagler County plates. It was his third day on the road. He needed a shave, clean clothes, and most of all, sleep. He was weary of the endless highway coming at him, the rush of trucks, the glare of headlamps, the blatting of horns, the sameness of the junk food he'd eaten at a dozen roadside diners.

He had spent most of his driving time on the journey south thinking through what had happened in Washington. The conclusion was unpleasant: because of his stupidity, Tom Crandon, Lennie Wurzel, and Butch Young were dead—perhaps even Genevevo, too. Caine had committed the cardinal sin: he had vastly underestimated the enemy, rashly assuming they were unaware of his involvement. He was now faced with the inescapable realization that not only had the opposite been true right from the start, but that he, too, had been a target when Tom Crandon was killed. And when that did not work, they had painted him Red instead.

There could have been no other reason for Dick McClelland's turning on him. His instincts told him that the only source for such an accusation was Avranilosa, but there had been nothing in the interrogation summary . . . Then he remembered Kingly's unwonted tension, Betty Torre's uneasy smile, McClelland's questions. Whatever the Cuban had said had been expurgated before Kingly showed the summary to Caine. They had been waiting to see how Caine would react. When there was no reaction, Kingly had decided to give him to the Company, or to the NSA, which explained the military types waiting at the airport. They would have driven him out to a helicopter on the tarmac and he would have spent the next six months under interrogation. While Frederic Drosdow got on with what he had come to America to do.

Why not call him by his real name, Andrei Guchkov?

The bastard had taken every trick so far. Whatever his true intent was, it was big enough for him to have sacrificed quite a few agents-in-place. Such actions would require sanction at the highest level at Red Center in Moscow. Could all this have been done merely to entrap a small-time CIA coding clerk? It seemed a long way less than likely, but if it wasn't that, what was it?

"How much further is it?" Lynda asked, breaking into his reverie.

"Thirty miles, give or take a few."

They had been driving along the Tamiami Trail for about an hour and a half. The dun-and-green saw-grass wetlands of the Everglades were behind them now; they would soon be out of Big Cypress National Preserve. They passed a roadside eatery with a fifteen-foot-high beer can advertising Budweiser. On the apron was a battered old Lincoln Continental; on top of it was a cutout alligator with the word GATORBURGERS painted on it.

"Half an hour," she said. "Do you want to talk, Caine?"

"What about? Drosdow?"

"Whatever."

"That's not his real name," he said. "His real name is Andrei Ilyich Guchkov."

"A Russian? He's a spy?"

"That's what all this is about, Lynda: espionage, not drugs. Tony Genevevo was killed because he found that out."

He tried to explain it to her, not really expecting her to understand. He told her how Drosdow—Guchkov, he was sure of it now—had posed as a drug dealer, using Avranilosa as his guarantor. Whatever his plans were, they were important enough that he could not allow Genevevo or the ISS men to jeopardize them, so he used Avranilosa to convince Baca that the simplest solution was to get rid of all of them.

"Then when he realized Baca's hit men hadn't succeeded in killing me, he painted me Red."

"You said that before," Lynda said. "What does it mean?"

"Sorry," he said, smiling. "Trade jargon. When you accuse someone of working for the other side, it's called painting them

Red. Somehow Guchkov knew the CIA was going to put the screws on Avranilosa—maybe he even engineered it—and fitted me into what he told the Fat Man. With the result that I am now on the CIA's books as a probable KGB agent, which will make me flavor of the month with the FBI.''

He didn't add that Kingly would certainly have put him on AI—Apprehension Imperative—status, permitting anyone from ISS to take him by any means short of actually killing him.

"What has all this got to do with what's happening on Marco Island?''

"Drosdow is trying to recruit a man named Paul Bogdanovich. To do that, he's using a technique that's known in spookspeak as a honey trap, or sometimes a swallow's nest. It means using a woman to seduce the target man—''

"So that's why Tony was so excited that night when I told him about Drosdow going to Key Largo to look at a swallow!''

"That's right. He knew that if Drosdow and Avranilosa were talking the way he thought they were, one or both of them were agents.''

"And you think Drosdow will be in Marco?''

"I hope so.''

"I hope so, too,'' she said fiercely. She looked at him. "There's more to it than that, though, isn't there?''

"What do you mean?''

"I want this man caught. I want him to pay for what he did. But it's more than that with you. There's another reason: something personal, isn't there?'' Lynda said.

"Yes,'' he said, "There is.''

It didn't seem likely that Guchkov would have remembered his name, but it was possible. Caine had been a very lowly field agent in West Berlin then, part of a team that was bringing over a defecting East German HVA agent named Anatoli Shadrin. Caine and his partner, Jerry Hadfield, went to a *Treff* in a house on the other side that looked out on the parish cemetery of the

Sophienkirche. Through its grimy windows, you could see the Wall looming ominously at the end of the street.

They had no inkling that Shadrin had been rumbled, or that the GRU *rezident* at the HVA in East Berlin—Captain Andrei Guchkov—had persuaded General Markus Wolff to make an example of them by fitting a bomb to Caine's car timed to go off after they had returned to West Berlin. The *boyeveya* sent to do the ''wet job'' botched it, and instead of exploding with the agents in it, the trembler didn't trip until two days later, when Caine's wife Jenny started up the Opel to run down to the commissary.

''Look,'' Lynda said. Up ahead of them was the long, rising curve of the Collier Boulevard Bridge. A sign beside the road said MARCO ISLAND WELCOMES CAREFUL DRIVERS. Down at the public boat ramp, a crew of suntanned kids were putting a sailboat into the water. Pelicans watched with wary detachment.

''Well, here we are, Caine,'' Lynda said, turning to face him. ''What happens now?''

''I'm going to buy you some coffee,'' he told her. ''Then I'm going to tell you what you need to know about Andrei Ilyich Guchkov. And then you're going to work.''

21 "You ever heard of Carl Sigman?" he said.

"Sure," Lynda replied. "He writes songs."

"Somebody told me when he got the music for the theme song for that movie *Love Story*, he tried about fifteen different lyrics, but the studio turned them all down, told him to try again. He was all out of ideas, and he turned to his wife, and he said, 'What am I going to do?' And she said, 'Try again.' And he said, 'Where do I begin?'"

"And lo, A Song Was Born," she said. "Point, please?"

"I feel the same way. Where do I begin?"

"You said you figured Drosdow had bought a place somewhere on the island?"

"He wouldn't rent."

"Then we hit the realty offices," she said.

"Saying what?"

"We'll tell them we're looking for our dear friend Fred Drosdow, who invited us down here for the week, only we lost his address on the way."

"Well," Caine said. "You seem to have the gift."

They drove along the broad, palm-lined expanse of North Collier Boulevard until they spotted a Chamber of Commerce sign outside a building next to the starkly modernistic First Bank of Marco Island. A helpful lady named Fran Gilbert loaned them a phone book and gave them a map of the island

and a list of realtors. Five hot and tiresome hours later, they got lucky.

The Pearson & Leach Realty office was on San Marco, right next to the Deltona Building. They told their story to a handsome blond woman in her mid-forties whose name was Jill Leach.

"We tried the Chamber of Commerce," Lynda said. After so many performances, she knew her lines perfectly. "And the post office. The only other thing we could think of was to make the rounds of the realty offices, describe Fred, and hope for the best."

"Bright blue eyes, you say?" Mrs. Leach said. "Almost violet, right?"

"Pockmarked face, slight accent," Caine confirmed. "That sure sounds like Fred."

"I remember the man," Mrs. Leach said, "but . . ." She shook her head, going through a card index. She frowned. "Ah, here it is. I knew the name wasn't the same. It isn't Drosdow. It's Ziegelmann. Victor Ziegelmann. Number 5, Alamo Court."

The reason she remembered the transaction so well, she told them, was because not only had the man known exactly what he wanted, he had a bank draft waiting to cover the full cost of the house plus agency fees and title registration. The whole transaction had been finalized in two days.

"Well, gee, that couldn't be Fred," Lynda said. "I guess he must have a double. You've been very kind, Mrs. Leach. Thank you very much for your help." She turned to Caine. "C'mon, hon, we'll just have to keep trying."

Jill Leach came to the door with them. They thanked her again and and got back into the car. He headed south on Heathwood Drive.

"You know what?" he said. "You're terrific."

"Shut up and drive," she replied.

Everywhere they looked they saw boats: big, small, sail, power. The whole island was one vast marina. Seen from the air, it would look like one of those enlarged microscope photographs of a snowflake, each tiny frond branching into jetties, landings, and cutely named "courts." The Rotary Club map they'd picked up at the Chamber of Commerce indicated that any thoroughfare ending at water's edge was called a court.

He made a left on San Antonio Drive. Alamo Court was third on the right. The Texan theme was continued in the names of the others: San Jacinto, Goliad, and Austin, on which new homes were being built. Each court was effectively a three-hundred-yard peninsula jutting into Roberts Bay. Each cul-de-sac had eight houses on it, surrounded by rectangles of artificial-looking fescue grass with carefully sited shrubs and trees. Caine turned the car around at the end of San Antonio and drove back the way he had come.

"Aren't you going to go and look at the place?" Lynda asked.

"Did you see that blue Safari parked on the corner?"

She twisted around in her seat. "I see it now."

"Mirror windows," he said. "Nobody in the cab."

"So?"

"Surveillance truck," he said. He drove straight along Winterberry to South Collier, then turned south. Condominiums stood like rows of roseate dominoes facing the pink white beach, monuments to a collision between fantasy and greed, distinguishable one from the other only by their romantic names: Princess del Mar, Royal Seafarer, Summit House, Club Regency, Surf Club, the Palms. The colored sails of boats and surfboards made kaleidoscopic patterns on the bright turquoise water.

The public boat ramp was at the far end of South Collier, looking out to Henry Key. Caine rented a dinghy with an outboard Evinrude for an hour, started her up, and pushed off into Smokehouse Creek, negotiating the turn into Roberts Bay, which was really a lagoon, never more than half a mile across.

"Where are we going, Caine?" Lynda asked.

"We need a better look at Alamo Court than we were going to get from the street," he told her. "Nobody takes any notice of two people pottering about in a boat."

As they drew closer to their destination, on the northwestern edge of the bay, they saw a twenty-four-foot twin-engined Seabird riding at anchor about twenty yards offshore. Caine eased back on the throttle and let the little dinghy idle northward. On the site where the new houses were going up, workmen in yellow hardhats moved about.

"Well?" she said.

"Van in the avenue, covering the front. Fast boat here in case he leaves this way. See the powered inflatable tied to the stern? Any move he makes, they can follow. They've probably got watchers on the building site as well. At night, they'll pose as security guards."

"Who is 'they'?"

"CIA. FBI. Or both."

He thought of the computers feeding their information into the inexhaustible maw of "Bubbles," the $17.6 million Cray-2 computer at the NSA. Everything Bogdanovich had ever done, every transaction he had ever effected, every ticket he'd bought, every subscription he'd ever taken out, all the fine hairs of the strands of his life would be in there now for reevaluation. There would be nothing about him, his family, his friends and acquaintances, the books he read, the trips he had taken, the mail he received, his bank, his phone, his taxes, his social security records, that would not be scrutinized in the search for that one denominator, common or otherwise, that would tell the searchers they were on the right track.

The little boat rocked gently in the water as Caine thought it through. The moment he went anywhere near the house, tapes would start to turn, shutters begin to click. They'd have a make on him ten minutes after the pictures were FAXed to Langley. So he had to make contact some other way; and once again, inescapably, Lynda was it. Nobody was looking for her yet.

"Why the long face?" Lynda said.

"Just thinking," he said. "We can go back now."

"Do we have to?"

"We can take a ride, if you like."

"I like," she said. He revved the engine up, and the little boat scooted over the water. The breeze was soft and refreshing. Lynda leaned back, her eyes closed, face lifted to the sun. Caine took the boat through the neck of the lagoon and out into the open water of Caxambas Pass. Ibis flew overhead in line astern. When the boat was in the lee of Henry Key, Caine cut off the engine. The only sound he could hear was the sound of water lapping against the hull. The setting sun bounced flashes of light off the windshields of cars moving along South Collier Boulevard.

"What was she like, Caine?"

"What was who like?"

"Your wife."

"How did you know—?"

"Someone once told me men over thirty are either married or singular."

"I'm not . . . singular."

"I never thought you were. What happened—divorce?"

"No. She died. She was just a kid. We'd only been married two years."

"I'm sorry."

"It's all right. It was a long time ago."

"Was she beautiful?"

"Beautiful? No, not really. But she had an honesty that shone out of her, that made her attractive. She wasn't tall. Five three, five four. Very slim. She had green eyes, very fine brown hair that frizzed up when she washed it."

"Where did you meet?"

"At a dance."

"I can't imagine you going dancing."

"That was the only time I ever went."

"Then how—?"

"I was sharing a flat with a guy. He arranged to meet a girl at a dance, but he didn't want to go alone. So he asked me to go with him, as a favor. Jenny had a friend . . . well, you can guess the rest."

"Her friend was your friend's date."

"Which kind of threw Jenny and me together. I liked her, she liked me. We made a date for the following Sunday. I didn't think she'd show up. Neither of us ever went out with anyone else after that."

"Love at first sight?"

"Not quite," he said. "She didn't want to get married. She wanted to travel: work on a kibbutz, the Greek islands, Africa. But I talked her into it. I was being sent to Germany, and I asked her to come with me."

"How . . .?"

"How did she die? She was killed by a car bomb that was meant for me." His voice was harsh. Lynda put a hand to her lips, her eyes wide with shock, and she fell silent. Waves slapped the side of the boat. After a while, Caine smiled at her. "It's all right, Lynda," he said, more gently. "It was ten years ago. I've done all my grieving."

"It was Guchkov, wasn't it? That's why you want him."

"That's why."

"I remember that anger, David. I remember what I felt when my husband died in 'Nam. Like he'd gotten himself killed on purpose, to make life more difficult for me. It was so irrational. And yet I couldn't help it. I suppose I needed to be angry at someone, something. Otherwise it was all so pointless. Such a waste.''

"Yes,'' he said softly. "I was angry. For a long time. I'd forgotten how angry till I saw Guchkov's face in that dossier. Then it all came back.''

"And now?''

He shook his head. "Not anymore. Angry men make stupid mistakes. You can't afford to make mistakes with a man like Guchkov.''

The sun was down low over the Gulf now, tinting the sky with ribbons of pink and red. He started up the engine and headed for the boat ramp.

"Time to go back to the real world?'' she said.

"I don't usually talk so much,'' he said.

"You didn't mind? That I asked about her?''

He shook his head. "I don't mind. You're easy to talk to, Lynda.''

"Thanks for the boat ride.''

"Next time we'll do it properly.''

"I'll hold you to that.''

He turned in the boat, then made a call to the post office from the booth outside. They told him the mailman delivered to the Alamo Court neighborhood around mid-morning.

It was safe to assume that the watchers would have someone at the post office opening any mail addressed to the house, just as it was safe to assume they were listening to the phones. While there was no way around the latter, there was a way to circumvent the readers.

"What now?'' Lynda said as he came out of the booth.

"We'd better check in someplace,'' he said. "How about the Marco Beach Marriott?''

"I only have a two-thousand-dollar credit line, Caine. Two

rooms at the Marco Beach Marriott is going to knock a big hole in that if we're here for any length of time."

"We'll just have to wing it, Lynda. Come on, let's get over there. We've got an early start tomorrow, and you've got to look your best."

"Why?"

"You're going to flirt with a postman," Caine said.

"Hi," Lynda said.

The mailman touched his cap, not stopping.

"I wonder if you could help me?" Lynda said.

"What's the problem, ma'am?" He was a tall, thin, fit-looking man with a short beard that made him look older than he probably was. Lynda guessed his age at about thirty.

"I got myself a little lost," Lynda said. "I wonder if you could help me out?"

"Glad to," the man said. "Where you trying to get to?"

"I'm trying to find the public library," she said. "I seem to have taken a wrong turning someplace."

"Library's on Winterberry," he told her. "Where's your car?"

"Over there," she said, gesturing vaguely.

"Okay, here's what you do," the man said. "This here is San Antonio. Drive west till you come to a stop sign, make a right. The next intersection, you make a left. That's Winterberry. The library is two blocks along on your right. You can't miss it."

"Well, thanks, uh . . . what's your name?"

"Owen."

"First name or last?"

"First. Owen Davies."

"This job must keep you pretty fit, Owen."

"I do some running."

186 •

"I thought it must be something like that. What kind of distances do you go?"

"Six, eight miles a day. Sometimes more."

"You run on the beach?"

"Right," he said. "Listen, it was nice talking to you, ma'am. I got to get this mail delivered."

"I'm sorry, I'm holding you up," Lynda said. "Thank you for your help, Owen."

"Y'welcome," he said.

He had gone about ten yards when she called his name. He turned, frowning.

"You dropped this," Lynda said, handing him Caine's letter.

"How the hell. . . ?" he muttered, looking at it. He riffled the bundle he was carrying, shaking his head. He jammed the letter in with the others, thanked her, and went on his way. Lynda went in the opposite direction, walking fifty yards to where Caine sat waiting in her car.

"Mission accomplished," she said.

"Let's hope it works."

They drove up to the Island Plaza Shopping Center and had breakfast in a coffee shop. Lynda said only snowbirds were dumb enough to pay seven dollars for an egg in resort hotels. She ordered croissants with her coffee. Caine took blueberry muffins. She told him he should eat more. He said, 'Yes, Mama.' The coffee was hot and strong. Pretty girls with long tanned legs giggled at the counter.

"Do you think he'll show?" Lynda asked.

"I'm working on the assumption he's expecting someone to contact him. Let's hope I'm right."

"But. . . ?"

"Go ahead."

"If he's under surveillance, they'll spot you the moment he makes contact with you."

"Think you're pretty smart, don't you?"

"But not as smart as you, huh?"

'Just you wait and see.''

He paid for the breakfast, and they walked over to the Winn-Dixie supermarket. He bought a pair of swim trunks, a bath towel, a pair of Ray Ban sunglasses, sneakers, and a straw hat. Lynda picked out a pair of short shorts in blue denim and some cheap sandals, and T-shirts for both of them with the words "Marco Island" set around a garish orange sunset and a palm tree. They changed clothes in the rest rooms and went back to the car. On the way, Caine "stressed" the straw hat, giving it a well-worn look.

It was only a short drive from Island Plaza to Tigertail Beach. They got there shortly after ten. It would be the best part of an hour before they could expect Bogdanovich. They sat and listened to the radio while they waited.

A bunch of shouting teenagers were playing volleyball on the beach, and further over, two sun-bronzed hulks in cutoff jeans were tossing a Frisbee at each other with a fine display of pectorals and trapeziuses. Near the water's edge, kids were splashing about and screeching. A golden labrador dashed into the water and out again, barking. Girls nearby squealed as the dog shook himself dry. A long-haired, bearded proselytizer pushing a ten-foot wooden cross on a single wheel went from group to group, inviting them to open up their hearts and let in the sweet music of Jesus Christ.

"Shall we dance?" Caine said.

They walked down to the water's edge, feet crunching on the wide swathe of broken shells on the high-water mark. Shell hunters searched in the shallows, picking up and discarding, their faces intent and serious. Caine singled out a kid of about fifteen standing shin deep in the water, a net bag of shells slung from his waist. He wore bathing trunks and one of those mass-produced baseball caps. On the white panel at the front were stenciled the words CHISUM TRAIL RIDE, 1980, and in smaller letters, ROSWELL, N.M.

"Ten bucks for your shells," he said. "What do you say?"

The kid took off the baseball cap he was wearing. He squinted and rubbed his head.

"You crazy, or what?"

"What," Caine said, and showed him the ten. The kid handed him the bag, took the money, and walked off, looking back once. Caine stood in the shallows, the warm water swirling at his feet.

"You look like you've been here all morning," Lynda said, joining him.

"That's the basic idea," he said.

"You know anything about shells?"

"I used to."

He tried to remember all the exotic names shellers gave to their treasures: pectins, jingles, boat shells, sunrays, Scotch Bonnets, Jewel Boxes, Lion's Paws, Cups and Saucers, Cat's Eyes. He looked at his watch: five after eleven.

"Okay, this is the plan," Caine said. "I've sent Bogdanovich a picture of you, and a note that says his life may depend on his meeting you here. I just hope to God it didn't spook him."

"What do I do?"

"We've got to get him away from his watchers long enough for me to talk to him. If they see me, we're cooked. So it's up to you. Think you can do it?"

"How will I know it's him?"

"He'll ask you if you've found any yellow rough scallops. You say they're the hardest ones of all to find. But you've got some other stuff if he's interested. He'll ask you what the hell all this is about."

"And then?"

"You tell him you've got proof his life is in danger, and if he'll walk across to your car, you'll show it to him. He'll probably be chary. He won't want to get in any car with a total stranger. Tell him he doesn't have to. Point out that the car is right over there in the open, where nothing can happen without a hundred people seeing it."

"And where will you be?"

"In the car, on the floor. So make sure he's close enough to hear me. Think you can do it?"

"Good job you brought me along, Caine."

"The thought had occurred to me." He grinned.

He pulled the straw hat down over his face and ambled up the beach, leaving her standing in the water, the bag of shells in her hand.

When he got to the car, he looked back. A man was working his way slowly up the beach. Every so often, he would stop and talk to one of the shellers. Caine checked the crowd for a watcher but could see no one obvious. They'd be out there someplace, though. The man drew level, looked at Lynda with appreciative interest, then walked on by.

Caine stifled a curse. Wrong man. The man walked on about ten yards, stopped, turned back and spoke to Lynda.

"I don't suppose you've come across any yellow rough scallops, have you?" He was tall, but thin and weedy-looking. He wore a white cotton tennis shirt, black Pegasus shorts, and carried a pair of Adidas tennis shoes with white tube socks tucked into them.

"They're the hardest of all to find," Lynda said. "But I've got some other stuff if you're interested."

"You the one sent the photograph?" Bogdanovich said. "What is all this about?"

"Tell me how interesting the shells are," Lynda said. "Make like you never saw one in your life before."

Bogdanovich did as he was bidden, picking up the shells one by one and examining them like a diamond cutter looking over an uncut stone. "Who are you?" he said, his voice almost inaudible. "What do you want?"

"You see the white Toyota parked over there?"

"What about it?"

"What I want to show you is in it."

"What is this, lady?" Bogdanovich said. "What are you after?"

"Look, you came this far. Trust me for another couple of minutes, okay? I couldn't bring what I want to show you down here. It's in my car. Just walk over there with me. You don't have to get in."

Bogdanovich frowned, then gave a curt little nod of assent. They walked up the beach to where the car was parked. Lynda noticed that one of the windows was rolled all the way down. Bogdanovich stood by warily as she opened the door.

"Bogdanovich, can you hear me?" Caine said. The man outside jumped visibly.

"Wha—who is that?" he stuttered.

"Drosdow sent me."

"Who's Drosdow? Who are you?"

"Where's the woman?" Caine said.

"You mean Eva?" Bogdanovich frowned.

"She's a plant, Bogdanovich. You know what a honey trap is?"

"Are you crazy, or what?"

"That's the second time today I've been asked that. Who owns the house? Who told you to come to Marco Island?"

"You'd better tell me who the hell you are, mister."

"Somebody has set you up, Bogdanovich. Your own people have got you under intensive surveillance. Didn't you know?"

Bogdanovich looked as if he had been kicked in the belly. His pasty skin went gray, and for a moment Lynda thought the man might pass out.

"Are you . . . who are you?" Bogdanovich managed.

"I told you, Drosdow sent me."

"I don't know any Drosdow."

He was looking around him edgily, as if he was convinced Caine was mad, and Caine was beginning to feel as if he might be. The more they talked, the less sense anything made. Something was vastly wrong.

"Listen to him, Mr. Bogdanovich," Lynda said. "He's telling you the truth."

"How do you know my name? What do you want?"

"Let's start over," Caine said. "The woman who brought you down here knows you work for the Company. She works for Russian intelligence. Her job is to compromise you so Drosdow can recruit you as a spy."

"You are crazy!" Bogdanovich said angrily. "Woman, Russian intelligence? I'm down here on vacation with my wife, for Christ's sake!"

"Listen, Bogdanovich," Caine said urgently. "I know it must sound insane to you, but I swear what I'm saying is true. Hear me out, okay?"

"I'm listening," Bogdanovich said.

"My name is David Caine. I work for a security firm called International Security Systems. You ever heard of it?"

"Nope."

"I was assigned to a case in Florida. It concerned a Company operation headed up by a Domestic Ops agent, Frank Forsyth. Name ring any bells?"

"I don't know who the hell you are, mister. And I'm not discussing my business activities, with you or anyone."

"All right, all right. Look, I know you work at the CIA. Let me assume you might know the name, and cut a long story short. Forsyth got onto a man named Frederic Drosdow who is probably a Russian intelligence officer. Drosdow sold drugs to raise finance for a honey trap. Let's also assume you know what that is. The swallow was a woman named Katja. The location was the house you are staying in. And the target was a senior Company coding clerk named Paul Bogdanovich. And that's why, right now, you are under intensive surveillance, probably by the Office of Security. They think you've been lured down here for entrapment. The fact you brought your wife may have thrown them a little, but that won't last long."

"You're one of them, aren't you?" Bogdanovich said, a wary look in his eyes. "This is the old double-whammy play, right?"

"Sure," Caine said scornfully. "And Lynda is Mata Hari in disguise."

"I've nothing to hide," Bogdanovich said defiantly. "I haven't done anything wrong."

"They haven't got round-the-clockers on you because they think you stole a few paper clips, sunshine," Caine told him. "You better talk to me."

"Why should I even listen to you?"

"Who else have you got?"

Bogdanovich thought about that for a while. Caine saw him scan the beach furtively from beneath lowered eyebrows, looking for watchers. "What did you say your name was?" he asked.

"David Caine. International Security Systems."

"And what do you want?"

"I want to find Frederic Drosdow."

"I told you, I never heard of him."

"All right," Caine said. "We've talked long enough. Take the shells, give Lynda some money. Meet me at the Marco Bay Marina tomorrow morning at nine-thirty. Bring your wife. Eva, you said?"

"I don't understand any of this," Bogdanovich said. He looked suddenly haggard, worried.

"Tomorrow I'll charter a boat. We'll go for a cruise, talk, try to figure this out. Okay?"

"The marina, maybe," Bogdanovich said. "If you think I'm going out on a boat with you or anybody else, forget it."

"Nine-thirty," Caine said. "Just be there."

Bogdanovich walked back down the beach. Caine tried to

spot the watchers and failed again. All he could see were brashly confident American kids, mindlessly enjoying the world's highest standard of living, waiting their turn with the American Express Gold cards and the Cadillac Sevilles.

"Okay," he said to Lynda. "We move fast now before they can get a car up here. Walk down the beach till you come to Bayside Court. Walk up to Collier Boulevard. I'll pick you up on the corner."

He watched her go, waiting to see if anyone would come over to check out the car. No one came near. As he had suspected, the watchers had been caught flat-footed. One of them would stay with Bogdanovich. If there were two, the other would tail Lynda on foot. He grinned at himself in the driving mirror. "Home, James," he said.

He drove over to Collier and turned south. As he coasted to a stop at the corner of Bayside Court, he saw her coming. She ran the last ten yards and jumped into the car. They didn't speak until she pulled into the parking area at the Marriott.

"What do you think, Caine?" she said. "Did he buy it?"

Caine shrugged. "I think so. He looked pretty worried."

"He looked sick," Lynda said. "As if he'd been betrayed."

Caine shook his head in disbelief. Then he took her face in his hands and kissed her on the lips.

"Holmes," he said, "you amaze me!"

She stared at him in astonishment.

"What did I do?" she gasped.

"It'll come to you," he replied.

When they were about an hour out, Hank Valdes broke out some Coors. The owner of the *Sea Wind* was a barrel-chested man with skin as brown as leather, a grizzled beard, and a luxuriant thatch of black hair liberally streaked with gray. He wore a T-shirt that bore the legend JOGGERS DO IT WITH THEIR EARPHONES ON.

The two women sat in deck chairs on the stern and watched the island dropping away. The sun was hot through the breeze of their passage. Valdes busied himself checking the leaders and swivels on the unused fishing equipment. The size of his fist made the beer can in it look small.

"Is there anything you'd like, Mrs. Bogdanovich?" Lynda asked the woman sitting beside her. Eva Bogdanovich was petite and dark, attractive in a soap-powder commercial sort of way. Her face was set and tense.

"Nothing. Thank you."

"Don't be afraid. There's nothing to be frightened of."

"I don't understand what all this is about."

"What did your husband tell you?"

"He said we had to go on this trip. That it was something to do with his work."

"That's all?"

"We have a family agreement. We never discuss his work."

"Did he tell you that you have been under surveillance the whole time you have been here on Marco Island?"

Eva Bogdanovich's eyes widened with alarm. She looked from right to left, as if seeking escape. "He . . . he said you'd ask me questions. He said not to tell you anything."

"But if you know nothing about his work, what could you tell me?"

"Who are you?"

"My name is Lynda Sanchez. I run a small restaurant on Key Biscayne called La Paloma."

"Then why. . . ?"

"Why am I here? I've wondered that myself once or twice. Let's just say we're trying to help your husband, Mrs. Bogdanovich."

"Help him?"

"He's in some sort of trouble. Espionage."

"Oh, God," Eva Bogdanovich said. Lynda looked at her more closely.

"Didn't you know?" she said.

"I told you, I don't know anything."

"Talk to him, Mrs. Bogdanovich. Try to make him realize we're the only ones who can help him."

"I don't know what you're talking about." Eva Bogdanovich stood up and went across to the rail, leaning out so she could see her husband sitting on the prow of the boat with Caine. They had been out there since soon after they sailed, more than an hour ago. "How much longer are they going to stay up there, anyway?" she said, irritably.

"Do you know who owns the house you are staying in?" Lynda asked. Eva Bogdanovich turned to face her, frowning.

"Of course I do," she said. "A friend of Paul's at work. A man called Marty Fielder."

"He told you that?"

"Of course."

"It's not true, Eva," Lynda said. "We talked to the realtor who sold it. The house was bought by a man who called himself Victor Ziegelmann. His real name is Frederic Drosdow."

"I . . . we don't know anybody called Drosdow. Or Ziegelmann. Are they going to sit out there for the whole trip?"

"Caine is trying to convince your husband that he wants to help him."

"You keep saying that. What has Paul done?"

"Here they are," Lynda said. "Ask him yourself."

Bogdanovich's face was stiff and sullen. He clambered into the stern well and sat down on one of the deck chairs. Caine sat opposite him. Eva looked at him and then at her husband.

"Paul," she said. "What's wrong? They keep saying you're in some kind of trouble."

"You don't understand," he said.

"Let's all go sit up top," Caine suggested. "It's cooler up there, anyway."

They went up to the flying deck. Valdes had rolled back the canopy so there was plenty of breeze. If by any chance Bogdanovich's watchers had put sneakies aboard, the sound of the wind and the waves was more than enough to ruin whatever they might pick up, Caine decided.

"How much has he told you, Eva?" Caine asked. Eva looked at her husband. He avoided her pleading eyes.

"She . . ." Eva gestured toward Lynda. "She says the house doesn't belong to Marty Fielder, Paul. Is that true?"

He did not reply. "She says it belongs to a man named Frederic Drosdow. Who is Frederic Drosdow?"

"He is a Russian military intelligence officer," Caine told her.

"Russian?" she said. "Here? In Florida?"

"The Russians have lots of agents working in Florida, Eva," Caine said. "Most of them are Cuban, but by no means all of them."

"How would he know about us? We know no one like that."

"That's what I keep hoping Paul will tell me."

"Paul?" she said, saying his name the way she had before, with a note of pleading in it.

"No!" he said sharply. "He's trying to get me to incriminate myself. You think I'm stupid?"

"What do you mean, incriminate yourself?" Eva said, her face suddenly pale beneath the tan. "How could you do that?"

"Tell her, Paul," Caine said.

"There's nothing to tell."

"You've been betrayed, Paul," Caine said. "They're throwing you to the wolves to protect someone—or something—much more valuable."

"You're crazy!" Bogdanovich said hoarsely, but the conviction had gone out of his voice. The gray pallor they had seen before had again taken away his color.

"If he's crazy, why are we under surveillance?" Eva said.

"How do we know it's the Office of Security that's watching us?" he snapped. "We've only got his word for it."

"Who else could it be?" Caine said.

"Why are they watching us at all?" Eva asked very quietly.

Bogdanovich shook his head. "I'm saying nothing," he said doggedly. "Nothing!"

"You were already working for them, weren't you, Paul?" Caine said softly. "That's how they knew you. What did they tell you—go to Marco Island, wait until you're contacted, something like that?"

"Tell her, Paul," Lynda said, putting her hand on his. He looked out at the unchanging ocean. Tears glistened in his eyes.

"You're expendable. You knew it from the moment I told you about the honey trap yesterday. That's why you agreed to come out on the boat with us. You knew we were the only hope you had."

"Why?" Bogdanovich whispered. "Why me?"

"They probably have someone else who can do what you were doing for them. You became a liability."

"Are . . . will you help me, Caine?"

"If I can. You've got to help me first, Paul."

"I'll be finished. You don't know."

"Then don't lie down and let them do it to you. Fight back."

"Who are you talking about?" Eva said angrily. "Who is 'them'?"

"The Russians, Eva," Caine said.

"Oh, God!" she whispered. "Oh, God, no."

By the time they got back to the marina that evening, Caine knew just about all there was to know about Paul Michael Bogdanovich. Born in St. Paul, Minnesota, he was one of the four children of Harold Bogdanovich, a naturalized Czech refugee who had a General Motors dealership in Golden Valley. Usual middle-class family background of high school and college. Faced with the prospect of going to Vietnam, Paul had embraced the offer made to him by a CIA recruiter who came out to the University of Minnesota; his fluency in Czech made enrollment in the Company's Junior Officer Training Program simple.

Caine knew the induction routine pretty well, but he let Bogdanovich talk about it at his own speed. It was all part of the debriefing technique, which varied only slightly from individual to individual. Caine's job was to make him relax, to allay his fears the way you do with a child: tell me the truth and nothing bad will happen to you. Once in a while he would throw in a deliberate error to see if Bogdanovich would correct it.

Enrollment in the CIA in those days began with a series of interviews and tests which took place at Quarters Eye, near the Potomac in Washington. It was an exhausting, nonstop program that made no concessions to normal working hours or physical needs. You grabbed a sandwich from one of the blind stands—all Company snack concessions were run by blind people—between punishing sessions with the Wechsler, Guilford, Minnesota Multiphasics, Rorschach, Strong, Kuder, and the rest of the tests. After more interviews, you signed an all-embracing secrecy agreement and were assigned to the Personnel Pool at 1016 Sixteenth Street. There you folded maps and competed in crossword-puzzle contests until your final "technical interview"—spookspeak for a polygraph test.

When you passed the lie-detector test—and only when—you got a provisional clearance to handle secret material. After a session on what was euphemistically called the Farm—the Company enclave at Camp Peary, near Williamsburg—Bogdanovich was assigned to East European Radio Transmissions as an analyst, reading radio traffic intercepts picked up by the NSA listening station at Menwith Hill, in Yorkshire, England.

"Menwith," Caine said, raking through the cold ashes of old memory. "Primary targets Western and Eastern Europe, and Russia east of the Urals."

"Let me ask you something, Caine," Bogdanovich said. "How do you know all this?"

"How did it happen, Paul?" Caine said, ignoring the question. "Did they come to you, or did you go to them?"

"Who are you, Caine? Who do you work for?"

"You know I can't tell you that."

"How do I know I can trust you?"

"If I was hostile, I wouldn't be helping you, Paul," Caine reminded him. "You'd already be dead."

"You could still do it," Bogdanovich said. "After you've got all the information you want."

Caine shrugged. "That's a risk you're going to have to take," he said. Bogdanovich looked at his wife.

"You've got to trust someone, Paul," she said.

"I did," he said bitterly. "Look where it got me."

Eva reached across and took his hand in hers. "Tell him," she said.

He took a deep, deep breath and then let it out slowly. "All right," he said. "I'll tell you."

"Go right back to when it first started," Caine prompted.

"Everything seemed to go wrong all at once," Bogdanovich said. "One minute everything was fine, the next . . . There was an appropriations cut, they said they were closing down my section. They told me I could take retirement on half pay or a downgrade in salary. I didn't have any choice. Then . . . it was . . . funny, really," he said, staring out at a gannet swooping above the turning waters of the boat's wake. "I was driving a Maverick back then. The transmission went. You remember, Eva?"

"I remember," she said.

"I went to a car dealer in Pimmit Hills, just to look around. I couldn't afford what they had, we'd just bought the house, I didn't want to borrow. Then I got talking to this guy who was there. We went and sat in a coffee shop together and he told me maybe he could help me, he knew a guy who loaned money at very low rates to government employees. He gave me a number to call. I called the man and he arranged to meet me."

"Where?"

"In the lobby of the Hay-Adams."

"Didn't you suspect anything?"

"No. Yes. Yes, now that I look back on it, I think I must have. But I think I'd already decided, in my mind, if this was a pitch, I was going to listen to it. Especially after what happened at work. I thought, If that's how they repay me for twelve years, screw them. I guess I was ready to talk to someone, and that someone came along."

"What happened then?"

"He asked me how much I needed, and I told him four thousand. He said he could handle that, no problem. He counted out four thousand dollars in hundred-dollar bills, right there in the hotel lobby. I couldn't believe it. I said, 'How do I pay this off,' and he said, 'Don't worry about that, I'll be in touch.' Then he was gone. It sounds incredible, but that's what happened."

"Let me guess what came next," Caine said. "Your friend had a friend he wanted you to meet."

"Right," Bogdanovich said. "He called me at home, asked me if I could help him out, he had this friend who was being investigated by the FBI. He said the friend would gladly pay a couple of K to see a copy of his dossier."

"You got it?"

"You wouldn't believe how easy it was. I mean, most of what the guy wanted he could have gotten himself under the Freedom of Information Act."

"Then what happened?"

"He asked me for some other things. It was mostly routine stuff. I couldn't believe the kind of money they were prepared to pay for what I was giving them. They could have read most of it in the *Washington Post*.

"What was the name of the man you were dealing with?"

"He called himself Alexei. His real name is Stepan Lykov. He's a third attaché at the Kremlin in Washington."

The vast new Soviet embassy high on its hill, dominating the entire Washington skyline, was known as the Kremlin to civilians and military alike.

"How long did the honeymoon last?"

"Is that what they call it? A year, maybe two. Then Alexei told me that from now on his requirements would be more specific. He would give me assignments to fulfill, and I would fulfill them. Like he was a goddamn general talking to a PFC."

"You did what he told you?"

"I had no choice. They had photographs of me accepting the money. It was do what they said, or—" He made the slit-throat gesture with his finger.

"All right," Caine said. "Let's get down to details. Alexei told you to come to Marco Island?"

"He told me to apply for ten days' leave. Fly to Miami, stay one night at the Marriott, then drive out here. On the first day I had to go to a designated booth in the Island Plaza Shopping Center, call a Miami number, and say 'Pimmit'—that's my code name—'in place.' After that, he said I was to wait until I was contacted."

"You were probably talking to a tape recorder," Caine said. "Or a hand-on phone."

"What's that?" Eva said.

"Bookies use them. You can set up a telephone so when anyone calls that number, it hands the call on to another phone. If anybody traces the call, all they get is a phone in an empty room. Obviously, all they wanted was to put you in place. They set you up, Paul."

"Why?" he said hoarsely. "I gave them everything they asked for. Always, everything."

"You've served your purpose. The Comrades are through with you."

"You . . . you mean they . . ."

"Look at it from their point of view. You're no use to them anymore. What happens next will depend on how much you know about them. If it's more than they want the Office of Security to find out, they'll kill you. If not, they'll let OOS take care of you."

Bogdanovich gulped noisily. "There's a unit in Special Operations. They sometimes . . . If you've become an embarrassment to the Company, they take care of it. It's called incineration. You just disappear. All the records, everything. You don't know what they can do."

"Oh yes I do," Caine assured him.

"Are you going to help me, Cainc?"

"I'll try," Caine said. "If I can clear this thing up, I might be able to do something. But you've got to help me first."

"How?"

"I want you to write down everything you can remember giving them. Do you understand? Every single thing you can remember."

"But . . . that would take hours!" he said. "Hours!"

"Then sit up all night," Caine said unsympathetically. "It's your life that's on the line, remember. Look, I need that information, Paul. If you come through, we'll get you out of this. Lynda will take you back to Miami. No one will look for you there.''

"Why do you want this Drosdow?"

"You know why."

"I mean, why you? You're not CIA, you're not FBI. Why are you involved in this?"

"You know I can't tell you that," Caine said. "You're just going to have to trust me."

"Trust," Bogdanovich sighed. "Who can you trust?"

"Will you do it?"

"I want you to take care of Eva," Bogdanovich said. "She didn't know about any of this. If anything happens to me . . ."

"We're going to try and make sure nothing happens to either of you," Lynda said. "Aren't we, Caine?"

"If Paul comes through for me," Caine said.

"All right," Bogdanovich said. "I'll do it."

"There's writing stuff in the cabin," Caine said. "Go below and get started. Hey, Hank! Valdes!"

"Yo!" Valdes said from below.

"I think we might try some fishing now.'

"Great!" Valdes said. "All of you?"

"Paul's got some writing to do," Caine told him. "But the ladies and I might take a crack at it. What do you say, Eva?"

Her smile was very bright and tight and brave.

"Okay," she said. "Okay."

24 "I give up," Harry Lloyd said, stubbing out his cigarette and lighting another. "This whole damned take makes no sense at all!"

Caine's reappearance, especially with the Sanchez woman in tow, had thrown them. Apparently, it had thrown Miami, too: Bensen's perplexedness had been almost tangible. He had promised them he would get right on it and get back to them. Since then, silence. Bensen was probably waiting for instructions from Langley. Maybe Langley was waiting for word from God.

"One thing's for sure," Balfour said. "There's no honey trap going down here. My bet is that Caine is taking Bogdanovich someplace to meet Drosdow."

"In a boat?"

"Maybe they want to be sure they're alone. Maybe they have to go to the same place every day and wait."

"I don't buy that," Forsyth said. "Anyway, why would Drosdow put himself at risk to meet Bogdanovich? What could Bogdanovich know that would interest him?"

"Why are there more questions than answers, Grandpa?" Lloyd said in a Mel Blanc voice.

"So, what are we supposed to do?" Balfour said.

"We wait," Forsyth said. "For Bensen."

"What a nice change," Lloyd remarked savagely.

The unease simmered in Forsyth's mind like soup. Even though it had been he who first made the connection between

Bogdanovich and David Caine, he still felt unhappy about it, NSA dossier and movements survey notwithstanding.

There was enough circumstantial evidence to point to Caine's being a Comrade: he'd had plenty of dealings with them while he was in Army intelligence in Germany. They could easily have turned him then. His profile was close enough to what Avranilosa had heard. All the same, a few things still bothered Forsyth. If Caine was the Comrade, how come the NSA could establish no link between him and Bogdanovich prior to their meeting on Marco Island? If Caine was supposed to be leading Bogdanovich into a honey trap, how come he'd let him bring his wife?

The thing that bothered him most of all was that Caine had run, which got him a Most Sought classification and made NSA's Office of Security even more anxious to know what he was up to. Usually, if one of their agents was blown, the Comrades had him on an Aeroflot Tupolev to Sheremetyevo before you could say *Tovarich*. In Forsyth's experience, a good agent never ran when he knew he was blown: a pro knew there was no place to hide. Yet Caine, who was if nothing else a pro, had run. And as if that were not enough, he had turned up at what he must have known, or at very least suspected, was a surveilled location.

The special link line to Miami gave its discreet bleep and Balfour picked up the handset. He grimaced and put his hand over the mouthpiece.

"Megacreep," he announced.

"Yes," Forsyth said into the phone.

"Anything new?" Bensen sounded aggrieved, as if all this had been done specifically to upset him. Caine had chartered a boat called *Sea Wind,* owned by a local man named Hank Valdes. Valdes had been checked out; he was clean. So why had Caine and the Sanchez woman gone cruising with Bogdanovich and his wife? Coast Guard surveillance reported they hadn't landed anywhere, hadn't picked anyone up. What were they doing out there? They sure as hell weren't interested in fishing.

"Nothing."

"No sign of Drosdow?"

"None. And none of anyone who might remotely be the swallow. What do we do, Donald?"

"The head office says let go. Let them run."

"What?"

"You heard me. Lift the surveillance. We're out of the picture, as of now."

"Would you care to spend twenty seconds explaining why?"

"I'm just passing on the word. They say we're to take no further interest, we take no further interest. Other arrangements are being made."

"What other arrangements?"

"Negative. You don't need to know."

That again, Forsyth thought disgustedly. The old need-to-know principle. You weren't supposed to know more than was necessary to carry out your compartmentalized little function. The guy above you knew a little, but only a little more. And so on, all the way up the line.

"Jesus, what a waste," Forsyth said.

"It's not my decision, Frank."

"You fought like a lion, right?"

"What?"

"I want my protest logged."

"I'll make a note of it," Bensen said curtly, and hung up before Forsyth could say any more. Not that there was any more to be said. Someone up the line had made an Executive Decision. Good, bad, or putrid, that was it.

"I've got bad news and bad news," he said to Lloyd and Balfour as he put down the phone. Lloyd shrugged.

"In that case, give us the bad news first."

"The party's over. We're off this take."

"You mean it?" Balfour said disbelievingly. "Bensen told you to drop it?"

"Right down the toilet," Forsyth said. He walked out into the garden at the rear of the house on San Antonio Avenue they were using as a base. A soft breeze was coming in off Roberts Bay. He looked up and saw ibis flying overhead. He took a deep breath, then slowly let it out, letting his own tension dissipate with it.

There was no more he could do. All the unanswered questions were going to remain just that, unanswered, at least as far as he was concerned. Maybe one day he might learn what finally happened; more likely not. The price of freedom is eternal fuck-ups, he thought. He went indoors.

"You guys roll all this up, okay?" Forsyth said, putting on his jacket. "I'll be back in a while."

"I thought you said we're off this?" Lloyd remarked.

"You know how forgetful I am," Forsyth said.

25 "Let me ask you a question, Mitch," Drosdow said, leaning back in his chair. "What would you do if you had a million dollars?"

They were alone in the big house. Kate was ostensibly visiting a friend in Baltimore. The servants had been given strict orders not to disturb them. The phones were switched off, the alarms switched on. Drosdow sipped his Rémy Martin and watched Butler Mitchell's face, as easy to read as a child's primer.

"God, what a thought. A million dollars."

"What would you do with it?"

"First thing, I'd take early retirement," Mitchell said. "Then I'd take off. Around the world. A first-class suite on the *QE2* to Southampton. London. A box at Ascot, Centre Court at Wimbledon, stay at the Connaught. Then on to Paris, the Ritz. Go to all those restaurants I've read about: Taillevant, Ledoyen, Lasserre, the Tour d'Argent. I'd buy a car, something fabulous, a Ferrari, or a Lamborghini. Drive to Nice, over to Florence, Rome. A suite at the Hassler looking out over the Spanish Steps. Athens, Cairo, then Arusha in Tanzania. A safari to Kilimanjaro. I've always wanted to see Kilimanjaro, ever since I saw it in that movie, with Gregory Peck and Susan Hayward."

"Ah, yes," Drosdow said. "Life can be beautiful when you've got money. Better than prison, Mitch?"

"Prison? Who's talking about prison?"

"It's an interesting subject," Drosdow said.

"I can take it or leave it," Mitchell said uncomfortably, not liking the turn the conversation had taken. Drosdow smiled. He'd like it even less, presently.

"Lot of blacks in the prisons in this part of the world," he said ruminatively. "That right, Mitch?"

"I expect so," Mitchell said with a shrug.

"Be pretty bad for a white man in there with all those blacks. I hear they do terrible things, gang rape, beatings."

"What the hell is this, Fred? One minute we're having a pleasant conversation, the next you're talking about gang rapes in black prisons."

"Which would you prefer?"

"What do you mean?"

"If you had to choose between a million dollars and going to prison?"

"You're not making sense, Fred."

"Indulge me," Drosdow said. He got up and went across to his desk. He opened the drawer and took out a large manila envelope. From it he took a batch of documents which he spread on the table. The red classification stamps looked like wounds: HANDLE VIA COMINT CHANNELS ONLY. TOP SECRET VIPAR.

Mitchell stared at them uncomprehendingly. He edged up to the table as if the documents were cobras that might strike him. He touched them gingerly.

"How in the name of God did you get these?" he whispered.

"Suppose I said I got them from you?"

"It would be a damned lie! I've never given you—"

"Of course not," Drosdow said briskly. "You know that, and I know that. But suppose you had to try and convince M-5?" M-5 was the Office of Security at the NSA, the fiercest and most diligent security organization in government service.

"They'd believe me," Mitchell said. "They'd know I never . . ." His voice tailed off as Drosdow's smile widened.

He thought of the little "favors" Drosdow had asked him to do over the few weeks that he'd known the man: first, the restricted directory, then items more sensitive: an organizational chart, a list of top-ranking NSA personnel. Never anything that seemed like . . . well, wrong.

"What's all this about, Fred?" he said, suddenly deeply uneasy.

"I'm sorry to have to do this, Mitch," Drosdow said. "I'd hoped we could make it last a lot longer. But I'm under pressure. My people are ready to move, and that means I have to give them what they want."

Mitchell frowned. "Your people?"

Drosdow sighed, as one might sigh at a child's inability to comprehend a nuance. He tossed a sheaf of checks and receipts on the table.

"Your gambling debts," he said. "All paid off. The checks were all drawn on an account at Manufacturers Hanover Trust, but deposits in those exact amounts came from the Narodny Bank—you know what that is, I assume?"

"You're . . . some sort of spy. Is that it?"

"An old-fashioned word," Drosdow said. "But it will do."

Mitchell shook his head stubbornly. "Whatever it is you want, I won't do it."

"I was hoping not to have to go this far," Drosdow said. He pushed a button by the side of his chair. A screen slid down from a slot above the fireplace. Drosdow pressed another button to dim the lights.

"What the hell is all this?" Mitchell said, making his tone belligerent. Drosdow made no reply. The screen lit up; the number nine in a circle appeared. Then the film started to run, counting down. The scene was a bedroom.

"Jesus Christ!" Mitchell whispered, recognizing it. The film ran on. The figures in the well-lit bedroom performed their predictable arabesques until their predictable conclusion. The screen went blank. Drosdow switched the lights back on. He looked at Mitchell. The man's face was stricken, colorless. His lips moved, but for a few seconds no sound came out.

"There are seven films altogether," Drosdow said. "Plus, of course, a great many still photographs."

He gave it a moment to sink in. The bronze Ansonia winter and summer clock ticked softly in the silence.

"Kate. . . ?" Mitchell managed hoarsely. "Is she. . . ?"

"Kate knows nothing about my . . . loyalties," Drosdow said briskly.

"You expect me to believe that?" Mitchell said bitterly.

"Kate is a young woman in love. She thinks you're a wealthy man and that you'll probably marry her." Drosdow watched the American closely. Mitchell wanted to believe it: he could see it in the man's eyes.

"You used her? Your own daughter? Why?" Mitchell said. "Why?"

"Come, come, Mitch," Drosdow said impatiently, "you're not as naive as that."

"You—" Mitchell's color came back. Anger lit his eyes. A vein throbbed in his temple. "You bastard. Oh, you fucking bastard!"

"Spare me the gutter talk," Drosdow snapped. "You're facing the most important decision of your life. Don't let emotion cloud it."

"No!" Mitchell said. "A few favors, yes. I didn't mind that. But I won't be a spy. You hear me? I won't!"

"Just as you wish," Drosdow said, pouring himself another cognac from the Waterford decanter on the sideboard. "I trust you understand the implications of your refusal?"

"What do you mean?"

"Copies of everything here, the films, the documents, all of it, will be sent to your wife—oh, yes, we know all about Cathie, Mitch—and to the director of the National Security Agency," Drosdow said.

"I'll tell them about you," Mitchell said. "They'll see how

you trapped me. All this." He waved a hand to encompass the house, all of it.

"You have been removing secret materials from the National Security Agency," Drosdow said relentlessly. "And you knew it. What difference if you go on doing it?"

Mitchell dumbly shook his head.

"Think carefully," Drosdow said. "One sight of this material and you'll be finished. Your wife will take you for every penny you possess, and the NSA will break you, Mitch. They'll put you in the worst hellhole of a Federal jail they can find, and they'll throw away the key. You'll spend the rest of your life playing wife to some lifer."

"I don't believe you. It wouldn't be just me. What about Kate? She'd go to prison, too."

"That's right."

"You bastard," Mitchell groaned.

"You're repeating yourself," Drosdow said impatiently. "You told me yourself you hated them, Mitch! You said they'd held you back for years, never given you the recognition you deserved. What loyalty do you owe people like that?"

"I wish I'd never laid eyes on you," the big man said, putting his head in his hands. Dry, racking sobs burst out of him.

"Stop that!"

Drosdow's voice was like a pistol shot. Mitchell sat up, surprise, and for the first time, fear in his eyes. Drosdow nodded. At last, the American realized just how deep was the water he was in.

"Is it really that hard a decision to make?" he said. "What did the NSA ever do for you, anyway? I'm offering you a straight choice: A million dollars in your hand. Everything you've always wanted. All the good things: money, travel, clothes. And a beautiful woman to share them all with. Do it, Mitch. Do it, or I give you to M-5."

"I . . . you've got to let me think," Mitchell said. "I've got to think."

"No," Drosdow said grimly. "You decide tonight."

He let the silence lengthen. It didn't make any difference how Mitchell said it, as long as he said something. He waited.

"I . . . what would I . . . have to do?" Mitchell said. Drosdow smiled.

"Have a drink," he said. "You look as if you need one."

26 By the time Valdes turned the *Sea Wind* south into Marco Bay, Bogdanovich had filled ten pages of a legal pad with his sloping scrawl. Glancing through it, Caine was astonished not so much by what the Comrades had asked for as how much Bogdanovich had been able to supply. For all his low-grade status, masses of sensitive material passed through his hands for pretransmission coding.

Caine decided not to give Bogdanovich and his wife any time to reconsider: he insisted that instead of going back to the house on Alamo Court, they should come to the Marco Beach Marriott.

"We've got two rooms," he told them. "Paul and I can sleep in one, Lynda and Eva in the other."

"Why do we have to do that?" Bogdanovich said pettishly.

"I want you to finish those lists tonight," Caine told him. "Then you'll be ready to leave first thing in the morning."

"Leave?" Eva said.

"You're not going back to Alamo Court," Caine said.

"But all our things are there, clothes, everything!"

"I want you out of Marco tomorrow, Eva," Caine said. "In case whoever sent you down here decides it would be simpler to just remove you from the picture."

Bogdanovich had that sick pallor again. "You really think they'd do that?" he said like someone who feels he has been unfairly treated.

"All I know is, you're at risk. I want to get you someplace you won't be."

"Like where?"

"I don't know yet. Maybe we can get Valdes to take us up the coast—Sanibel, Sarasota, Cedar Key. When we got there, you could jump ship. Lie low until I can clear this up."

"Using what for money?"

"I could get some money to you," Lynda said. "Enough to live on."

"Suppose I turned myself in?" Bogdanovich said. "Told them all I know?"

"They already know all you know, Paul."

Valdes brought the *Sea Wind* in toward her berth at the marina. Caine could see people on the apron in front of the coffee shop and wondered if Forsyth was among them. Maybe he'd been out looking for them in Gullivan Bay. It was a big bay.

They said so long to Valdes and walked down the jetty. Caine and Lynda stood watching as Paul and Eva Bogdanovich walked over to their Citation. Caine turned away as Bogdanovich got into the car and started the engine.

The explosion was flat and sudden.

He felt the warm movement of air past his head as he spun around, knowing what he would see before he saw it. The Citation was lying on its side, burning furiously. A thick, heavy pall of oily smoke lifted in the still air . . . *and he tried to get close enough to pull her out, screaming her name over and over, but they pulled him away, they dragged him kicking and fighting away from the burning Opel, his hands seared by burns he did not even feel* . . .

"Jesus!" he heard someone say in an awed voice. "Did you see that?"

People were running into the parking lot from the marina, shouting. A police car whooped past with all its lights flashing. The cops piled out, rushing to the blazing wreck with portable fire extinguishers.

"David?" Lynda said very faintly.

He took her in his arms, and she buried her face against his chest. He felt the shudders running through her body. He put his arm around her shoulder and walked her away. The chances of anyone being alive after that explosion were zero. He pushed through the crowd which had gathered, another unanswerable question going on and off in his brain like a neon sign. They had put a bomb in Paul Bogdanovich's car.

But who were they?

Nobody locked their cars on Marco Island, which made it childishly easy for Caine to hot-wire a Mecury Cougar and get the hell away from Towne Centre. Lynda's little Toyota could stay in the marina parking lot until kingdom come as far as he was concerned: for all he knew, there was a bomb under that, too. He glanced at her: she sat beside him, staring sightlessly at the road ahead of them, her arms folded tightly, her shoulders hunched. She had not spoken since saying that one word after the car blew up.

Caine drove over the bridge and north to Naples, reputed to have more millionaires to the acre than any other town in America. It was one of those places where they renovate hundred-year-old houses and call them monuments, all white clapboard and fretwork balconies. When they got there, he checked into the Edgewater Beach Inn on Gulf Shore Boulevard. When they got to the room, Lynda came into his arms, weeping.

"Hold me, David, hold me, hold me," she sobbed.

He put his arms around her and held her tightly, intensely aware of the warm strength of her body against his own. After a while, the tremors ceased. She lifted her head and looked up at him, her eyes dark and unreadable. Her lips found his fiercely, demanding. She kicked off her shoes. He picked her up and carried her across to the bed.

"Yes," she said, throatily. "Yes, yes, yes."

Their lovemaking was urgent, eager, without tenderness, fueled by a need deeper than love.

When it was over, she cried again, but more softly this time. He held her in his arms and said nothing. After a while, she stopped crying. She got up and went into the bathroom. He heard water running. When she came out, she had washed her face and combed her hair. She looked pale and sad.

"I didn't expect this," she said.

"Neither did I."

"How do you feel about it?"

"Like in that Sondheim song: sorry-glad."

"Yes," she said. "Yes."

They were silent for a moment. He touched her bare shoulder.

"I'm sorry you had to see . . . what happened."

"Who did it, David?"

He shook his head. "I don't know."

"It was so . . . brutal. So pointless. Would . . . our people have done something like that?"

"They do."

"It's horrible."

"Did you think it was some sort of game?" he said, more harshly than he had intended. He saw her flinch and was sorry for what he had said, but he did not apologize. Instead he went over to the telephone and had room service send up some food and a bottle of Jack Daniels. They watched the late news as they ate, the TV creating a no-go zone into which they could both retreat without talking.

A Russian dissident was being exchanged at the Glieneckebrücke in Berlin. The commentator explained who all the people getting in and out of cars were. Russian soldiers stared stolidly at the cameras.

"Frederick the Great used to travel to his palace in Potsdam over that bridge," Caine remarked. "Not many people know that."

"Have you ever been there?" Eva asked.

"Yes," he told her. "About twelve years ago. We were bringing one of our agents out. Normally, civilians can't get within half a mile of it."

In the background, Caine saw the gold Mercedes that belonged to Wolfgang Vogel, the East German lawyer who arranged such exchanges.

"Who's paying your fees, Wolfie?" he said to the flickering screen. And who, for that matter, was financing the return to Israel of the dissident, who had doubtlessly been ejected penniless from Russia by the KGB?

He took the lists Bogdanovich had written and spread them flat on the floor in front of the sofa. Lynda watched the rest of the news. Among the agents being returned to the East were a Czech husband and wife who had spied for Prague while the man was a contract translator for the CIA. They had airline tickets to Zurich in their pockets when the FBI arrested them. They had sold their Manhattan apartment for four hundred thousand dollars, and had been planning to use the money to settle comfortably in Switzerland. Their life would be somewhat less glamorous in Moscow, he thought.

He poured himself a healthy measure of Jack Daniel's and sipped it as he started reading Bogdanovich's notes. Lykov's shopping lists had included a predictably catholic range of requirements: they ranged from the very specific, indicating a formidable degree of existing intelligence, to the very vague, meaning the Comrades were trying to get a handle on something they knew very little about.

It was easy to understand why Lykov had asked for information about an Air Force general who'd been killed while testing a MIG-23 jet at Nellis Air Force Base in Nevada; they wanted to know where the jet had come from, and what it was being tested for—or against. Lykov had also asked for any documents referring to the Aurora project, code name for the new B-1 Stealth bomber under development by Rockwell International;

Bogdanovich had provided him with information about its stingray shape and the revolutionary 'skin' which absorbed, rather than reflected, radar waves aimed at the $620 million plane.

Bogdanovich's lists emphasized the Russian preoccupation with American high technology. There were requests for details of the $100 million complex being built in New Mexico to test laser-beam weapons; for an update on the progress of phased-array radar; for information about the Goodyear radar satellite; for the specification of the Cryptag scrambler used on Company computers, and the new speech-activated STU-II scrambler phones.

Equally predictable was the Kremlin's interest in the disposition of investigations into Russian espionage. Lykov had asked for information on the present whereabouts of the twenty-three Soviet-bloc spies who had been exchanged in Berlin in June 1985. He asked for status reports on the all-in-the-family spy case involving Navy veteran John A. Walker, Jr., his brother Arthur, his son Michael, and his old Navy crony, Jerry Whitworth. He wanted details of the case of Svetlana Ogorodnikova, who had involved an FBI agent named Richard Miller in a classic honey trap recruitment, and Ludmilla Kondratjeva, who had testified against Miller and was found dead in her car in the surf near Malibu.

There had been a flurry of requests in August 1985 while the KGB defector Vitaly Yurchenko was in American hands, and a lot of other names which would have been familiar to anyone who read a weekly newsmagazine—Jonathan Pollard, Edward Howard, Ronald Pelton, and Larry Wu-Tai Chin, who killed himself by putting a plastic bag over his head while awaiting sentence. There were others Caine assumed were espionage suspects who had been arrested without a great deal of publicity. The last request Bogdanovich had received from Lykov had been for information on a KGB colonel named Viktor Gudarev, who had defected with his son and a woman friend in Athens late in February 1986.

Caine looked up to find Lynda watching him. On television, Robert Mitchum was being driven somewhere by Jane Greer. It took Caine a moment or two to remember the name of the film: *The Big Steal*. Mitchum is supposed to have stolen an Army payroll. He's being hunted by William Bendix. What was the name of the suave guy who was supposed to be Greer's boyfriend? Knowles. Patric-without-a-*k* Knowles.

"Almost finished," he said.

"This thing has gone a long way away from Tony Genevevo, hasn't it?"

"A long way."

"Will whoever killed Paul and Eva try to kill us, too?"

"Quite possibly. If they find us."

"I'm scared, David."

"And I'm sorry I got you into this, Lynda."

"It's not your fault . . . what happened."

"In a way, it is. In a way, everything that has happened is my fault."

She was silent for a long moment, looking at him. It was as if she was making her mind up about something. He thought of the way he had embraced loneliness after Jenny died, and wondered if Lynda had done the same when she lost her husband. She got up and came gracefully across the room, bending down to kiss him on the lips, once, twice, her dark hair falling like soft rain around his face.

"What's that for?" he asked her.

"Openers," she said.

27 "You son of a bitch!" Forsyth said.

Bensen blinked, swallowing noisily. "That's enough, Forsyth. I'm not going to sit still while you call me names. As chief—"

"Chief!" Forsyth fumed. "You knew Special Ops was going to take Bogdanovich out, you bastard! You *knew*, and you didn't even see fit to tell me."

"It was a policy decision. Langley—"

"Yeah, yeah," Forsyth gibed. "They had one of those seventh-floor brainstorm sessions where everyone talks integrated reciprocal mobility and ultimate logical necessity and shit like that. And you gave them the green light."

"It was taken out of my hands," Bensen said. "The executive decision was maximal demotion. I told them Bogdanovich was our only lead to Drosdow. They said forget Drosdow. They told me to close the whole thing down."

"The hell we will!"

Bensen shook his head wearily. "Have you got anything I could use as an argument?"

"Nothing. Not a damned thing."

"Then we leave the whole thing to the FBI, including Avranilosa and his little band of brothers."

"Let them take them, and welcome," Forsyth said. "That's small potatoes, Donald."

"Oh, I wouldn't say that," Bensen bridled.

No, you wouldn't, Forsyth thought. You wrote it up as the biggest espionage coup since we captured Major André. You can't unwrite it, even though the scalp hunters were beginning to wonder if maybe Avranilosa was a plant after all.

"I want one more crack at Drosdow," he said.

"Negative. How many times do I have to tell you? As of now, the FBI has jurisdiction."

"Donald," Forsyth said slowly, "you are full of shit."

Bensen blinked, like a priest encountering blasphemy. He buttoned his jacket, then unbuttoned it again. He moved a piece of paper from one side of his desk to the other. Malice flickered in his eyes.

"You never learn, do you?" he hissed. "All right. All *right!* I've taken all I'm going to take from you, Forsyth. I'm going to get your ass transferred out of here to somewhere so far away you'll have to use drums to get a message out."

"Well, well," Forsyth said. "It bites."

"You sour-tongued bastard, you think you're clever, don't you?" Bensen flared. "You think you're a cut above the rest of us. You don't want to play by the rules. You want to strap on your six-guns and clean up, like the goddamn Lone Ranger. Being nice to you doesn't work. So now I'm going to try it the other way—see how you like that. You are suspended from duty until further notice. Am I making myself clear?"

"Transparent," Forsyth said.

"Then get the hell out of my office!" Bensen snapped.

"My pleasure," Forsyth said. He got out of the Brickell Avenue building as fast as he could and went back downtown to the Vanguard office, where he sat at his desk, smoking cigarette after unwanted cigarette, his face a furious mask of concentration.

Nobody spoke to him. The grapevine had already transmitted the news of his collision with Bensen, and people kept away from him, as if he had a communicable disease. Forsyth wasn't even aware of the atmosphere in the office. He had decided what he was going to do before he even got there. No matter what Bensen did or didn't do, he was not about to give up on the Drosdow case. He wanted that turkey so badly it made his teeth ache.

But everything known about the man had been checked and double-checked, and they were still batting zero. Immigration had traced the forms filed by Drosdow when he landed at Miami International. They listed a false address in Bogotá as his home and gave as his Miami address the Omni International. The hotel's records showed Drosdow had stayed there on four separate occasions, paying in cash. Nobody recalled anything about him. Just another anonymous guest/room/service unit, processed through the machinery of the hotel as impersonally as a rivet in an assembly plant.

Avranilosa was no help. Never having seen the girl Drosdow was to meet in Key Largo, he was unable to give them a description that the dossier computers at Langley and Fort Meade could use. No trace of either Drosdow or the woman had been left at the Holiday Inn. Cross-checking of the date turned up only a Mr. Smith and a Miss Jones who had stayed in poolside rooms one night and paid cash for their accommodation.

Subsequent to the events at Marco Island, every facet of Bogdanovich's life had been reexamined. His spot-check ratings had always been Alpha One; even the deep scans had failed to indicate anything untoward. Yet it was beginning to appear as if he had been passing classified material to the GRU for some time. Among the relevant documents he had handled was the dossier on ISS that Forsyth had requested after Genevevo's murder.

There was some kind of link there someplace, but no way could Forsyth put a finger on it. No trace of a link between this man Caine and the CIA analyst could be found. And since Bogdanovich was already selling classified material to the Comrades, the whole idea of honey-trapping him became ludicrous nonsense. Yet they had watched Caine establish contact with Bogdanovich, taking him out on the boat and—Forsyth guessed—pumping him. Then came the word: lay off. He saw why now, of course. Those cold-eyed bastards in Langley had decided the simplest way of closing the case was to take Bogdanovich and Caine out of the picture. They'd taken care of Bogdanovich all right. Forsyth had been on his way into the parking lot at the marina when the bomb went off. There had been no sign of Caine or the Sanchez woman since then.

He didn't buy the idea of Caine as a Comrade anymore. He riffled through the ISS dossier again, as if somehow the information it contained on Caine would suggest a new approach. Of course, it did nothing of the sort. A good degree at Cambridge, straight into Army intelligence. Service in England, Canada, Germany, Northern Ireland. Married to Jennifer Bruce, who had died in a car-bombing in Berlin. Anything there? It might be worth checking. He made a note, then went on reading. Caine had resigned from government service in 1980, joined International Security Systems, transferred to America a year later. Home in Cherokee Triangle, no permanent female companion, bills paid on time. Clean as a whistle.

Forsyth ran a hand through his hair, yawned, and rubbed the scratchy stubble on his chin. I need a shave, he thought. And a shower, and a clean shirt, and a large Black Label, not necessarily in that order. He lit another cigarette and doggedly went back to his digging. There had to be something, somewhere, even though everything he had fed into the magic box so far had come out zilch.

He tried cross-referencing names, ages, descriptions, locales, places of origin. There were no common denominators for the computer to isolate. Drosdow didn't match up with any existing profile on the Langley, Fort Meade, or FBI computers, and neither did Caine, and neither did anyone else. No one named Frederic Drosdow had flown on any commercial airline within the continental United States during the last thirty days. No credit-card company had any record of him, nor could any bank account be traced. The payment for the house on Marco Island had been effected by a cashier's check, for cash paid into the Republic National Bank in Miami, using Avranilosa as a referee and his home as an address.

Dead end after dead end.

Come *on,* Forsyth told himself. His brain felt like a bowl of oatmeal. The lines of text on the computer monitor swam before his tired eyes. He knew what he ought to do was go right back to the beginning, start over. The thought was deadening. He got up and stretched. The office was emptying out as the day shift ended.

Three and a half hours later, he found what he had been looking for: the piece of information all the computer trawls had missed. Among the many visitors logged at Avranilosa's home was a well-dressed man of about fifty. He had dined with the Fat Man and Frederic Drosdow at a Key Biscayne restaurant that night. Not just any Key Biscayne restaurant, but the one managed by Lynda Sanchez. Avranilosa's guest caught an early plane next morning. It had been established that his name was Harold Percival, a realtor from Easton, Maryland. The appropriate checks were made: Percival's standing in his home town was impeccable. Since Genevevo had no knowledge then or later of Drosdow's intentions, Percival had been eliminated from the investigation.

Got you, you son of a bitch, he thought.

Something less than two hours later, showered, shaved, and wearing a fresh Sea Island cotton shirt and a dark blue Palm Beach suit from Jordan Marsh, Forsyth leaned back smiling in his seat as Eastern's Flight EA 198, a Boeing 737, climbed like a homesick angel into the evening sky over Miami. For no reason he could think of, he found himself humming an old Bill Haley song: "See You Later, Alligator."

28 There was no mistaking the cold, alien feel of a gun muzzle against the back of the neck. Dick Mc-Clelland froze in the driver's seat of his Mercury Cougar, stifling a curse. Mugged outside my own apartment at nine-thirty in the morning, he thought disgustedly.

"All right," he said. "Don't do anything stupid. I'll hand you my wallet. Just take it easy, okay?"

"Do what I tell you. Drive!" an unnaturally hoarse voice commanded.

McClelland half turned, frowning, a protest forming in his throat. The man jammed the gun muzzle even harder against the base of his neck.

"Drive, I said!"

McClelland put the car in drive and moved off down Devonshire Place toward Connecticut Avenue. He stopped at the junction.

"Which way?"

"Drive into the zoo," the man in back said.

McClelland made a right and drove down the hill, then turned in through the gateway of the National Zoological Park.

"Head for the parking lot," the man behind him said. "Park off to one side someplace."

There was nobody in sight. The zoo had opened only a few minutes earlier. McClelland silently cursed his bad luck as he coasted to a stop on the far side of the parking lot.

"Switch off and put the keys on the passenger seat," the man said. "Then turn around."

McClelland did as he was bidden, turning warily. He let out his breath in a great gust of relief and anger.

"You!"

"I'm sorry, Dick," Caine said with a wry grin. "There wasn't any other way of doing it. I couldn't be sure how you'd have reacted if I just came up to you in the street."

"You can put the gun away," McClelland said coldly. "I'm not armed. What do you want?"

"I need some help, Dick."

"You can say that again. Don't expect any from me."

"Dick, you've known me for a long time," Caine said. "Give me a break. Trust me, just for a few minutes."

"Give me one good reason why I should."

"I will. Look, I'm going to put the gun away. Promise me you won't try anything."

"Trust me," McClelland said sardonically. "Just for a few minutes."

"I want you to listen to my side of it," Caine said. "Will you?"

"Do I have a choice?"

"You called me a traitor. That day at the airport. Why?"

"You know the answer to that one."

"Tell me anyway."

"I'll tell you nothing."

"You've got to give me a chance, Dick. I know you think I crossed over, but it's not true."

"Then why did you run?"

"The moment you called me a traitor, I knew someone had fitted me up. Why, how, didn't matter. I knew I wasn't going to find out sitting in a locked cell talking to a squad of dredgers."

"Go on," McClelland said. His training had reasserted itself after the first brief burst of anger. His feelings about Caine were

228 •

not important. The first imperative was to listen and extract what he could from the situation.

"Tell me this," Caine said. "If I'm a spy or a defector, why am I still around?"

It was a telling point. If Caine had been an agent, he would have run to the only place he could have gotten help. If one of their operatives was blown, the Comrades usually had him on an Aeroflot flight to Moscow within hours.

"If you aren't, why didn't you call Mother?"

"Nobody would have believed me," Caine said. "And anyway, I knew Kingly would change all the systems."

McClelland neither confirmed nor denied the guess, although in fact it was true. Kingly had made swinging changes in the wake of what was seen as Caine's defection, moving swiftly to render obsolete as much as possible of what Caine might be telling the Russians. These precautions taken, Kingly flew by Concorde to London for what were euphemistically referred to as "urgent management consultations" but which everyone knew meant a security review. London was paranoid about inside jobs, and nobody wanted another inquiry like the stringent review of the security services carried out in 1985 by Lord Bridge of Harwich.

When Kingly returned, signals flew thick and fast. The six remaining ISS consultants were recalled and replaced. McClelland, promoted to deputy director, sent cleaning squads to each of the regions. Anyone who had been in active contact with Caine during the preceding year was debriefed. Close associates underwent polygraph tests and intensive interrogation. Every case in which he had been involved was reviewed. A completely new team was sent to replace the one Caine had led, the members of which were transferred to nonsensitive duties. Then, and only then, was Station Two returned to Active status.

"Tell me just one thing, Dick. Who said I was Red?"

"What difference does it make?"

"It was Avranilosa, wasn't it? Kingly expurgated the dossier before he gave it to me."

"If you say so."

"It had to be him. What I haven't figured out yet is why."

"It couldn't perhaps be because it was true?"

"He lied to them, Dick. He was programmed to lie to them."

"What reason would he have had to lie?"

"Let me put it another way: he was telling them what he believed to be the truth. So if they gave him polygraph tests, did all the business, he would come out clean. But he'd been programmed, Dick. By someone who wanted to be absolutely certain we were out of the picture."

"And who was that?"

"Andrei Guchkov. 'Viktor.' Alias Fred Drosdow."

"David," McClelland said. "Do you seriously expect me to believe all this?"

"All right, tell me: have they found him?"

"Why do you want to know?" The second imperative was to say as little as possible; let the man talk. Nod. Agree. Say only what had to be said. *Listen.*

"You remember I was going through his dossier that day, just before you drove me to National?"

"I remember," McClelland said. And I also remember Kingly saying you probably pulled it so you could tell the Comrades what we knew about Guchkov, he thought.

"I knew it was him. Everything fitted: the descriptions, the timing of his arrival, everything."

"Why didn't you say anything then?"

"Because I couldn't be sure."

"Or because you preferred we not make the same connection?"

"Let me run something past you," Caine said. "What if Guchkov's defection was a blind? Look what he gave us: a few small-time agents who'd probably served their purpose anyway. Look what he got in return: a conducted tour of Five and Six operations, a breakdown of the Berlin station, a new legend, a bankroll. What if all that was part of a plan, right down to his disappearance?"

"It's a lot of what-ifs."

"I'll offer you a bet," Caine said. "Guchkov flew from London to one of the European capitals. Rome would be good. Madrid or Lisbon would be even better. From there he could get a flight to South America. Did they get a fix on him?"

McClelland hesitated. "He took an Iberia flight to Madrid, then another out of Barajas to Montevideo. No sign of him after that."

"He probably went to ground in the GRU *residenz* at Bogotá until he was ready to move. They gave him his new legend—Frederic Drosdow—and set up the connection in Miami with Avranilosa. The Fat Man is the go-between in the drug sale Guchkov used to finance his operation—the cynical bastard would enjoy that, it would amuse him. Then at the critical juncture, he discovered that Avranilosa was under surveillance."

"By Genevevo."

"Right. My guess is that, accidentally or otherwise, Genevevo got on to Guchkov, or what Guchkov was really up to. Avranilosa, pushed by Guchkov, egged Saturnino Baca to take Genevevo out. His people spotted mine while they were setting up the hit, and Guchkov made a preemptive decision to take us all out. He didn't give a damn what happened. He'd probably foreseen the possibility. Anyway, he was walking away from it. Nobody even knew he was there."

"And what about the money?"

"It was partly to finance a honey trap. Guchkov told Avranilosa enough to make him—and us—believe it was on Marco Island. But it wasn't. The whole Marco Island setup was a decoy operation, and it worked beautifully. We all homed in on another no-hoper, a Company coding clerk named Paul Bogdanovich who'd been selling secrets to the comrades in Washington. Somebody put a couple of pounds of plastic explosive in Bogdanovich's car."

"Which somebody?"

"I lean toward Langley."

"You think the Company killed this Bogdanovich?"

"And his wife. Probably Domestic Operations' way of closing the file. Permanently. That way there'd be nothing to advertise the fact that they'd been operating on American soil."

"They didn't try for you?"

"I don't know. I left my car where I parked it. When they realize I'm not going to pick it up, they'll disarm it."

"You don't even consider the possibility that Guchkov might have been behind it?"

"Why would he bother? While you've been chasing me, and I've been chasing Bogdanovich, and the boys from Domestic Ops have been chasing their tails, that bastard has been getting quietly on with whatever it is he really came to America to do."

"Do you have any idea what that might be?"

"Yes," Caine said. "That's why I braced you, Dick. I need your help."

"Suppose I were to entertain this . . . theory of yours," McClelland said. "Although there isn't one good reason on God's green earth why I should—what would you want?"

"What I want to know is on the computer somewhere, Dick," Caine said. "Somewhere in our surveillance reports on Genevevo, in Avranilosa's ITS, there's a name we haven't considered because it didn't seem germane. That name will tell us where to look for Guchkov."

"That's it?" McClelland said. "You don't know the name, you don't know where it is. But you want me to find it. Is that what you're saying?"

"It's the only thing I can think of," Caine said.

"You could come in."

"It would take too long," Caine said. "Even if I could make Kingly believe me."

"What makes you think I believe you?"

Caine grinned. "A woman knows these things," he said. "Will you do it?"

"How would I contact you?"

"You don't," Caine replied. "I'll find a way to contact you. It's safer that way. And Dick, don't let anyone at ISS know what you're doing, or why."

"You must be joking," McClelland said. "If I were to report seeing you and taking no action, I'd be under security arrest before I finished saying it."

Caine opened the rear door and got out. McClelland wound down his window.

"When will I hear from you?"

"Tomorrow. Between ten and noon. And . . . thanks, Dick."

"Sure," McClelland said, and drove off.

PART THREE
FIRE

Red Center was ready. Guchkov was ready. And
so was Mitchell.

They had nursed him—correction: Kate had
nursed him, pretending loving concern—through the cold-sweat
coda that followed every freshman spy's first foray into espionage. Mitchell had been as jumpy as a kitten, walking into
his office each day filled with the dread certainty of immediate
apprehension.

Nothing happened. Guchkov would have been vastly surprised if anything had. Mitchell had been most carefully selected. The stuff he brought out was worthless, of course. The
real reason Guchkov wanted it brought out was to prove to
Mitchell that he could do it without being detected.

The next, equally predictable phase was euphoria. This was
the point at which control became vital: overconfidence was far
more dangerous than fear. They nursed him through that, too—
Guchkov with encouragement, Kate in other ways.

Mitchell had told her, of course. She handled it brilliantly.
She made the man believe what Drosdow had already told him,
that they would both go to prison for life if he balked, that he
had to do it for their safety, for their future. She told him how
fine he was, how brave. She made Mitchell feel strong, confident, daring. And he discovered the power in what he was
doing: the power of knowing what others did not. He swung all
the way from fear to a sort of elation. He was going to have a

million dollars. He was going to ditch his wife and live with Kate. He really believed it.

Now Guchkov was ready for the kill. He smiled: an apt word, in the circumstances. Red Center's laser satellite was at pre-launch status AOW: Awaiting Open Window. The final phase had begun.

He booked a table at the Tidewater Inn in Easton, and after drinks at Highfield the three of them drove over there for dinner. Kate saw to it that Mitchell got most of the second bottle of Chardonnay as Guchkov led the conversation around to computers.

They already had a good idea of the environment in which Mitchell worked; a question here, there, and it was not difficult to piece together from what he had told them and what they already knew. Beneath the NSA headquarters complex at Fort George Meade was an air-conditioned labyrinth, several city blocks long, housing the largest concentration of computer and data-analysis equipment in the world. Along aisle after gold-carpeted aisle ran serried rows of hardware: front-end interfaces, mass storage units, a brain so enormous that it could perform in nanoseconds calculations that would take an army of mathematicians decades.

Until recently, the biggest number crunchers at the NSA had been Carillon and Loadstone. Built by Cray Research in Minnesota, Loadstone—which had provided only half the agency's capacity—could transfer 320 million words a second—say twenty-five hundred books of three hundred pages each—and could accommodate forty-eight disk storage units holding perhaps 30 billion words, each word retrievable within eighty-millionths of a second.

GRU knew most of this already, from published sources. What was important about the information was that Mitchell was telling it to them, further confirmation of Guchkov's control.

The other half of the NSA "brain," Carillon, was made up of

five quad-redundant IBM 3033s attached to laser printers that could produce hard copy at sixty thousand lines a minute. That was the state of the NSA art until "Bubbles," the new Cray-2 supercomputer, came on line in June 1985. It was about this machine that Guchkov now encouraged Mitchell to talk.

"Astonishing though it is, Bubbles is only a stopgap machine," the American told them. "Seymour Cray is already working on an even bigger baby, which we expect to be on line around 1988."

To coincide with the inauguration of the Spacetrack system, no doubt, Guchkov thought, making a mental note.

"It doesn't seem possible," he said. "I read somewhere that the Cray-2 had a top speed of over a million flops a second."

"It's a million two, actually," Mitchell said.

"Flops?" Kate frowned.

"Floating point operations," Guchkov said benevolently. "Calculations. How much faster is it, Mitch?"

"Six to twelve times faster than Loadstone, forty-to-fifty thousand times faster than a business computer. What took a year to do in 1952, we can now do in a second. You should see that baby go, Fred!"

His enthusiasm was genuine. Like most computer people, he had an inbuilt conviction that the subject was ordinarily death to conversation. Fred and Kate were "in the business," as it were, so he could assume a more informed interest on their part.

"How many of them are there?" Guchkov asked.

"There's one in the agency think tank at Princeton, another at NASA's Ames Research Center."

"That's the one in Mountain View, California?"

"That's the one."

"How big a memory has this thing got?"

"Two billion bytes. The Cray-3 will have eight billion."

"That's astonishing. It must be a hell of a thing to look at."

"It doesn't look much like a computer, I'll give you that." Mitchell smiled. "It looks like a cross between a recreation-room bar and a fish tank. It's just . . . different from everything else, different the way a modern fighter is from a World War One biplane. There's a whole new area of thinking that goes with it. We're talking analog optical computers now, Fred. We're talking multiprocessing, light-sound interaction and charge-transfer devices. We're discussing achieving more than a quadrillion—that's one thousand million million—multiplications per second. The research people at Chippewa Falls and New York University are into stuff the man in the street has never heard of: cryogenics, optical logic, magnetic bubbles, laser recording, kinetic activation. There are already machines that will convert the human voice into digital signals, others that will instantaneously transcribe spoken conversations . . .''

He was still going strong as they pulled to a stop in front of the house. Guchkov nodded and smiled, encouraging the man to talk himself dry.

"Come into the library and have a cognac," Guchkov said. "There are a few things I want to ask you about."

"If you men are going to keep on talking about computers, I'm going to watch TV upstairs," Kate said.

"I'm sorry, Kate!" Mitchell said contritely. "I just got so wound up, I forgot. Look, stay, we'll talk about something else."

"No, no, you men have your brandy and cigars. I'll . . . see you later, yes?"

She kissed him lightly and went out, the fur wrap slung over her elegant shoulder like a bullfighter's cape. Mitchell beamed bemusedly at her as she closed the double doors behind her.

"Tell me about Platform," Guchkov said as if it were the most natural thing in the world. He busied himself with the drinks so that he did not need to meet Mitchell's eyes.

"Went into operation at the end of 'eighty-four," Mitchell said, taking the glass from Guchkov and sitting down in one of the deep leather chairs in front of the fireplace. "How did you know about it?"

Guchkov evaded the question by asking another of his own.

"Security?" Mitchell replied. "Stringent. In fact, I'd go as far as to say Draconian. You know what DES stands for?"

"Data Encryption Standard. It's the national protection cipher system approved by the government for industry, banking, and some of the federal agencies."

"You do know your computers, don't you?" Mitchell said admiringly. "All right, if you know that, you know DES is based on what we call a 'key,' an extra-long string of bits whose combination varies from user to user. Like the grooves in a door key, say. Same basic pattern for everyone, but each with different teeth and valleys. This key goes into a series of super-complex mathematical formulas called S-boxes. When they combine with the key, they encode the data into indecipherable bits, and reverse the procedure at the receiving end."

"Difficult to break into," Guchkov suggested.

"But not impossible. The process of ciphering includes something called intense validation. That means the cipher has been tested by being bombarded with sophisticated cryptanalytic attacks by a team of experts. It's called a brute force attack."

"So you'd need super brute force to do what they couldn't."

"Right," Mitchell said. "Say you could put together a machine with a million special-search chips, each capable of testing a million possible solutions a second. That gives you a testing capability of a trillion keys a second. You know the DES uses a fifty-six-bit key, so the number of possible combinations is about seventy quadrillion. So it would theoretically be possible for you to break into any DES cipher in about ten or twelve hours. Twenty, max. That's if you had the hardware, of course."

"Could a machine like that be built?"

"All it takes is thirty, forty million dollars. The toughest trick is buying the technology without attracting attention. IBM and the NSA sleep in the same bed."

"Could a machine like that break into the NSA system?"

"Nope. NSA uses a hundred-twenty-eight-bit key," Mitchell said. "You'd need more money than there is in the world to build a machine that could break into Bubbles."

"What about intercept stations?" Guchkov asked, getting up and holding out his hand for Mitchell's glass. "Do they have the same equipment?"

"In effect, yes," Mitchell said. "Most of the signals picked up by the intercept stations are too sophisticated to be attacked on receipt. So they bounce them off a DSP to us, and we analyze them. We're the host to fifty-two separate computer systems around the world."

"What's a DSP?" Guchkov said, handing Mitchell another Rémy Martin.

"Defense Support Program. A type of satellite."

He launched into a monologue about the various types of communications satellites NSA used, and Guchkov nodded and smiled, only half listening. What was it Katja had said about the American? "He gives new meaning to the word 'interminable,'" she'd said, laughing that bitch's laugh. He wondered idly what she would do when all this was over. He'd grown to respect her in the time they'd been together: he admired professionalism above all else, and Katja Renis was a real pro.

While the American rambled on, Guchkov's mind slipped back to the day this operation had begun, so many months ago in Moscow. He remembered the day clearly, the pigeons foraging on the grass verges, the girls in their summer frocks smiling in the sunshine as he hurried through the city to the meeting of the Operations Executive at Znamenskaya Ulitza . . .

Of all the plans submitted to OE, his had been selected. That alone would have been a signal honor. To have been chosen to carry it out meant his reward would be even greater: a decoration, certainly; promotion perhaps as high as lieutenant general, with the material rewards that accompanied it: a new car, possibly a European one, a dacha in the country or an apartment at one of the Black Sea resorts.

He remembered how nervous he had been, that first day, facing the bemedalled Grandfathers seated around the shining table, their faces dour and unwelcoming. The meeting had been conducted by Colonel General Ivashutin, head of GRU. Also present were his deputy, Pavlov; Drachev, Guchkov's superior, head of the Second Directorate; Goliakov, head of the Sixth, Electronic Intelligence; Professor Doctor Chebriakov, head of space projects; Zotov, head of Information.

"With your permission, Comrade General?" Ivashutin nodded.

"Proceed, Guchkov," Pavlov interpreted.

"The initiative is to be known as Open Window," Guchkov began. "Its purpose is to secure, by or before this time next year, the successful covert launch of our assault satellite, Smert Ptyetsa."

"Yes, yes," old Goliakov said. He was famous for his impatience. "We've all read your briefing paper. Ambitious. Perhaps too ambitious, young man."

"We shall see," Pavlov said, urbane as ever. He nodded to Guchkov, who unrolled his map, thumbtacked it to an easel, and began his carefully prepared presentation.

"On Thursday, January 24, 1985, the United States Air Force launched its first secret space-shuttle mission. Unlike all previous flights, which had been predominantly civilian, this one was controlled by the National Security Agency. None of the conversations between the crew and ground control were broadcast; all were heavily encoded. Even the actual takeoff time and the intended trajectory of the shuttle were kept secret."

"Yes, yes, yes," muttered Goliakov testily. "We all know that, man. Get on, get on!"

The reason for all this secrecy, Guchkov continued, was Challenger's payload: a thirteen-and-a-half-ton spy satellite, which the shuttle was to place in geostationary orbit 22,300 miles above the Equator, between the Indian Ocean island of

Diego Garcia and Singapore. From this thirty-degree segment of longitude, and only this segment, it was possible for satellites to "see" the area in Russia used for space launches.

"The American satellite has processing capabilities greater than anything else in space," Guchkov said. "Its antennae are over a thousand feet in diameter. Any transmission on frequencies between one hundred megahertz and twenty gigahertz—a gigahertz is one thousand megahertz—whether it be radio, microwave, or radar, can be picked up by its forward dish antenna and simultaneously relayed by its rear dish to the appropriate window, or intercept installation on earth, and from there onward to the NSA."

"The satellite is called Big Bird," Ivashutin interjected. "It forms part of the American Spacetrack network. You will remember my mentioning it at our briefing in June. Although it is now their only spy-in-the-sky satellite, we cannot, must not underestimate its capabilities. If we are to launch Smert Ptyetsa undetected, we must neutralize that satellite."

"And this officer has found a way?" Zotov asked, speaking for the first time. He rarely smiled. He was a squat, dark man whom his staff called Gospodin Mrak, Mr. Gloom.

"Colonel Guchkov is one of our most outstanding officers," Ivashutin said. "His knowledge of the United States is encyclopedic, unrivaled. He speaks their debased language as if he had been born there. He has studied their history and is an acknowledged authority on their military and defense systems. Go ahead, Guchkov. Tell them your idea."

"Let us take a hypothetical case to begin with," Guchkov said. "We launch a satellite from Sary Shagan, or Kapustin Yar. Within a minute of liftoff, an American early-warning satellite spots the rocket plume and signals back to earth that a launch has taken place. The input is channeled via ADN—automatic digital network—to DEFSMAC at Fort Meade and simultaneously via the CRITICOM circuit to the White House situation rooms, the Pentagon, and NORAD in Colorado."

"Perhaps it would be as well if you translated your acronyms as you go along, Guchkov," Ivashutin said, concealing a smile. Old Zotov was glaring at the young officer in utter puzzlement, and Ivashutin knew he would die before confessing ignorance.

"I am sorry. DEFSMAC is the Defense Special Missile and Astronautics Center at NSA. CRITICOM is the Critical Intelligence Communications circuit. And NORAD—"

"I think you could assume we know that one, Colonel," Pavlov said.

"Yes, sir. NORAD—Air Defense Command at Cheyenne Mountain—tracks the missile's flight profile to make sure it is not on a threat azimuth. In due course, the satellite will send in telemetry intelligence that will inform the analysts what kind of rocket it was, how it was programmed, trajectory, and so on."

"So this spy satellite would detect our launch of the Death Bird within seconds, is that it?"

"Exactly," Guchkov said. "Let me ask Professor Doctor Chebriakov a question. If we could black out the American satellite at the moment we launch Smert Ptyetsa, what would the effect be?"

All eyes turned toward Professor Doctor Chebriakov, in charge of the most important Russian space project of the last decade, and arguably the most important ever. The Death Bird, Smert Ptyetsa, was a fifty-five-foot-long, thirty-seven-thousand-pound monster satellite packed with the most advanced laser weaponry yet developed. Laser technology was the one field where Russia was unquestionably ten years ahead of the West, and every bit of that technology had been incorporated into the design for the new "bird."

"Very simple," Chebriakov said jauntily. "We would totally dominate space and there would be nothing anyone could do about it."

If the satellite could be placed in orbit, he said, not only would Russia be able to neutralize every existing non-Soviet satellite in space, but she could also prevent any new ones from being placed in successful orbit.

There was a considering silence following this assertion. Complete Soviet domination of space would radically alter the balance of power between East and West. Every parameter of strike capability would have to be redefined. If the initiative was a success. But if it was not . . . Every one of them remembered the last time. Although not so much as a hint of the confrontation had reached the world's press, Soviet humiliation had been complete. The purges that followed were merciless. In their world, nobody ever forgave and nobody ever forgot.

"So we black out the American satellite," Zotov said. "And then?"

"Once our bird is up there, in orbit, the Americans will track her, of course, from space or from the ground," Guchkov explained. "They will wonder what she is. They may even ask us, but of course we will not tell them. But from the day that she goes into orbit, the American space program will be finished. Every time they make a launch, the Death Bird will destroy the payload. There will be no more spy satellites. Most importantly of all, the Americans will never be able to put into space the hardware to effect what they call 'Star Wars.'"

There was another considering silence. No one in the room needed to be reminded how much effort had already been expended, on the diplomatic as well as the espionage front, to sabotage in any and every way American progress with the machinery for the space-based Strategic Defense Initiative.

"The Americans are moving ahead very quickly with their research on SDI," Guchkov said. "The Pentagon has already constructed a $1.2 billion command center at Falcon Air Force Station, ten miles from Colorado Springs. Another $135 million Pentagon program is in hand to develop Mimic—a gallium-arsenide microchip that will process electronic signals at five times the speed of silicon, with twice silicon's resistance to radiation. The scientific adviser to the president has stated publicly that they will be ready to test the pulse-laser system within three years. That is the real reason for Initiative Open Window, gentlemen.''

"No one here doubts the necessity, Colonel," Zotov said. "Are you going to enlighten us as to your methods for realizing it?"

"My plan proposes a series of set pieces, each of which leads ineluctably to the next. I have prepared a dossier which enumerates those set pieces if you wish to read it. The end proposition is to obtain access to the National Security Agency computer system."

"You won't mind telling us how, I trust?" Drachev said sardonically. He didn't like having his protectorate taken out of his hands, especially by one of his junior staff. There was a dangerous precedent there. He had fought hard to gain control of Open Window, but Ivashutin had blocked every move he made.

"I spoke earlier of intercept stations," Guchkov said, following the chief's example and not allowing Drachev to rattle him. "The Americans call them 'windows.' You see them on the map marked in red. The most valuable of them, at Kabkan in Iran, was abandoned subsequent to the rise of the Ayatollah Khomeini. In 1980, the Americans entered into an agreement with the Chinese to build a new window in the Sinkiang Uighur Autonomous Region, close to our eastern borders; it is not yet operative. However, there are plenty of others, as you can see: at Asmara in Ethiopia, Sidi Yahia in Morocco, in Panama, in Puerto Rico, in Cyprus. The three most important windows however are those situated at Aurora, near Denver in the United States; at Menwith Hill, near Harrogate in England; and the least-known of them all, Pine Gap, near Alice Springs in Australia, in the heart of what is known as the Red Center."

There was an appreciative murmur of laughter as he took the spy-satellite photographs of the installation from the large artist's portfolio he had brought with him and pinned them to the board. Alongside them he thumbtacked the enlarged color photographs of the place taken by a GRU agent-in-place there.

With its radomes and supermarket-sized concrete buildings, Pine Gap looked like a moon colony dropped by mistake on the spinifex-covered scrub. Eleven and a half miles southwest of Alice Springs, he told the Grandfathers, on an unposted road off the main highway, Pine Gap was not marked on any map. No tourist brochure, gazetteer or guide book so much as hinted at its existence. No visitors were permitted, no aircraft allowed to fly within two and a half miles of it. Operating under the name of the Commonwealth of Australia Joint Defence Space Research Facility, the $500 million complex was the National Security Agency's most highly sophisticated intercept station.

"Since the Death Bird launch site at the Verkhoyansk firing range is inside the field of vision of the new American satellite, the information would be relayed to this station, Pine Gap, and then onward by satellite to the NSA. It is this link we propose to interrupt."

"All very well," Zotov said dourly. "We've all read your paper, Colonel Guchkov. Very clever. But what's it all going to cost, eh? How much of my budget is this going to gobble up?"

"The operation will show a profit of thirty million dollars," Guchkov said. "It is self-financing, Comrade General. I am following Lenin's dictum that the capitalists will sell us the rope we need to hang them. That is why it has been planned as it has: my 'defection' to the British, all of it."

"Too many things to go wrong, if you ask me," Zotov said, sourly. "Far too many things to go wrong."

"I, for one, think it is a remarkable piece of work," Ivashutin said forcefully. "Exceptional."

"Couldn't agree more" old Goliakov said, and banged his stick on the floor. To Guchkov's surprise, the others began applauding. Even Zotov joined in, although his face was taut with anxiety because of his faux pas . . .

By God, what a moment that had been, Guchkov thought.

That night, after the formal adoption of his initiative, he had gone out and got wildly, gloriously drunk. He picked up a woman in the Ukraina Hotel, a bosomy blonde on an Intourist package from Stockholm. She wasn't what he'd have called subtle, but she was willing, healthy, and energetic. The next morning the silly cow had wanted to take his photograph on the Kalinin Bridge . . .

"What are you smiling at?" Mitchell said. "Did I say something funny?"

"I was thinking of something else," Guchkov said. His smile changed to that of a cat stalking through long grass.

"Your new shift begins tomorrow."

"That's right."

"There is something I want you to do. This will be your last task for me."

"What do you mean?"

"If you successfully complete your assignment, you will be paid that million dollars we once talked about."

"What do you want me to bring out?"

I don't want you to bring anything out. I want you to take something in."

"I . . . don't quite understand."

"Mitchell, you and I know that no single person could penetrate the NSA computers from the outside. It would require a comprehensive knowledge of the system and its peripherals that no single person could have, even those with the highest security clearances. There is only one way to do it. A prepared program planted in the memory, to be triggered by an external command."

"You . . . you've got such a program? What is it for?"

"The program is ready and waiting," Guchkov said, ignoring Mitchell's question. "I want it put into Bubbles. Tomorrow."

Mitchell stared at him, dumbfounded. "I can't do that," he said, almost scornfully, like a child asked to do an adult task.

"You can," Guchkov said. "And you will. Bring proof to

me tomorrow that you have done what I ask, and I will give you one million dollars in cash,'' Guchkov said. "You can go away with Kate, anywhere in the world. Live like a king.''

"I don't know," Mitchell said hoarsely. "I don't know.''

You poor pathetic bastard, Guchkov thought without a shred of pity. All this time Mitchell had been psyching himself up to tell him that there were some secrets it just wasn't possible to bring out, only to find he was going to do the easiest thing there was: take something in. He had no doubt at all that Mitchell would do as he was bidden. There was no fight left in the man. He had been led by the cock to this point, drowning in greed and lust. There was no way out, none at all.

"Tomorrow," Guchkov said, and left him there.

30 Come on, damn you, Caine thought. It was three hours since McClelland had gone into the ISS office at Arlington. If anything was going to happen, it had to happen soon. He hated the game he was playing, but he knew no other way to go. He had had plenty of time to think on the way back north from Florida, a lot of time to formulate the plan he set up before he waylaid McClelland outside his Woodley Park home.

The whole thing hung on his reading of McClelland. Loyal though he might still be to Caine, he was more loyal by far to the Service. He would do what Caine expected him to do: he would tell Kingly that Caine was around, and he would tell him about Guchkov. Meanwhile, all Caine could do was chew his fingernails and wait.

He wondered where Lynda was. He had hated to leave her yet known that he must from the moment he found Miles Kingly's name among those Stepan Lykov had instructed Bogdanovich to watch for in the Miami traffic. What he had to do now, he could best do alone. So he left her still sleeping, her dark hair tumbled across the pillow, wanting to waken her, knowing he would not.

Instead, he had written her a note, hoping she would understand. Maybe she would; more probably she would not. She would feel used, hurt. She would be angry and bewildered and justifiably unforgiving. It was quite possible that they would never meet again, in which case it was probably better for both of them if she came to think of him as someone who made a brief mark on her life, like a bruise that would fade and be forgotten. So he went away silently, hating what he was doing, knowing he had no choice. He felt a pang of regret, a rare sensation: he had deliberately courted loneliness after Jenny died. He wondered whether he had been a better agent or a worse one because of it.

He was quite certain Lynda's apartment in Miami would be staked out. When she reappeared, they would go on alert, waiting for him to put in an appearance. While they were expecting him down there, they wouldn't be looking for him in Washington. He looked across at the anonymous frontage of the ISS office. "Come on, come on," he muttered.

The day preceding his encounter with McClelland, Caine had taken the Metro out to Takoma Park and walked back to Walter Reed Army Medical Center, where he took a Dodge Aries from the visitors area parking lot. He drove it south on Georgia Avenue to the six-block sprawl of Howard University. It took less than ten minutes to exchange the plates from the Dodge for those of a beaten-up Volkswagen Karmann Ghia convertible that looked as if it had been in its parking slot since Christmas. A quick visit to an Army surplus store and a filling-station accessory shop, and he was ready.

At twelve thirty-eight, the doors of ISS opened and Miles Kingly came out. He was wearing a pale blue silk Giorgio Armani suit, a cream silk shirt, tasseled loafers, and a narrow-brimmed straw hat. With him, wearing a flowery summer dress, was Betty Torre. Kingly looked right and left, then walked briskly down the street, his hand at Betty's elbow gently guiding her along.

A hundred feet behind them, Caine cut diagonally across the street. He was wearing a combat jacket, faded blue jeans, and a pair of Nikes. Like the Duracell tube bag slung over his shoulder, he had picked them up the day before at the surplus store.

In addition, he had not shaved for a couple of days. As disguises went, it was perfunctory, but it was effective. Kingly glanced at him and then away without any sign of recognition. Since the Vietnam Veterans Memorial near the Constitution Gardens pool had been dedicated in November 1982, combat jackets were a common sight on the streets of the capital. The veterans came in patient procession—ones, twos, dozens, coachloads—to see Maya Lin's black granite chevron, to reach out and touch the carved names of dead comrades. Caine looked like just another of them.

Kingly and Betty Torre stopped at the corner of Courthouse and Fourteenth, talking. Caine strolled by them on the opposite side of the street, heading for the Metro station. Even now, he kept on wishing he were wrong, but he knew he was not. Had he been wrong, the entire area would have been crawling with surveillance waiting for him to show. Their absence was further proof he no longer needed.

He watched as Kingly smiled, nodded, and abruptly crossed the street toward the Metro. Caine moved into his wake. Anybody who'd seen *The French Connection* knew the best place to shake a tail was in the subway. How Kingly expected to succeed wearing a pale blue silk suit was another matter. He had no option: he had not known when he dressed that it would become necessary.

Kingly turned and turned again. He crossed and recrossed his own path several times until he ended up on the westbound platform. When the train came, Caine took a chance and got aboard, watching warily as Kingly waited until the very last minute to get on. At the next station, Clarendon, he jumped out and hurried across to the other side. Caine ducked behind a billboard, and when Kingly took the next train back to Court House, he still had him in sight.

At Court House, Kingly stood for several minutes near the ticket machines, watching the passersby until he felt sure no one had followed him. Then he hurried to a pay phone. When he had made his call, he headed for the exit. Caine sighed and made his move.

"Hello, Miles," he said, falling into step alongside Kingly. Kingly stopped dead, his chubby face rigid with shock.

"I never saw you once," he said, as cunning replaced the fear that had filled his eyes.

"That was the idea," Caine said. "Let's go, shall we?"

"Go where?"

Caine ignored the question. He took Kingly's elbow much as Kingly had taken Betty Torre's and steered him out of the station into the bright sunshine. Kingly's eyes flickered left, right, left again. He was getting his confidence back.

"What are you going to do, Caine?" he said. "Pull a gun on me? Even you can't be as stupid as that. All I've got to do is call a cop. You're wanted by every law-enforcement agency in America."

"Shut up, Miles," Caine said wearily. There were lots of people on the street. Cars glided by. Kingly gave Caine a smile of feline challenge.

"I'm just going to walk away from you," he said. "And there's not a damned thing you can do about it."

"Try it, Miles," Caine said, "and I will hurt you very badly."

Kingly's confident smile dissolved, and fear washed the contempt from his eyes. Caine knew his weak spot. He was not just afraid, he was terrified of physical hurt. Without giving him time to think, Caine pushed him forward, and Kingly flinched, as if anticipating a blow. Smiling all the way, as if they were two old friends who had met in the street, Caine steered him to the stolen Dodge and pushed him in. Kingly sat slackly in the seat, his eyes watchful, empty, as Caine took out a set of handcuffs and locked Kingly's right wrist to the seat belt, then switched on the Sony cassette recorder he'd bought and put it on the dashboard in front of them.

"What do you think this is going to achieve?" he said pettishly.

"I want Guchkov, Miles. You just phoned him. Where is he?"

"You're crazy!"

"No," Caine said. "I was stupid. We all were. But not crazy. It had to be you, Miles. Nobody else could have done it."

"I tell you I don't know what you're talking about," Kingly protested.

"Just as you wish."

Caine headed across Key Bridge and up through Georgetown. He turned onto Wisconsin Avenue, driving around and then into the Naval Observatory. He parked in the campuslike grounds and turned off the engine. Kingly sat with his lips pressed together; he had not spoken during the entire journey.

"How long have you worked for them, Miles?" Caine asked. "Since Berlin? Or before that, even?"

Kingly ignored the question. Caine shrugged.

"I think I always knew," he said. "The flashy clothes you shouldn't have been able to afford. The access to information I couldn't understand. It was a setup, right from the start, wasn't it? That's why Guchkov was always so far ahead of us. You told him about Genevevo. They knew I was going to Miami before I did. We never made a move they didn't know about in advance. You let them kill our people. You were going to let them kill me, and when that didn't work, you fitted me up. You knew, of all people in the world, you knew if I saw the file on Viktor I'd make the connection. So you fitted me to look like a Comrade. You, all the time."

"I always thought you were one of the brighter ones, Caine," Kingly said. "But you're out of your depth here."

"We'll see. Where's Guchkov, Miles?"

"If you think for a second I'm going to tell you anything, you're a fool, like the rest of them."

"That's the way you see it—we're all fools?"

"All you've got is a conclusion. You aren't going to get far with that."

"You're right," Caine said. "That's why you're going to tell me everything you know."

"If you believe that, you're an even bigger fool than I thought, Caine. What are you going to do, kill me?"

"I've been giving it serious thought."

"If you kill me, you will never find Guchkov. And if you don't, you're a dead man!"

He was so confident, so sure. Caine tried to suppress his anger. One part of him hated what he was going to do to Kingly; another part of him couldn't wait.

"Where is he, Miles?"

"Oh, go to hell," Kingly said contemptuously.

"Last chance."

"Time is your enemy, Caine. And my friend. All I have to do is wait."

"No, Miles," Caine told him. "You're not going to play Scheherezade with me."

He got out of the car, opened the trunk, and took out a jerrican. He unscrewed the cap and sloshed its contents all over Kingly, who recoiled in horror as the stink of gasoline filled the car. There was no way he could know that the liquid Caine had doused him with was water, with enough gasoline in it to smell but not to burn. He watched in utter disbelief as Caine took a box of kitchen matches from his pocket.

"Jesus Christ, Caine!" he screeched, shrinking away but held in place by the seat belt.

"Where's Guchkov?"

Kingly shook his head, whimpering. Caine struck a match and Kingly put his hands in front of his face, screaming with fear.

"No, don't, Christ, don't, don't!"

A heavy, fecal smell mingled with the gasoline fumes. Caine shook out the match, nostrils wrinkling with disgust: Kingly had fouled himself. It was as if he had collapsed inwardly. Gone was the urbane, well-dressed man of moments ago. In his place, enveloped in terror, was a blubbering baby in a wrecked silk suit.

Caine struck another match.

"Easton, Easton!" Kingly sobbed. "He's bought a big house in Easton. Near Baltimore. Oh, Christ, put it out, put it out!"

"I want it all, Miles," Caine said remorselessly. This was even worse than he had expected, but he could not turn back now.

"Yes, yes, all right, yes, just don't . . . don't burn me, Caine, David, please, don't," Kingly jabbered. Once he began, it was as if he could not stop. Stinking, crumpled, abject, Kingly told Caine what he needed to know about Open Window, from the setting up of the cocaine deal in Miami to the big house on the shore of Chesapeake Bay. And as he did, the parameters of his own treachery became apparent.

"What's the name of the target officer at NSA?" Caine demanded.

"I don't know."

Caine shook the matchbox and Kingly whinnied with fear.

"I don't know, I don't know!" he whined. "Oh, Christ, look at me, look at the mess."

"Get out!" Caine snapped. "Get out of the car!"

Kingly got out, his right arm held in the car doorway by the fully extended seat belt, his eyes swimming in shame and self-loathing. The pale blue suit was ruined, wrinkled and stained with his waste.

"Oh, Christ," he wept. "Oh, God."

Caine opened the trunk of the big car. He took Kingly's arm, unlocked the handcuffs, and pulled him around to the rear of the Dodge. The man stank. Before he knew what was happening,

Caine stuck the stun gun against Kingly's sternum and pulled the trigger. In the same moment, he grabbed Kingly's lapels in his left hand, so that when Kingly's knees buckled, he was able to thrust him backward into the open luggage compartment. He slammed down the lid, got into the car, and drove back to Arlington with all the windows open.

He parked the Dodge on Calvert Street and walked up to the court house, where he used a pay phone to call Dick McClelland. The ISS operator was unable to conceal her reaction when he told her his name. Caine allowed himself an unamused smile as he pictured the trace machinery being set into operation, the tape reels turning.

"Sorry to keep you waiting, sir," the girl said. "We're having a little difficulty locating Mr. McClelland."

"You've got ninety seconds before I hang up, Dick," Caine said. "Cut in or I'll do it now."

"David?" McClelland's voice said. "Is that you?"

"Listen carefully, Dick," Caine said. "I'm only going to say all this once. Kingly is the Comrade. He's told me everything. He'll do the same for you when you pick him up. And if he won't, you'll find a cassette on the back seat which says it all for him."

"What in the name of God are you talking ab—?"

"He's locked in the trunk of a dark blue Dodge Aries, Maryland plates, license number JJB-2689," Caine said. "The plates don't belong to the car, by the way."

"Where is it?" he said. His voice had changed; now it was all business.

"Inside a one-mile radius of your office," Caine said. "If you send out the sweepers now, you ought to be able to find it in a couple of hours."

"He's not . . . damaged?"

"Only his pride," Caine said harshly.

"You say he . . . confessed? How did you—?"

258 •

"I threatened to set fire to him. He didn't know it was water mixed with petrol."

"Jesus, David!"

"Save your sympathy," Caine snapped. "He's garbage. As you'll see when you pick him up."

He hung up and walked away. The trunk of the Dodge had plenty of air in it. Kingly would survive until the sweepers found him, as long as he didn't choke on his own stench.

He took the Metro to Union Station, and in the men's room he discarded the combat jacket and jeans, changing to the pale gray London Fog windbreaker, dark wool slacks, and dark brown Hush Puppies he'd been carrying in the Duracell bag. He spent another twenty minutes getting rid of his beard, then went out into the crowded reservation area to find a fat pigeon.

Half an hour later, driving a Ford LTD he'd hot-wired at a meter bay on New Jersey Avenue, Caine was driving past the Air Force Transmitting Station west of Bowie on the John Hanson Highway. In his inside pocket was a wallet containing $194 in cash, $500 more in American Express traveler's checks, and a good selection of credit cards in the name of Desmond Briggs, a large, bespectacled man whom Caine had "accidentally" jostled in the station newsstand. Beneath his left arm, snug in its Myres shoulder rig, hung the Smith & Wesson ASP Tom Crandon had given him in Miami.

With any luck, he thought, he'd be in Easton by four.

31
Forsyth stayed overnight at the Hyatt Regency on Capitol Hill, which wasn't on Capitol Hill at all, but on New Jersey Avenue, opposite a Quality Inn motel. It was an unnecessary extravagance which he perversely enjoyed, a sort of the-hell-with-it gesture. And in a way, it wasn't entirely wasted, even if the dinner he bought his old friend Frank McCabe at Hugo's did not alter his long-held prejudice that the better the view, the worse the restaurant's food. At least the meal provided him with the opportunity to ask for a favor to be repaid, and he was able to drive a fully equipped Company car out to Easton the following morning.

He got there shortly after ten. Traffic was light, lighter in the town itself. A tabby cat strolled haughtily across Washington Street, curling up on the steps of the Seven Stars Hotel as he drove through. With so few people about, the eighteenth-century facades gave the town an eerie, time-warped atmosphere.

Easton was historic, with a capital letter, and Forsyth felt a surge of affection for it, and for the thousand places like it all over America, with their artsy-craftsy boutiques, the Puppens and Patchworks, the Little Rascals, the Country Punkins, the Lu-Evv Framing Shoppes. The pre-Revolutionary houses, taverns, and museums would all be staffed by charming, knowledgeable middle-aged ladies who could not only tell you what George Washington ate for breakfast, but probably every secret in town. He smiled. Life, liberty and the right to sell pomanders, Leatherette bookmarks, and spiral-bound souvenir jotters.

He parked the Cutlass and walked down Harrison Street to the offices of the Percival Realty Company, a block over from Magazine Alley. A bell tinkled as he pushed open the door. The outer office was light and airy, with enlarged photographs of splendid houses. At a desk facing the door sat a pretty young blond girl. Twenty-something, good figure, fresh complexion, bright smile. The sign on her desk said her name was Betty Adams. She made him feel a hundred years old.

"My name is Forsyth," he said. "I called from Washington."

"Mr. Forsyth," a voice said. The door to the inner office had opened. In the doorway stood a tall, spare man with weather-beaten skin and shrewd bright blue eyes. A light gray alpaca coat hung on his bony shoulders. He looked like he just stepped out of a Norman Rockwell painting of canny old Yankees around a potbellied stove, but his voice was soft with Southern cadences. "I'm Harold Percival. How may I help you, sir?"

"May I speak with you privately, Mr. Percival?"

He noticed Betty Adams's sharp look of small-town curiosity. Percival hesitated for a moment, then made a gesture.

"Come in, come in," he said.

His office was small and cluttered: a desk; a moquette-covered swivel chair; a couple of prints on the wall; a side table with an old Underwood sit-up-and-beg typewriter on it; a filing cabinet; and a set of shelves crammed with local directories, leaflets, and maps.

"How can I assist you, Mr. Forsyth?"

"Do you know a man named Frederic Drosdow?"

Percival frowned, unsuccessfully trying to conceal uneasy surprise. "Drosdow?"

"Or Pedro Avranilosa?"

"I don't believe so. They certainly don't sound like local people. May I ask you why you want to know?"

"I'm a government agent, Mr. Percival. I'm trying to trace Frederic Drosdow. Are you sure you don't know him?"

"Could I see some form of identification, Mr. Forsyth?"

"The agency I work for prefers not to show ID, sir. Unless you insist."

The unease he had discerned in Percival's eyes deepened. The old man looked at him and then away, out of the window. The prominent Adam's apple jiggled up and down as he swallowed.

Money, Forsyth thought sadly. They'd given him money to keep his mouth shut and now he thought the IRS was on his trail.

"Mr. Percival, this is a very serious matter," he said slowly. No need to give the old boy a coronary. "You do know Drosdow, don't you?"

"I . . . has he done something wrong?"

"You know him, then."

"He made it a condition of our transaction that it remain completely secret. He was most insistent."

"In other words, he paid you to keep your mouth shut."

"See here—"

"Look, Mr. Percival, I'm not interested in your finances. But it's imperative you tell me exactly what your dealings with Drosdow were. I promise you that what you tell me will not go beyond this room."

"If I have your word of honor on that. . . ?"

"You have, sir."

"A man called me. From Washington. Said he was acting on behalf of clients in Florida who wished to purchase a house in this area. They had a specific property in mind, and knew that I was the agent."

"Who was this man?"

"He told me his name was Miles Kingly."

262 •

"Go on."

"The arrangements were . . . unusual. The client wished to purchase the property outright, for cash. I would be paid my standard commission. After three months, the house was to be put back on the market. When it was sold, I was to deduct a further commission and pay the balance into a nominated account at the First National Bank in Baltimore."

"You didn't think that strange?"

"Strange? Yes, but perfectly legal."

"Of course," Forsyth said, and the old man flushed.

"They said if I would accept the commission, they would furnish first-class transportation to Miami, all expenses paid."

"And?"

"I met Mr. Drosdow in a house at Bal Harbour in Miami. The other man, too. What did you say his name was?"

"Avranilosa."

"They signed all the papers. I remember thinking how perfunctory they were, as if the house itself were an irrelevancy. Drosdow paid a deposit in cash. He gave me a briefcase with the money in it. They said the rest would be paid by banker's draft, and it was. I flew back to Washington, took care of the paperwork. That was it. The house was theirs."

"And is Drosdow living there now?"

"I believe so. I haven't been out there."

"Where is it?"

"It's on Route 333, about halfway between here and Oxford. A beautiful place, quite outstanding."

"How much did it go for?"

"Four million."

"Can you remember which bank the draft was drawn on?"

"Yes, of course. The Republic National Bank of Miami."

"Have you got any photographs of the place?"

"Highfield? Yes, certainly." Percival brought out an envelope from a rank of files in the middle drawer of his credenza.

He shook the pictures out and turned them so Forsyth could see them.

"Nice place," Forsyth said. "What about maps?"

"Of the estate? There are none."

"Here's a pencil," Forsyth said. "Draw me one. And don't leave anything out."

The dirt road ended at an ornate wrought-iron gate eight feet high, supported by twin stone pillars into which were chiseled the name of the house. A steel trapdoor on the right-hand one indicated the location of the recessed telephone connecting with the house.

Caine got out of the car and walked south along the six-foot-high stone wall. After about two hundred yards, it made a right angle down the gentle slope toward the river and disappeared into a dense, cultivated thorn thicket. He walked back to the gate and then north. This stretch of wall was much longer, perhaps half a mile. As on the other side, the wall was topped with angled brackets supporting wicked German S-wire with closely set, razor-sharp rectangular blades. Porcelain carriers indicated the presence of an electrical current, or an alarm, or both. Beyond the walls stood closely planted trees and rhododendron bushes. Through the gate he could see up the drive to where it bore right, into the trees. He could not see the house at all.

He walked back to the Ford and drove back up to the main road and on to Oxford. Once the sister port of entry to Annapolis, the little town had boomed briefly before the First World War, then returned to its pre-Revolutionary slumber. Today it was just a pretty residential village on an L-shaped spit of land pointing north into the Tred Avon River, with a couple of boatyards and a harbor used by watermen and weekend sailors.

He stopped at an Exxon station just outside town to buy a couple of things and get some directions. Following these, he drove to Applegarth's Marine Yard on Morris Street, picked up a couple more items there, then headed for Market Street. A sign outside the Waters United Methodist Church said Sunday worship was at 11 A.M. At the end of the street, fronting Town Creek, was a boatyard. A sign said SHORELINE YACHT SERVICES. ELI JOHNSON, PROP.

Caine got out of the car and walked over to where a tall, weather-beaten, skinny man of about sixty was hosing down a boat. He wore a faded denim coverall and a baseball cap that bore the legend BRINKMAN'S: WE'RE MUCH MORE THAN AN ICE-CREAM STORE.

"Like to rent a boat for a couple of hours," Caine told him.

"Plenty to choose from."

"You Mr. Johnson?"

"If I ain't, I better not be rentin' you any my boats."

He ambled on down the dock, and Caine followed him. He stood on the jetty and waved at one of the boats. "Try the Glastron there," he said, gesturing toward a metallic-finished speedboat with a Mercruiser engine. "Go ahead, start her up."

Caine gave him a surprised look, then stepped down into the boat. He switched on the pumps to clear the bilges, then operated the power tilt to lower the propeller into the water. The engine started first time. The skinny old man on the jetty grinned.

"Looks like you know what you're at," he said. "Switch her off and come up to the office. We'll do the paperwork."

"Suppose I'd just switched her on?" Caine said as he followed the old man into the cluttered hut that served as his office.

Johnson smiled mischievously. "I was watchin' you real close, son," he said. "I'd 'a stopped you."

"And kicked me the hell out of your yard."

"Somethin' along those lines," the old man said with a wheezy chuckle. Switching on the engine before making sure there were no gasoline fumes in the bilges was an easy way to blow the stern right off a boat. "Done much sailin' in these parts, son?"

"First time," Caine told him. "Don't worry, though, I'm no going far. Just up the river a ways."

"Only one thing you need to know, then," Johnson told him "Where you see reeds, keep well offshore. You git your prop fouled, it's hell's own job gittin' off. What you plannin' to do fish?"

Caine held up the Pentax 8 x 40 BWCF wide-angle binocu lars he'd bought in town. The old man shrugged.

"You one o' them bird-spotter fellers?" he said, like a mar who couldn't quite believe any grown man would want to watch birds as a hobby.

"What time do you close?" Caine asked as he pushed off

"Round nine. If I'm gone, just tie her up and put the key through the mail slot."

Caine took the boat out into Town Creek on quarter throttle and brought her bow around into the current. Then he eased the revs up till she was moving steadily through the water. Herring gulls wheeled overhead, watching his wake. At first, the shore line was low and wooded, with strips of shingly beach fronting expanses of marshy grass. Nearer to Trippe Creek, it rose in sandy bluffs. Then he came around the headland and saw the big house sitting grandly on its low hill, terraced gardens slop ing gently down to a natural inlet on the river with a jetty and a covered dock.

He hove to off the inlet. Using the binoculars, he could see the hull of a sleek-looking cruiser inside the covered shed. To the south, off to his right, stretched a strip of private beach with a barbecue pit and wooden bench-tables. Beyond and behind the beach lay open pasture, backed by tree-lined bridle paths. North of the dock lay formal gardens; beyond them the swimming pool glimmered in the late sunshine. Further back, a dovecote on what looked like a stable block poked up amidst the trees.

He checked his watch. About an hour till sundown.

It took Butler Mitchell about an hour to drive out to Easton from Fort Meade. Apart from the usual holdups, it was a pleasant drive. The Dodge 600 Turbo was still enough of a head-turner for it to be gratifying. He was looking forward to seeing Kate, glad all this was over. In the slim Prince Albert wallet in the inside breast pocket of his cream linen Gianni Versace suit were two open-dated first-class tickets to London and a draft of his letter of resignation.

He did not know and resolutely refused to think about what the program he had planted was for. Let the specially trained Tiger Teams, whose job was to detect unauthorized entry into the mainframes, worry about that. He had done what Drosdow wanted; once he got the money he had been promised, their relationship would be ended, which would suit him just damned fine. There had been altogether too many espionage cases recently, and he didn't want to be another. He had not missed the significance of the Senate amendment to the defense authorization bill which mandated execution or life imprisonment without parole for anyone convicted of espionage.

He threw off the thought. What was done was done, and as of tonight, he would be out of it. On the seat beside him was a Gucci document case stuffed full of travel brochures. As he drove along, carefully observing the speed limit and half listening to his tape of Barbara Cook, he turned over in his mind some of the things he planned to do when Drosdow finally paid off.

One million dollars. The thought of it hung in his imagination like a blimp over a football field. The interest alone would be more than a $120,000 a year. Imagine never having to lift a finger again if you didn't want to. Imagine all the things you could buy, all the places you could go, all the things you could do.

Rich. What a word it was!

He swung around Easton on the bypass, following Route 333 across Peachblossom Creek, past the Country Club, paralleling the old Easton-Oxford railroad line as far as Trappe Station. There, he turned right on a light-duty road that led down to Trippe Creek Lane, a dirt lane running down to the Tred Avon between thickets of gallberry, chokeberry, greenbrier, and sand cherry. When he got to Highfield, he opened the metal trap and reported his arrival on the intercom.

After a few moments, the locked gates clunked open and swung back. Smiling, humming a tune, Mitchell drove in. Not for so much as a second did it occur to him that anyone might be watching. Even had he been listening for it, it is doubtful he would have heard the *zizzz* of the motor drive on the Polaroid SLR 635 with which Frank Forsyth photographed him as he went by.

While the Polaroid prints developed themselves, Forsyth fed the details of the Dodge 600 Turbo into the onboard computer fitted to the dash of the CIA Cutlass. He was immediately linked via Domestic Ops to the Department of Motor Vehicles computer.

To obtain an operator's license in the state of Maryland, an applicant was required to sumbit his name, address, license number, thumb print, restrictions (such as whether the driver wore glasses, or could only drive with automatic transmission), race, weight, height, signature, sex, birthdate, and social security number. Photographs were optional, but usually supplied. The only information not on the records were the color of the applicant's hair and eyes which, with three good Polaroid shots blooming before his eyes, Forsyth hardly needed.

The DMV computer accepted his clearance, and the readout came through in a matter of seconds.

"Rhett Butler Mitchell. *Rhett Butler,* for Christ's sake," Forsyth muttered. "What the hell kind of name is that?"

Born at Plymouth, Massachusetts, on January 2, 1940, Mitchell lived at 2133 High Ridge Road, Laurel, Maryland. License number, as checked, RBM-7777, a Maryland vanity plate. Race, white; sex, male; weight, 172; height, 6 feet 1 inch. Social security number, 228-74-9132. No traffic violations.

Next stop, Treasury Department. Forsyth knew, as any rookie cop did, that the records of the IRS were sacrosanct. Unlike the rookie cop, however, he knew that while *most* of them were, *all* of them were not. He tapped another question into the computer: *Provide employer and occupation Rhett Butler Mitchell Social Security Number 228-74-9132.* He waited. After a while, the tiny screen blinked and the information zipped across it.

"Holy shit," Forsyth breathed. The man who had just gone into Drosdow's house was a deputy chief in the Office of Communications Security at the National Security Agency.

Caine ran the Glastron toward the private beach below the house. She grounded gently, with a soft, grating sound. He jumped out and splashed ashore, lashing the painter to one of the picnic tables. The bluffs concealed him from the house.

He ran, crouching, toward the dock, the plastic bag containing the stuff he had bought in Oxford clutched in his hand. There was no one in sight. He went into the covered boat shed. Inside it was a thirty-one-foot Bertram Flybridge, white, handsome, glistening. He noted with satisfaction that there was a telephone on the wall, near the door. The lapping water sent flickering birds of light dancing across the walls.

Working swiftly but cautiously, Caine rolled an empty ten-gallon oil drum into the well of the Bertram. He prized off the lid and dropped it into the water. Next he unrolled the ten yards of acetate curtain material and put it into the drum in an untidy pile, draping lengths over the sides of the drum and onto the decks of the cruiser. In a plastic bailing bucket, he mixed coal oil and sawdust, which he splashed on the curtains and on the decks. Then he soaked a roll of kitchen towels with methylated spirit and scattered them on top of the bunched curtains in the drum.

Across the top of the drum he now laid a length of plastic curtain rail. Taking a reel of cotton out of his pocket, he snapped off a two-foot length, tied one end to the rail and the other to a book of matches, the cheap, paper-covered kind. Nearly there.

He picked up the telephone and dialed 8222222. A nasal female voice squawked, "Oxford Fire and Ambulance. Which service do you requi-er?"

"Fire," he said.

When the Oxford Fire Department answered, he told them slowly and clearly that there was a fire at Highfield, on Trippe Creek Lane, and hung up before they could ask questions. All set.

He lit a cigarette. Carefully, deliberately, he opened the matchbook tied to the rod, wedged the unlit end of the cigarette behind the match heads and closed the flap, thus anchoring the cigarette inside the matchbook with the lighted end outside. Very slowly, he lowered the matchbook so that it hung suspended inside the oil drum. Then he went below, took the cap off the Bertram's fuel tank, and stuffed one of his meths-soaked kitchen towels loosely into the aperture.

He ran out of the dock and up the path toward the formal gardens on the left. Twilight was falling; there were lights on in the big house up the hill. He edged along the path between the gardens and the kidney-shaped swimming pool. He reckoned it would take about five minutes until the cigarette burned down to the match heads, igniting them and severing the cotton so that the burning matchbook would fall into the incendiary mixture. Give the resulting fire two or three minutes to reach the open fuel tank. Say eight minutes in all.

In the event, he was thirty-eight seconds off.

32

"Well?"

"No word yet, Colonel General," his deputy chief reported.

Ivashutin made an impatient gesture. It was 5 A.M. Moscow time, but he felt no fatigue. He was nearly eighty, and sleep was no longer important to him. He looked at the clocks on the wall of his office: they showed London, Washington, Tokyo, and Moscow time. It was 9 P.M. in the American capital.

"You have spoken to Washington?"

"Yes, sir," Pavlov said. "They have heard nothing."

"Damn the man!" Ivashutin said irritably, "He's done everything else perfectly. What's holding him up?"

"There's still time, sir. We still have three hours."

"I know that, damnit!" Ivashutin growled. The American spy satellite routinely photographed the missile site every twelve hours. With the missile on the pad, once that shutter clicked, the fat would be in the fire.

"He'll come through, General. Do you want some coffee?"

"To hell with coffee," Ivashutin said. "Bring me some cognac. And tell them to get me Professor Doctor Chebriakov on the phone at Kapustin Yar."

Pavlov hurried away, leaving Ivashutin staring at the large-scale map of the world on the far wall of his office. Don't fall at the last fence, Guchkov, he thought. There is too much at stake. Far too much at stake.

He had come a long way for a boy who'd begun as a volunteer in the punitive formations of the Special Purpose Units. He'd been nineteen then. Twenty-two when he came into Army intelligence. More than half a century—my God, where did the years go to? He was the last of a dying breed, the generation that had produced Brezhnev and Yuri Andropov, Chernenko, Kuznetzov. All gone now. There was a new breed in high office these days, pragmatic bargain makers with university degrees who worked for the system instead of making the system work for them. He didn't relish the thought of giving the gray men a chance to bring him down; he knew only too well with what zeal they would do it, and with what pleasure the Neighbors would assist them.

He looked around him. Unlike the strictly utilitarian cream-painted boxes most GRU officers worked out of, his office was ornately furnished, with Oriental carpets and embroidered sofas. The walls were paneled in mahogany, and the high windows, looking out over the courtyard, had no bars on them. On his antique desk, once the property of a wealthy sugar merchant in Sverdlovsk, was a battery of telephones: a direct line to the Kremlin, another connecting to the principal GRU stations throughout Russia, still another to the Ministry of Defense, and so on. The sixth telephone, which was white, connected him directly with his deputy chiefs: Pavlov, Bekrenev, Zotov, Meshcheryakov, Kolodyazhny, Milstein, and Sidorov.

The red scrambler phone purred; he picked it up.

"Is that you, Professor Doctor Chebriakov?"

"At your command, General."

"What is the present status of Smert Ptyetsa?"

"She is on the launching pad, General. Everything is in readiness. We await only your clearance to commence countdown."

"Countdown is twelve hours?"

"That is correct. Can you give me any indication when we will begin?"

"Not yet," Ivashutin said gruffly. "We're all as anxious as

you are to get started, Professor. But we can't give you a 'go' until we hear from our man in Washington."

"I understand. You will forgive my question. My enthusiasm."

"No apology necessary, my dear fellow. We're all tense. It's only to be expected. I'm sorry to have disturbed your sleep."

"I wasn't sleeping, General. I can't sleep. I won't sleep until our bird is flying."

"Your dedication is commendable," Ivashutin said. "It will not be forgotten."

"Thank you, General," Chebriakov said into the receiver, thinking how true Ivashutin's words were. If everything went to plan, what he had done would not be forgotten. The same would be true if everything went wrong. The only difference would be who was doing the remembering.

"I'll call you as soon as we get word," Ivashutin told him. "Don't worry. It won't be long. I'm sure of it."

I hope you're right, thought the scientist as he put down the telephone and looked out of his window. There on the featureless steppe, stark and ugly against the lightening sky, the F-2m launch vehicle with its huge payload stood within its mighty gantries, like an enormous futuristic skyscraper under construction. I hope you're right.

33 Guchkov detested guns.

Guns were for morons, assault groups, *boyeveya* squads, assassins. Brains were the most potent weapon, not firearms. Even so, he could not take the chance of encountering a situation where a weapon would make the difference; so he had chosen carefully. He wasted no time on the 5.45 PSM which was replacing the old 9mm Makarov throughout the Russian security services. Both guns were anyway a copy, and a poor one, of the German Walther PP. He gave serious thought to the fifteen-round 9mm Beretta selective-fire pistol which had replaced the old Colt .45 M1911 automatic in the U.S. Army, but in the end decided to go American because ammunition was so much easier to get.

There was a specialist firm in Wisconsin called Armament & Systems Procedures who made a very effective combat version of the Smith & Wesson M39 pistol. It carried seven rounds of 9mm Parabellum, was very light—just under one and a half pounds loaded—and although hard to obtain, had much to recommend it. In the final analysis, however, he opted for firepower and selected a .45 Detonics Combat Master Mark V, the one with the stainless-steel finish. Slightly heavier than the ASP, and carrying one round less, the pistol was like a smaller, lighter version of the M1911, but with the same stopping power.

He held the pistol in his hand now as he pondered the best

way of disposing of Mitchell. Guns were clumsy, noisy, and far from reliable. Ricin would be much better.

The Technical Operations Department of the GRU, Tyéchnecheski Dyéystvye, or Tyé-Dyé as it was known throughout the Service, had done enormous amounts of research into undetectable poisons: glycolates, shellfish toxins, curare extracts. No one had yet come up with a better one than ricin, which was derived from the seeds of the castor-oil plant, *Ricinus communis*. A slow-acting poison which took up to three days to kill, ricin induced cardiovascular collapse and all the external symptoms of a genuine heart attack.

He went to the locked cupboard beneath the staircase, to which only he had access. From it he took a long wooden box, and out of it lifted what looked like a target pistol. It was a 9mm Tokagypt, the Egyptian version of the Russian Tokarev TT33, extensively remodelled into what Tyé-Dyé called a nondiscernible microbioinoculator—GRU jargonese for a battery-operated gun which fired a poison pellet without the target realizing he had been hit. The poison itself was carried in a tiny mercury phial which dispersed on impact, leaving the deadly poison to slowly find its way to the heart.

He looked at his watch. Six-thirty. Mitchell would be arriving soon. He went into the huge circular foyer. As he did, Katja came down the stairs. She was wearing a Halston day dress and Magli sandals. Her golden hair was swept back in a style not unlike that of the English Princess Diana.

"What time is he due?" she asked, stopping at the foot of the ornate staircase like a model posing for a photographer.

"Anytime now," he said. He placed the Tokagypt poison gun between two books on a sofa table near the door and looked around.

"Are you ready?" he said.

"Yes. Everything is packed."

"Good. We'll leave as soon as I have disposed of Mitchell."

"With . . . that?" Katja inclined her head toward the hidden gun.

"Don't worry. He won't feel a thing."

"How long will it take?"

"Twenty-four, forty-eight hours. More than long enough for you to ditch him."

"Will I see you again?"

"It's a small world."

"You're glad to be going back, aren't you, Andrei?"

"Yes," he said. "I am."

He had already had more than enough of America. He detested its fat men and even fatter women, the pretentiousness of the architecture, the mindlessness of the television, the ghastly sameness of their food. He loathed the graffiti-defiled subways and the arrogant colored youths with their ghetto-blasters, the filthy, littered streets of the cities, the sidewalker hustlers who urged you to "check it out," the blatant whores who walked up and touched your genitals, the illiterate cab drivers, the lurching panhandlers, the street crazies. Americans worshiped only two gods, money and success. They could not lead, and they refused to follow.

He remembered an SS captain he had once talked to in the Hofbräuhaus in Munich. Forty years after the end of it, the man was still bitter about the fact that Germany had lost the war, and bitterest of all that they had lost it to Americans.

"Man for man, they were not in our class," he said, shaking his head at the memory. "As an army, they were a rabble. The only reason they won was because there were so fucking many of them."

Guchkov was looking forward to his return—triumphant return, he corrected himself—to the motherland. All he had to do now was to confirm to Red Center via the Washington embassy that the "logic bomb" was in place. As soon as that confirmation reached Moscow, the countdown to launch of *Shmert Ptyetsa* would begin. At T minus 12, the massive assault on the

American computer systems, orchestrated from the huge computer bunker beneath the Washington embassy, would begin. Triggered by remote satellite controls, accurate to a microsecond, the program would turn the American satellite into so much junk orbiting in space, and simultaneously wreak havoc in the computers at Pine Gap in the Red Center of Australia.

Long before then, Guchkov would have boarded the Aeroflot jet that would take him back to Moscow's Sheremetyevo Airport and a welcome befitting a hero of the Soviet Union. There would be kisses from the director, bear hugs from the Grandfathers, flowers from smiling children, a guard of honor. At the Aquarium, they would line up to shake his hand.

The GRU lieutenant who acted as a butler at Highfield came in and told him Mitchell was through the gate. Guchkov nodded and went to meet the American. The big Dodge came to a stop in front of the Palladian porch, tires crunching on the gravel. Mitchell got out, smiling. He was wearing a cream silk shirt, cream linen suit, and matching leather espadrilles. He looked, Guchkov thought, like a Harlem pimp.

"Well?"

Mitchell nodded.

"Let's go inside," Guchkov said. "I think this calls for a drink."

"I won't be staying long," Mitchell said. Guchkov smiled. How true, he thought. The sun was below the wooded bluffs across the river; he could see the lights of Bellevue, a mile away. Smoke lifted lazily into the air down at the dock; probably one of the servants burning trash.

"Kate's inside," he said, leading the way toward the house. As he did, the unmistakable sound of fire-engine sirens bored into the stillness of the evening, coming nearer. He frowned, sensing without knowing why that something was amiss. The sound of the sirens drew nearer. The wisp of smoke that he had noticed earlier had turned now into a roiling black pillar into which flickering fingers of orange flame lanced. He saw one of the servants running down to the dock, shouting. Then a mighty explosion assaulted his eardrums like roaring thunder.

He watched, transfixed, as the entire dock erupted straight up like a volcano, massive chunks of metal and wood burning and turning against the soft, purpling sky. He felt the blast hit him like a hot hand, heard the chittering crash as two of the big drawing room windows were blown in. Oleg, the butler, came running out of the house.

"The fire department is at the gates, sir!" he yelled. "What shall I do?"

"Let them in!" Guchkov shouted. There was no choice. Down at the dock a raging, leaping fire roared at the evening sky. He watched for a moment longer, stunned. Then he turned to see Mitchell standing in the doorway, gaping at the incredible scene.

"Get inside!" he snapped.

As he spoke, the fire department's huge red Mack truck roared past the house, churning up the gravel, gouging deep black tracks in the lawns as the driver shortcut the distance to the dock. Men ran, shouting, hoses unsnaked, challenging the inferno at the jetty.

"Wait in the library!" he said to Mitchell. "Go on, I'll be right there." He hurried across to the telephone. It was dead. Cold fingers of unease touched his nerve ends. This was obviously hostile action, but who was the enemy? Kingly had said Caine was back in Washington. But how would he know where to find Guchkov? He looked up to see Katja watching him, a frown puckering the flawless brow.

"What is it?" she said. "What has happened?"

He drew the Combat Master out of its shoulder holster and handed it to her. "He's in the library," he said. "Kill him. I'll get the car."

He went out of the front door, and Katja walked into the library. Mitchell was pacing up and down, fear painted on his face.

"Kate!" he said, vast relief in his voice. "What the hell's going on?"

"I don't know," Kate said. "It doesn't matter. We have to get out of here. Is the program in place?"

"What about the money?"

"There's no time for that now. Is the program in place?"

"What program is that, Mitchell?" a voice interposed.

Katja swung around. A man had come into the room on soundless feet, a tall, well-built blond man wearing a gray windbreaker and dark slacks. Mitchell stared at him, a bewildered frown on his face.

"Who the hell are you?" he growled.

"It's Caine," Katja said. "Caine, isn't it?"

"And you're the swallow. Katja."

She smiled and produced the gun that had been concealed by the folds of her dress. Mitchell gaped at her, paralyzed, his jaw slack with shock.

"You know what happens now, Mitchell," Caine said. "She kills me, then she kills you. There's no payoff. There never was going to be one."

"Kate?" Mitchell gasped.

"What did you do for them, Mitchell? What was the program she was talking about?"

"Kate?" Mitchell said again.

"Mitchell, they've double-crossed you," Caine said urgently. "Tell me what you did."

Mitchell shook his head. "You wouldn't . . . Kate? You wouldn't do that?"

"You damned baby," she said, and shot him through the heart. Mitchell cartwheeled backward, crashing into the ornate fireplace. Like a tigress, Katja swung around, turning the gun on Caine, but he was already diving to one side. Her first shot missed completely. She had pulled the trigger for her second shot when the bullet from Caine's ASP hit her on the bridge of her freckled nose, hurling her backward like a rag doll to fall in an ugly heap. Her wild unaimed shot smashed into Caine's lower body and drove him back, yelling with pain, against the fine mahogany bookcase, the ASP skittering away.

Caine dragged himself to his feet. His body felt as if it was on fire. He could not see clearly, and his movements felt as if he was wading in treacle. After a moment's dizziness, his vision cleared. He saw Mitchell lying in front of the fireplace, the spattered blood on the walls. The man's arm moved. Caine lurched across. Mitchell was staring up, his eyes drowning in agony.

"Pock," he said. Blood came out with the word.

The cream linen suit was spattered with blood, a ghastly mess. Caine ripped the jacket open and took out Mitchell's wallet, shaking its contents onto the rug.

"What?" he shouted, shaking the dying man. "What am I looking for?"

Mitchell tried to speak. Another gob of blood trickled from the writhing lips.

"Goddamn you, Mitchell, what?"

"Copy," Mitchell said clearly. Then he was dead.

Caine picked up a strip of card perhaps eight inches long and three wide. He knew enough about computers to know that the hieroglyphics on it were some kind of program. He put it into his pocket and lurched out into the hall. His hip felt as if someone was playing a blowtorch on it. He reeled and almost fell, bringing down a table near the door. A weapon clattered on the tile floor. He knew what it was: they'd taken poison guns off Russian agents before. Grimly ignoring the searing rushes of pain driving through his entire body, he picked up the Tokagypt and staggered outside.

At the dock, it looked as if the firemen were getting the blaze under control. He could see men walking up toward the house across the terraced formal gardens. He turned to his left and saw Guchkov in the Mercedes 380SEL convertible on the concrete washing apron in front of the garage, engine running.

Guchkov saw him in the same moment. He saw the Russian's

startled expression, saw the car leap forward as Guchkov rammed his foot down. The car spat gravel and earth backward as Guchkov swung the wheel to turn onto the drive. He missed it by a yard and the big car spun onto the grass, tires whining as they sought purchase.

"Guchkov!" Caine screamed. Guchkov smacked the shift into reverse and came at him backward, engine screaming. Caine fell out of the vehicle's path, lying helplessly on the ground as Guchkov swung the car side-on, cursing, his face a sweating mask of desperation. Caine pulled himself up to a sitting position, bent his good right knee, and, steadying both arms on it, fired the poison pistol. It made an insignificant sound: *bnfff!* Guchkov made a quick, irritated gesture like a man brushing away a wasp. In an instant that seemed like an eternity, Caine saw Guchkov look at the weapon in his hand and knew that the Russian realized what had happened to him.

"That's for Berlin, you bastard!" Caine shouted. "That's for Jenny!" He had no idea whether Guchkov heard him.

Now he saw blue lights flashing among the trees bordering the main driveway. Guchkov saw them, too. He wrenched the Mercedes around, roaring away from the house in a flying shower of gravel, scouring extended S-grooves into the drive. He skidded off the drive between the huge oaks bordering it, sliding on the grass, fishtailing back onto the drive behind the police cars as they slammed to a stop. Down the drive, the Mercedes roared as police officers piled out of their vehicles, firing wildly at the vanishing taillights. His face a rictus of frustration and terror, Guchkov raced toward the main gate. A telephone, a telephone: the thought hammered in his mind like a pulse. If he could reach a phone, the satellite would go, and there was still a chance that his people could save his life.

The gate loomed into view. He saw there was a police car standing in the road outside, and another one, an unmarked tan sedan, parked at right angles to it. Two patrolmen stood talking to a civilian. Guchkov jammed the gas pedal to the floor, and the Mercedes powered forward, hurtling through the gateway like a juggernaut. The policemen leaped for safety as the Mercedes whiplashed past their Mustang with a smashing of grinding metal and glass, then slewed wildly on the grass verges on the far side of the road, tearing clods of earth out of the ground as Guchkov fought to control the car.

Over the roar of the engine, he heard the sound of shots, the spang of bullets hitting the coachwork of the car. He wrestled the Mercedes back onto the road, snatching a look in his mirror to see the men running back toward their car. He roared up Trippe Creek Lane, heading for Route 333. Maybe there was still time.

Maybe.

34

When the four-vehicle motorcade bringing the Sewer Squad arrived, Forsyth came out of the house to meet them. The fire department had gone; a pair of Oxford PD Mustangs were still slewed in the turning circle in front of the Palladian porch, blue lights flashing, radios squawking. Down at the dock, the blackened wreck of the big Bertram lay on its side in the water. The officer in charge of the clean-up unit identified himself to Forsyth and looked around in wonderment.

"Hanrahan, Logistics Twelve," he said. "What the fuck went down here? It looks like World War Three broke out."

Forsyth shrugged and pointed with his chin at the burly, gray-haired police captain coming out of the house. Hanrahan nodded and strode across to confront the big policeman, whose ID shield gave his name as Captain David James. Hanrahan flipped open his own ID wallet. The police chief stared at it for a moment, then spat on the ground.

"I might have known," he said disgustedly.

"Give me a rundown, Chief," Hanrahan said. "What have we got here?"

"Out here we got that," James said, with an angry gesture in the direction of the burned dock and the wrecked boat. "Inside, we got a dead NSA officer, an unidentified woman with the top of her head blown off, and half a dozen servants who won't even tell us their names without talking to the Russian embassy. That's what we've got. You want to tell me what it means?''

"You got an ID on the NSA man?"

"His name is Butler Mitchell," Forsyth said, coming across to join them. "I notified NSA as soon as I made him, coming in. They're sending an M-5 squad out. Should be here before long."

"You'll find what was in his pockets on the table in the hall," James said. "The bodies are in the library. I sound like a goddamned Agatha Christie movie. On the physical evidence, somebody else was wounded in there. We've got three different blood types. We've also got two guns, a .45 and a .38 ASP. Three shots fired from the .45. One of them killed the NSA man. The woman was killed with the ASP. Could be she wounded whoever killed her. You want to talk to the ME?"

"Maybe later," Hanrahan said. "Thanks a lot, Chief. You can get your people out of here now. We'll take over."

"What do you think, I'm just going to walk away from this?" James said. "I've got TV people, newspapers banging on my door. My report—"

"Don't file it till you hear from us, Chief," Hanrahan said. "Okay?"

James looked at him for two long seconds, then decided against whatever it was he had been about to say. Hanrahan went into the house, and Forsyth followed him. The marble-floored foyer was circular, perhaps forty feet in diameter. Twin staircases bent upwards to a gallery. It looked like a set for *The Merry Widow*. They walked through to the library. Beautifully furnished, and lined with mahogany shelving, it was dominated at the far end by a Victorian marble fireplace on which stood a gilded clock with two figures representing winter and summer. Above it hung a painting of a river scene. In front of the marble fireplace lay the body of Butler Mitchell, his cream linen suit incarnadined. The woman lay in an ugly sprawl about ten feet nearer the door, the Chinese carpet beneath her stiff with coagulating blood.

"Jesus!" Hanrahan said. Shaking his head, he crossed the long room, squatting on his haunches to examine the bloody smears on the bookcase and the floor where Caine had fallen. A chalked circle showed where a bullet had been dug out of the wood. Hanrahan made a mental note to collect it from the Oxford police.

"You gonna talk to the servants?" he asked Forsyth.

Forsyth shook his head. "They'll all be Russians," he said. "We won't get a peep out of them, neither will M-5. They'll plead diplomatic immunity."

"You're probably right," Hanrahan said glumly. "All right boys, come on in."

A team of men in gray coveralls appeared in the doorway. There was no change in their expressions as they saw what was waiting for them in the library. Like men who have worked together many times before, two of them went across to where Mitchell lay. They unrolled a heavy black plastic body bag, unzipped it, rolled the body in, and lugged it out of the room. Another pair did the same with the body of the woman. A trolley was wheeled in, stacked with cleaning solutions, pails, rolls of muslin, stain solvents—in fact, everything the team would need to remove every trace of what had happened in this room. For their pains, they were called the Sewer Squad.

"What's your reading of this, Forsyth?" Hanrahan asked. "You think your Russki friend was wounded?"

"He didn't drive as if he was."

"He won't get far."

He doesn't need to, Forsyth thought. Drosdow would only need to make one telephone call. His people would send out a team to pick him up and spirit him away to some Russian safe house. From there, they could put him on an Aeroflot plane or one of a dozen other airlines without anyone ever knowing he'd left the country. Or, if it was realized that his work had come to nothing, they might simply incinerate him.

"You got to report to the director when you get back to town, Forsyth," Hanrahan told him. "I'll handle this end. You can take off any time you like."

"Sure," Forsyth said, allowing himself a grin at the thought of his impending interview with the chief. They wouldn't know whether to give him a medal or set fire to his ass.

He walked down to the dock and stood for a while staring at the wreckage, without really seeing it. It was almost dark. The lights of Bellevue looked pretty across the mile of water between. He played back the scenario he had constructed, testing it for flaws. Someone had got to Highfield by boat, probably rented in Oxford: they could check that easily enough. Beached it over yonder. Set fire to the dock and the boat in it. Cut the phone lines. Went in after Drosdow. Who . . . what? Killed Mitchell and the girl, and wounded someone . . . someone else? Who?

Was it you, Caine? he wondered. And if it was, where the hell are you now?

35

The Central Medical Establishment doctor who dressed Caine's wound was a harrassed-looking Scot with a tired smile. He had deft hands and a casual professional attitude that inspired confidence. He gave no name; nor did Caine ask for one. They both knew the rules.

The doctor told him he was in a private hospital. Although he was not supposed to, Caine knew that the Service maintained a maximum-security clinic on Old Court House Road, not far from Wolf Trap. The doctor told him that he'd lost a lot of blood before they got him there, and that the Service surgeons had to work hard, and fast, to save him. The heavy slug from Katja Renis's automatic had torn a hole in Caine's body low on the left-hand side, chipping a splinter out of his pelvis, burning past the large intestine and tearing apart the external oblique muscles. The doctor told him he was a lucky man: he'd have his own built-in weather forecaster for the rest of his life.

"Every time there's rain in the air, you'll have a wee twinge there, laddie," he predicted. "Probably get a job with the Meteorological Office when you retire."

"How long have I been here?"

"Three days."

Three days since the reckless race back toward Washington in Mitchell's car, fighting to stay conscious long enough to make the rendezvous in Annapolis.

"I can't remember meeting McClelland," he said. "But I suppose I must have."

"You're here, aren't you?"

"Can I use the telephone?"

The doctor smiled and shook his head. "Not till the dredgers are done with you, laddie," he said. "They'll be here tomorrow, so get some rest. You'll need it."

The next day, the debriefing officers from Station One arrived. They gave no names either. One of them was about fifty—tall, thin, unsmiling, precise. He took all the notes. The other man, although much the same age, was positively tubby, with dark hair, wide frank eyes, a ready smile, and an ingratiating manner. He handled the Uher portable reel-to-reel recorder they brought with them and asked most of the questions. It was impossible to avoid thinking of them as Laurel and Hardy.

"Let's start at the beginning, shall we?" Laurel said, unsnapping the lock of his EIIR briefcase and taking out a Parker ballpoint. He was all business. Hardy smiled benevolently at Caine, as though to say, "Don't take it to heart, he's always like that." He radiated sympathy; he made you want to confide in him. Caine bet himself no money at all that they were the best dredging team in the Service.

"Bloody marvel, you are," Hardy said as if in admiration. "One-man crime wave. Stolen cars, credit-card fraud, interference with the U.S. Mail. Then blowing up half of Easton. You've given us a lot of headaches, Caine. A lot of oil has had to be poured on a great deal of troubled water."

"Costly, too," Laurel put in. "Very costly."

"Are you going to tell me what happened?"

"All in good time, Caine," Laurel said. "All in good time."

They spent three days with him, long, punishing twelve-hour days of questions and more questions, going over again and again every aspect of the Guchkov assignment, from Caine's initial involvement in Miami until the final moments at the big house in Easton. As Caine had thought, they were very professional and very, very thorough. He was glad he had nothing to hide from them.

As well as being professional and thorough, they were also fair: as the interrogation progressed, they told him more and more of what had happened subsequent to his getting the computer program to Dick McClelland that bloody night.

The moment Caine handed over the program for the logic bomb, an ISS cover operation was set in motion. Caine was whisked away to the secret clinic near Wolf Trap. Mitchell's car, which he had appropriated to make the drive to the rendezvous, was spirited away to a Service workshop from which it would emerge with a totally new identity. McClelland himself raced back to the ISS bureau in Arlington and spent the next half hour on the scrambler line to London.

At seven-thirty the following morning, Sir James Bamford, the head of ISS, called a crisis meeting with the Joint Intelligence Chiefs, who concurred that their first priority was to urgently apprise NSA of the situation while at the same time concealing the role of ISS in uncovering it.

To ensure this, they decided to inform the director of the National Security Agency that a British security officer named Kingly had been identified as a Soviet agent. Under interrogation, he had revealed the existence of an ongoing Russian initiative code-named Open Window whose purpose was to suborn and recruit a senior NSA officer named Butler Mitchell. Mitchell had been used by Russian military intelligence to plant a logic bomb inside the NSA computer network. A copy of the program had been found in Kingly's possession, and this was transmitted to DIRNSA. His reaction to this intelligence was electric: within two hours of his receiving the program from Cheltenham, the logic bomb had been located and removed from the system.

Intensive analysis of the GRU computer program indicated that its function was to neutralize on command the American reconnaissance satellite known as *Big Bird III*, in geostationary orbit above Diego Garcia in the Indian Ocean, and to trash reception and transmission from the tracking station at Pine Gap for a period of approximately fifteen minutes.

"What for?" Caine asked.

"We're coming to that," Hardy said.

Crash-program inspection of current satellite and aerial reconnaissance photographs showed unusual activity on the missile launch site at Kapustin Yar. A new type of satellite, whose capabilities and functions were not known, was ready for launch into clandestine orbit.

"It was not unnaturally assumed that since the Soviets had gone to so much trouble to effect a clandestine launch, the satellite's capabilities were inimical to our interests," Laurel added dryly.

"So that was it," Caine said. "That was what bothered me. I couldn't figure out what Mitchell could possibly bring out of NSA that was worth so much money. But Guchkov didn't want him to bring anything out. He wanted him to take something in."

"By George," Laurel said sardonically, "I think he's got it."

"What's happened to him? Is there any word yet?"

"No trace of him anywhere. He could have made it to the Kremlin in Washington," Hardy said. "If you're right and you hit him with that microbioinoculator, they'd have got him out—they couldn't run the risk of an autopsy. We're still checking."

"Who was the girl?"

"Her name was Katja Renis. Czech refugee, been working in the School of Foreign Service at Georgetown University since 1973. Clean as a whistle until all this."

"One way and another," Hardy added, "the Comrades are in some disarray. I suppose you get the credit for that at least."

Analysis of the logic-bomb program also made it possible to establish the parameters within which the Soviet missile launch must take place to achieve optimum lift-off and orbit. These were projected as, respectively, within eighteen, forty-two, or sixty-six hours from the receipt of the signal activating the program. Acting on the premise that the countdown might commence almost at once, certain secret contingency plans involving Air Force pursuit planes carrying air-to-air missiles were immediately put into effect.

Then, less than six hours later, with the planes in the air and visible to Russian radar, the American ambassador to Russia was admitted by his own urgent request to the presence of General Secretary Mikhail Gorbachev, to whom he presented a strongly worded note from the president of the United States. With the letter came a copy of the GRU logic-bomb program that had been planted in the NSA computers by Butler Mitchell. The presidential note stated unequivocally that if the launch planned by the Soviet Union were now to take place, the United States would feel itself at liberty to use all means at its disposal to destroy the missile.

Simultaneous with the destruction of the missile, all the details of the Russian initiative—with emphasis upon the GRU's role in smuggling sixty million dollars' worth of cocaine into the United States—would be released to the world press. This would indubitably result in a grave, and possibly permanent, setback to plans for arms-reduction talks at Geneva, and détente between East and West. The secretary general's immediate response was requested.

"What happened?" Caine asked his interrogators.

"The launch has been indefinitely postponed."

"So we win."

"Win, lose, draw. They're only words. We do what we have to do. So do they."

"You mean, no medal?"

"That's a good one," Hardy said to Laurel. "Eh?"

Laurel allowed himself a thin smile, as if he severely rationed them. "It certainly is," he said. Caine almost expected him to add "Ollie."

"What about Kingly?" Caine asked. Laurel's wispy smile disappeared, and his eyes became almost furtive.

"Of course," Hardy said. "You wouldn't have heard."

"Heard what?"

"Hanged himself in his cell," Hardy said. "During interrogation." The words did not match the evasiveness in his colleague's eyes. Caine did not pursue it. The British security services had their own equivalent of the CIA's "maximal demotion."

"Poor Miles."

"Don't waste your sympathy on him, Caine," Laurel said, stiffly. "We still don't know how badly the treacherous bastard has compromised your organization." It was the first time Caine had seen either of his interrogators show emotion. Laurel obviously felt very strongly about treachery. Perhaps that was why he was such a good interrogator.

Caine got up and walked over to the window. He was still weak, but the wound was healing well. "Have we got much more ground to cover?" he asked.

"Not much," Hardy replied. "We're nearly finished."

"Any idea when I can return to active duty?"

"When you get out of here you'll be going back to London for redeployment," Hardy told him. "You've had much too high a profile to be any use here any more."

"Will I have to fly straight back to London? Or would I be allowed to take a few days' leave first?"

"Where?"

"Miami?"

Laurel looked positively pained.

"I thought not," Caine said. "What about New York, then?"

"We'd have to get a reading on that," Hardy said. "Why do you want to go to New York?"

"To see a lady."

"Mmmm," Laurel frowned. "That wouldn't be Lynda Sanchez, would it?"

"Tricky, Caine," Hardy said. "Having you back on the street so soon."

"I could always resign," Caine said brightly. "Then you wouldn't be able to stop me."

"That's a good one," Hardy beamed, looking at Laurel. "Eh?"

They left soon afterward. Caine ate, slept, ate, waited. For the first time, he was allowed to see the newspapers. One of them contained a brief item datelined Moscow that announced the unexpected retirement of General of the Army Pyotr I. Ivashutin and his replacement by a rising young star in Soviet military circles, Lieutenant General, now Colonel General, I. M. Drachev. The item went on to speculate that Ivashutin, known to be director of Soviet Military Intelligence, had been relieved of his command for reasons not yet known in the West.

Time dragged by. Caine read a couple of the paperbacks that had been brought in for him, did his physiotherapy, and waited. Three days after his interrogation, a nurse came into the room pushing a trolley. On it was a phone.

"There's a call for you," she said, and went out. Caine picked up the receiver. The remembered prim voice of Laurel came down the line.

"You're cleared for repatriation," he said. "Thought you'd like to know."

"I'm accredited again?"

"With the not surprising exception of duty in the United States."

"What about New York?"

"Sanctioned. Three days, no more."

"Oooh, yer luvly," Caine told him.

"Aren't I, though," Laurel replied dryly. "By the way, the chief asked me to pass along some news. We finally found out what happened to your friend Guchkov. He's dead, Caine. Circulatory collapse on an Aeroflot flight from Washington to Moscow. Classic ricin poisoning symptoms. They made an emergency landing in Berlin, but he was dead before they touched down. So you did get him. I'm to tell you the chief said 'well done.'"

Berlin: Caine smiled grimly at the irony. In his mind's eye, he saw again the desperation on the Russian's face as he wrestled with the wheel of the Mercedes, the sick certainty in his eyes in the moment that he realized what Caine had shot him with. Had he heard the words Caine shouted after him? It didn't matter one way or the other. The bastard was dead and that would have to do.

He got Lynda Sanchez's number from Information and called her. Her voice was guarded and anything but friendly.

"What do you want?"

"I want to see you, Lynda. To explain what happened."

"I know what happened. And I don't plan to have it happen again," she said.

"What about all the money I owe you?"

"Send me a check."

"Lynda, Lynda, talk to me. Give me a chance to make it up to you."

"Where are you calling from?"

"I'm in Washington. I'm taking the Amtrak to New York tonight. Why don't you fly up and join me?"

"Just like that?"

"I'll take you to every musical in town."

"You walked out on me, Caine. You just disappeared."

"I'll take you on that boat ride I promised you. All the way to Staten Island. How about it?"

"Look, you've got me flustered. I'm not used to that. Let me get back to you. Where are you staying?"

"Call me this time tomorrow at the Carlyle in New York."

"The Carlyle? Are you rich, Caine?"

"Didn't I just tell you I'd take you for a ride on the ferry?" he said. "The last of the big spenders, that's me. Come on, Lynda. Fly up here. It'll be my treat, the whole schmear."

Lynda Sanchez thought about that. "It sounds terribly sinful."

"Let's hope you're right," he said.

He hung up, then sat for a long time looking at the telephone, surprised he had actually called her. She was the first woman he'd felt remotely attracted to since Jenny died. He thought back to the few days they had spent together, remembering Lynda's warmth and resourcefulness, her direct, no-nonsense approach to life. He remembered her walking across the parking lot in the Dadeland Mall. Nothing noisy, but everything in the right places . . .

He pushed the button for the nurse. She went out and came back with a Samsonite soft-top suitcase full of clothes, a wallet containing credit cards, a driver's license, and an acetate envelope containing ten twenty-dollar bills and two thousand dollars in traveler's checks. As he got dressed, he thought about sharing New York with Lynda Sanchez. They would both have ghosts to exorcise there. It would be restorative; it might even turn out to be more. That was as much as anyone could hope for. In his business, you only allowed yourself one dream at a time.

19